KEEP ME POSTED

KEEP ME POSTED

Lisa Beazley

 NEW AMERICAN LIBRARY

NEW AMERICAN LIBRARY
Published by New American Library,
an imprint of Penguin Random House LLC
375 Hudson Street, New York, New York 10014

This book is an original publication of New American Library.

First Printing, April 2016

Copyright © Lisa Beazley, 2016
Penguin Random House supports copyright. Copyright fuels creativity, encourages diverse voices, promotes free speech, and creates a vibrant culture. Thank you for buying an authorized edition of this book and for complying with copyright laws by not reproducing, scanning, or distributing any part of it in any form without permission. You are supporting writers and allowing Penguin Random House to continue to publish books for every reader.

New American Library and the New American Library colophon are registered trademarks of Penguin Random House LLC.

For more information about Penguin Random House, visit penguinrandomhouse.com.

LIBRARY OF CONGRESS CATALOGING-IN-PUBLICATION DATA:

Names: Beazley, Lisa, author.
Title: Keep me posted/Lisa Beazley.
Description: New York: New American Library, 2016.
Identifiers: LCCN 2015038157 | ISBN 9781101989869 (hardback)
Subjects: LCSH: Sisters—Fiction. | Letter writing—Fiction. |
Self-actualization (Psychology) in women—Fiction. | BISAC: FICTION/
Contemporary Women. | FICTION/Sagas. | FICTION/Literary.
Classification: LCC PS3602.E265 K44 2016 | DDC 813/.6—dc23
LC record available at http://lccn.loc.gov/2015038157

INTERNATIONAL EDITION ISBN 978-1-101-99171-8

Printed in the United States of America
10 9 8 7 6 5 4 3 2 1

Designed by Kristin del Rosario

Penguin
Random
House

To sisters everywhere, especially mine.

ACKNOWLEDGMENTS

Thank you . . .

To Erika Mailman. Writing this was fun because of you.

To my agent, Marly Rusoff, for her most excellent guidance. Thanks also to Julie Mosow and Michael Radulescu.

To my wise and delightful editor, Claire Zion, and the good people at the Berkley Group, including Kara Welsh and Jennifer Fisher.

To my grandparents, Ben and Pat Beazley and Julie Wood, for making reading and writing the thing we all do.

To my parents, Mike and Julie Beazley, for filling my childhood with books (Mom) and adventure (Dad), and for a lifetime of pure and unconditional love and support.

To Jeff, Sarah, and Kate, for being the kind of people who led me to write a book in which the happy ending involves moving in with your adult sibling.

To my husband, TJ Kling. I couldn't ask for a more selfless and generous partner. I'm tremendously grateful for all of the weekends you let me hide away with my laptop while you keep our world spinning.

To my beloved children, Grady, Seamus, and Arlo, for making me feel all the feelings—mostly the good ones—on a daily basis.

To Agnes Laurente, for taking such loving care of my family and my home so that I can write.

ACKNOWLEDGMENTS

To the talented writers who worked alongside me in Erika's class, especially Leslie Cauldwell, Brett Singer, Ellen McGarrahan, Emily Bond, Elizabeth Cockle, Rosanne Dube, Beth Dougherty, Lynne Hoerauf, and Lucie Patrowicz.

To the mommy bloggers. Your wit, generosity, and honesty helped to shape Cassie.

To my friends, aunts, uncles, cousins, nieces, nephews, and in-laws. I'm lucky to be surrounded by such smart, funny, and interesting people. If my characters are any good, it's because I know you.

KEEP ME POSTED

CHAPTER ONE

Later—much later—I would regret pretending to be asleep when Leo sidled up to me in bed that night. Not that it was an isolated incident; it's just that the timing stands out as an apropos kickoff to what would be the year everything went pear-shaped.

"'Night, Cass," he said, coming in for a kiss. When I didn't turn toward him, he planted a soft peck behind my ear and lingered for a few seconds.

"Niii," I mumbled, my sleepy voice more indicative of my state of mind than my level of alertness. In fact, I was wide-awake and mentally scheduling my morning to somehow fit in packing and an activity to exhaust the boys before sticking them in the car for our eight-hour drive.

Sadly, I'd reached a point where when faced with the options of sex or hours of sleepless anxiety, I chose the latter. Would I like some kissing and breast caressing? Nah. I think I'll formulate snarky retorts to made-up potential insults for ten or fifteen minutes. How about an orgasm or two? No, thanks! I'm good mentally going through my inadequate wardrobe, trying to figure out what to pack for five days of holiday merrymaking with my family. Fall asleep sexually satisfied and with a grateful-and-therefore-more-likely-to-wake-up-first-with-the-kids-in-the-morning husband? I'll pass. My restless legs syndrome should be kicking in anytime now, and I'm due to be pacing and stretching in the living room.

So steeped in ennui was I that doing something guaranteed to relieve stress, boost endorphins, and strengthen my marriage—all without leaving my bed—seemed like just another chore.

It's not like we were going in for lengthy acrobatic sessions. Quite the opposite, I'm afraid. The tired-parent sex between Leo and me had become what I thought of as a battle for the bottom, with one person (the winner) lying there while the other (the loser) expended minimal effort from the top. My tactics had recently moved beyond polite and passive maneuvering to actual deceit. If you think I'm exaggerating, listen to this one: I told him it was suddenly easier for me to orgasm from down there. (It wasn't.) So that caused a whole other set of problems.

When I was sure he was asleep, I retrieved the iPad from under the bed and opened the Kindle app to read some of my novel. Within a few pages, predictably, my restless legs drove me into the living room, where I could pace, still reading. There was just enough mess-free floor space to make it about three small steps, so I switched to a march-in-place move, periodically shaking out my legs. My mind wandered to Christmas, and I grabbed a pen to write the letter "S" on my hand, hoping it would remind me to pack the scarf I had bought for Leo weeks ago and stashed in a spare purse in my closet. Then, with a flash of panic, I remembered that I'd never placed my online order for the boys' gifts. My shopping cart had been filled for at least a week, yet completing a simple transaction was beyond my bandwidth: This was far more frustrating to me than my lousy sex life. With very few responsibilities other than keeping my kids alive, not being able to tick simple things off my to-do list was an endless source of chagrin.

I closed my novel and switched to Safari, then paid the rush charges to get the Batcave, Buzz and Woody costumes, and some books and puzzles to my parents' house in Ohio by Christmas Eve.

When I checked my e-mail for my order confirmation, I had a rare treat—a message from my sister. Rare because her electronic-communication habits are those of someone twice her age: She checks her e-mail once every two weeks or so and eschews all social media. A treat because she lives in Singapore, and I hardly ever see her or talk to her—and because I adore her completely.

Cassie—

Arrived at Mom and Dad's yesterday. Loopy with jet lag. Baked cinnamon bread with Grandma Margie today— exactly what I needed to get into the Christmas spirit. Now bring me some figgy pudding! Tried to talk her out of this last-Christmas nonsense, to no avail (sniff). Can't wait to see you!!!

> Love you.
> —Sid

Buoyed by her cheer, I popped an Ambien and went to bed happy after all, anticipating a reunion with my dear sister.

CHAPTER TWO

Sid and I had taken to calling it "the last Christmas" because Grandpa Joe and Grandma Margie announced that they were done hosting. They wanted their children to start taking turns holding Christmas Eve. It was getting to be too much work for them, they said. My parents and aunts and uncles had taken the news in stride, but Sid and I were in mourning; Christmas as we knew it was over.

To us, Christmas *was* Joe and Margie. The Old English–soap smell of their house mingling with the aroma of a roasting turkey and all the trimmings, the giant tree in their double-height foyer, the big round coffee table filled with snow globes . . . It's everything a family Christmas should be. Imagining the alternatives—fending off Aunt Faye's three rambunctious Great Danes while listening to Mannheim Steamroller on repeat; anxiously following the boys around Aunt Linda's overheated little ranch house with breakable and expensive Chihuly-esque sculptures on every surface; Mom's and Dad's utter uselessness in the kitchen—had me contemplating a trip to the Bahamas next December.

My sister and I adore Grandpa Joe and Grandma Margie. Sid is only fifteen months older than me, so we have many of the same magical memories of making cookies and paper dolls with Grandma Margie and reading—always reading—with Grandpa Joe. At his feet, we'd listen to anything. Margie's maiden name was Quinn, and my twin sons, Joey and Quinn, are named for her and Grandpa.

Something about being in their home puts everyone on their best behavior. Probably because Joe and Margie are the epitome of good behavior. You'll sometimes catch them at these gatherings, just the two of them, regaling each other with stories that *can't* be new, the other hanging on every word, asking questions, and then finding something kind and witty to say at the close.

Leo and I have been together only five years, but if he starts in on a story I've heard, I'll hold up my hand and go, "Yeah, yeah, I know this one. The dog dies." But whenever I'm around Joe and Margie, I try to behave like they do—with courtesy and old-fashioned grace.

We are big on traditions. The men always get red sweaters from Margie; the women, gloves and socks. We do a choreographed routine to "The Twelve Days of Christmas." This last bit makes you think really hard before bringing that special someone home for the holidays. In fact, it's rumored that my cousin Lizzy was dumped over it. One theory is that this guy took one look at her mom—my aunt Faye—doing her "lords a-leaping" with abandon, caught a glimpse of his future, and headed for the hills. It was beyond corny. But I think it's the corny traditions that separate the interesting families from the boring ones.

One year when Sid and I and our seven cousins were all in our twenties, we started another tradition: boxed wine. Everyone in the cousin generation brought wine, and it had to be in a box. For years, that meant Franzia white zinfandel, which gives the worst morning-after headaches of all wines. But then better wines started coming in boxes, and it became a contest of who could find the fanciest or best or most expensive box of wine. Despite our best efforts, a box per cousin always resulted in a surplus of wine, and the half-empty containers could be found stashed throughout Joe and Margie's house year-round.

So last Christmas, *the* last Christmas, I was hitting the box pretty hard. I was feeling all warm and fuzzy by the time we'd finished "The Twelve Days of Christmas," and then Grandpa Joe announced that he had something he'd like to read to us. This wasn't unusual. He found a way to read aloud at any gathering—usually a Molly Ivins column or a passage from Thurber or Bud Trillin, as we called Calvin (we considered him to be a family friend since Joe and Margie had many years ago been at a dinner party where he was in attendance, and I had passed him on the street in New York a handful of times, even exchanging a nod once or twice). But this time he announced that he'd found a stack of letters from the early days of their marriage, while he was in the coast guard and Grandma Margie was juggling two under two at home, my dad and my aunt Faye. Sid and I exchanged a look that said, *Swoon!* and perched ourselves at Grandpa Joe's feet like a couple of kids, although, of course, we were well into our thirties.

The letters did not disappoint. Grandma Margie wrote about sweet and funny and maddening things the kids were doing, the kind nurse at the hospital who would play with Faye and hold Dad while she dropped off jars of extra breast milk she had expressed for the orphans, and the hard time she was having as a Chicago girl understanding the accents of their new neighbors in Bar Harbor, Maine. Grandpa Joe wrote about the comically loud snoring of his bunkmate on the boat and how his heart leaped when he could see the lighthouse in the harbor, because it meant he would be coming home to her and the kids soon.

Enchanted by the romance of it all, I privately lamented that Leo and I had never once exchanged a letter. Why would we? We'd never been separated for any amount of time, and even if we had, there were half a dozen ways to reach him and get an immediate response. I tried to imagine my eventual progeny being anywhere near as impressed by our quotidian communication. "Get milk," "Coming home soon? May kill the children," and the like. It was a depressing thought and made me long for a simpler time, a time when we might not have been able to text back and forth all day long. I wondered if we'd been missing out on the sort of intimacy that could have come from simply catching up at the end of the day. By the time Leo arrived home from work each day, we'd been in near constant contact. In some ways, it made me feel close to him, always knowing where he was and what he had for lunch. But it also made it easy to spend most of our evenings busy on our respective iPhones.

Later that night, back at Mom and Dad's, Sid and I lounged on the big brown sectional in the basement, listening to old mixtapes on an ancient paint-splattered jam box, the container of Y+B Malbec still on tap at my side. Leo was upstairs putting the twins to bed on the floor of my old room. As extremely active three-year-olds, Quinn and Joey were so exhausted at the end of every day that if you could get them to just stop moving, they were asleep in minutes. It's harder than it sounds. We figured out a maneuver likely used in state-run homes for troubled youths and animal shelters, where you kind of held them and pinned down every extremity at the same time. When you're putting them to bed by yourself, as is often the case, there are a couple of ways to go. With both of them on the floor, I would lie down between them on my stomach, looking like a frog that had splatted on the sidewalk as my left arm and leg restrained Quinn while my right arm and leg covered Joey. Singing—loudly—was the only way to keep them quiet. They each got a request. Quinn usually chose "Tomorrow" from *Annie* and Joey, "Show Me the Way to Go Home," the drinking song from *Jaws*. (Not that they'd ever seen either movie.)

Leo was less flexible than me, so his plan was probably to slip Joey his phone while Quinn wasn't looking to let him flip through pictures and get Quinn to sleep first and then move on to Joey. The songs they requested most from him were "Cripple Creek" and the theme from *Cheers*.

I was starting to feel guilty because he had been up there for nearly an hour. But we had an arrangement: He always did bedtime when we visited my family, and I did it when we visited his. Leo was the youngest of four boys in the Costa clan, so I was usually happy for a break from that frat party, but I knew he was looking forward to catching up with Sid and her son, River, too. They'd been living in Singapore for seven or eight months, and there was little chance we'd see them again before next December. Sid's husband of two years, Adrian, hadn't come with her and the kids. He had meetings, she told me.

"On Christmas?" I asked.

"Yeah. His meetings are in Jakarta. Unfortunately, they don't stop everything for Christmas in a Muslim country," she explained.

Sid's son, River, who was seventeen, was watching *A Christmas Story* upstairs with my dad. Lulu, who was eight months old, slept peacefully attached to Sid's breast. Mom was in her room fast asleep.

"Ugh! Cass! How beautiful were those letters?" Sid said. "It kills me that Lulu will never really get to experience Christmas at Joe and Margie's."

"Just Like Heaven" by the Cure was the next song on the tape that Emily Van Wey had made for me when I got my driver's license.

Instead of acknowledging what she said, I sang along and absent-mindedly scrolled through Facebook on my iPhone.

"What are you always doing on that phone?" she said. I wished I had been scanning the headlines on CNN or even playing Tetris, but I let her peer over my shoulder at my Facebook feed of "Happy Holidays" status updates.

Suddenly she gave a little snort, and then, because Lulu was still sleeping on her, whispered, "You're Facebook friends with Tommy Saronto?"

"I'm Facebook friends with half the people we went to elementary school with and pretty much everyone we went to high school with," I said.

"Oh my God, he has five kids?"

"Yep. Clara, Ava, Ella, Will, and Tommy Jr." I felt a little embarrassed that I knew my sister's eighth-grade boyfriend's kids' names.

But she had moved on. "Whoa, look at Tara Lockshin."

"Yeah. Those boobs are new."

"She's so tan. Where does she live?"

"Over near Bowman Mall."

"How do you know all of this?" Sid looked genuinely shocked.

"I don't know. It just kind of seeps in. I mean, when I need a break from the kids, I scroll through Facebook and, you know . . ." I trailed off, hoping to move on. Our quality time was turning into a junior high school reunion, and I didn't want to share my sister with all of these people.

But Sid—dinosaur that she was, without a Facebook account or even an idea of what Twitter or Instagram or Pinterest were—was thoroughly entertained by my knowledge of these people's lives. To her, *I* was the novelty act. She turned it into a game, and I, being quite tipsy, played along.

"All right. Hannah Canary. Go."

"Radiologist. Daughter named Devina. Loves Jesus."

"Correct," she said in a game-show-host voice, scrolling down. "Becky Applebee."

"She's on the Colorado Springs city council. Married to an architect. Has triplets. One of them is . . . um . . . diabetic!" I shouted a little too triumphantly.

I nailed a few more, and then Sid said, "Okay, Cassie. You are starting to scare me. This is not healthy."

"Oh, everyone does it. You're, like, the only one who's not on Facebook."

"Well, according to River, Facebook is for old people . . . Oh dear, what happened to Jamie Walton?"

"No idea. He was such a sweet little boy."

Sid is about three notches kinder than me, and around her I sometimes rein in my darker humor. But I could have shared some real zingers on the topic of Jamie Walton, our childhood next-door neighbor, whose profile picture was him, shirtless, draped in ammo.

Actually, Sid and I shared the same basic outlook on many things, but we differed in demeanor so much that we could say the same exact thing to a person and leave them with wildly different impressions. The two summers we waited tables together at Don Pablo's Mexican Restaurant really brought those differences into focus. I turned out to have a real gift for it—multitasking, food and drink, and pleasing people being among my strong suits. But Sid's other gifts meant that she made more in tips every night. I would be killing it in my section, turning table after table of satisfied diner, and look over to see her squatting down next to a booth, chatting away like she was out with old friends while the other tables in her section sat with empty chip baskets or margarita glasses. I tried to cover for her, refilling waters or salsas and running her food as often as I could. But any frustration her customers were feeling evaporated as soon as she returned her attention to them. The way she always touches you when she talks to you or looks you right in the eye and smiles like you're sharing a secret—those things turned out to be worth about sixty extra bucks a night.

Handing me back my phone, she said the thing that got me: "You probably know more about these strangers than you know about me."

"That's not true!" I immediately shot back while simultaneously wondering if she was right. "Hey, if you're feeling left out, just get yourself on Facebook."

"Nah," she said, gazing down at Lulu. "It's not my thing."

I felt annoyed with myself for not being cool enough to be above the whole thing and blurted out, "I can't stop looking at it! I don't like to get behind. It's like a sickness."

She just giggled.

Then, in an effort to get her to see my side of things, I tried, "But occasionally there is a little gem . . . like . . ." I scrolled through my news feed, looking for something witty or astute with which to impress her, but all I found were generic holiday wishes and photos of kids I didn't know.

"Oh, never mind," I said, tossing my phone onto the table.

In my defense, it had been a rough year. After months of layoffs and salary reductions, the magazine where I'd worked for seven years had finally folded just before the holidays the year before. Leo and I had decided that with the magazine industry the way it was, and with child-care costs the way they were, I'd stay home with the boys, just until the economy recovered. I figured I could pick up freelance writing assignments to keep myself in the game and bring in some money and, eventually, find another job. But I hadn't so much as sent a single work-related e-mail, attended a networking event, or even updated my LinkedIn profile since the day late last year I brought home that cardboard box of desk accoutrements. Likewise, the urban planning, architecture, and real estate news that used to occupy much of my headspace went completely disregarded. Since my Twitter identity was so connected to my job as managing editor of *City Green* magazine, I gave that up too. But Facebook was still there for me, a sort of bridge between my old and new lives.

Without my commute time to read the *Times*, I rarely knew what was going on in the world. Even our *New York One* time in the morning had given way to *Sesame Street*. Before I knew it, Facebook and the odd *Daily Show* became my main sources of news.

On the occasion that I did catch a few minutes of real news, there was hardly any context for me, and so I became uninterested. After a while, the only world events that resonated with me were unspeakable tragedies (like school shootings or child abductions), celebrity marriages or divorces, and weather phenomena.

I could foresee a future in which my role as a full-time mother contextualized the world, where topics like poverty, education, food, and gun control could be made more real when viewed through my mom eyes. But despite my substantial efforts to land this job, I'd undertaken my occupation as a full-time mother somewhat reluctantly and couldn't quite bring myself to rally around the mommy causes du jour.

So maybe I got a little carried away, but Facebook was the one thing I found that distracted me from my daily grind just enough to keep me sane.

Lulu stirred, and Sid stood up and started swaying with her to "Here's Where the Story Ends" by the Sundays, which, because our last name was Sunday, was on every high school mixtape anyone ever made for us. I sipped my wine and stared at my sister, thinking that it was like we were the same person but she had been dipped in some kind of effervescent fluid.

Lulu was sleeping by the end of the song, and Sid carefully lowered her next to me on the musty couch. When she looked up and met my eyes, she wore a satisfied grin, like she had just figured something out. Then she said—slowly, definitively—"I've got it. Let's be pen pals."

It wasn't really a question, but she perched herself on the edge of the couch next to me, awaiting an answer. Having continued to imbibe at a steady clip since we'd come down to the basement, I was drunk enough that I had to close an eye to see just one of her. She handed me her glass of water, taking my wine for herself now, and I drank the water as she laid out the plan she'd formulated during the Sundays song.

"It's perfect. It's been impossible to talk on the phone with me in Singapore. Let's not even e-mail. Just the letters. Maybe when we're old we'll read some out loud to our grandkids—how cool would that be?" Switching to a singsong voice, then, "I think we have a new tra-di-tion."

Sid is like a female Bill Clinton. I say that with the authority of someone who once met him. One of the things about growing up in Ohio is that you have plenty of opportunities to meet presidential candidates. He was jogging with his Secret Service guys at the park where Sid and I walked our neighbor's dog for twenty dollars every Saturday morning. The dog, a golden retriever named Thumper, led us over to a small mutt among a cluster of people taking pictures. We knew he was there, because we'd had to go through a security checkpoint on our way into the park, but we weren't expecting to have an impromptu chat with him. Yet suddenly, there he was, leaning down and patting Thumper's head and saying something about him being a "beautiful animal," cameras clicking all around us. I can't remember much about anything else he said, but I do remember feeling like we were friends—like he'd be all, "Of course I do! How have you been?" if I ever called him up and said, "Remember me from the park outside of Columbus, Ohio? I had the golden retriever?" I felt he saw me— really saw me, even though Sid was standing right next to me, which typically rendered me invisible—and I wanted to say the right thing to let him know I was cool. He said something about "young people" being our country's most important asset, and he nodded right at me, like *I* was our country's most important asset. I felt sparkly and impor- tant for days afterward.

Sid has a similar effect on people. I've seen it hundreds of times. When people were around her, you could feel them yearning to lock in the friendship. There was this photo booth at the mall, and in middle school, if anyone was within forty feet of Sid and that booth, they would persuade her to go get pictures taken together, so they could tape the strip of black-and-white images up in their locker or on their mirror at home as proof of their association.

In high school, her turns of phrase and affectations became part of the common vernacular. She used to do this thing when someone paid her a compliment, where she'd kind of comically, kind of sweetly, kind of ironically say, "Ooooh, kitten," and suddenly every- one was saying, "Oooh, kitten," all the time.

People assumed I was jealous of her, or that I felt inferior, and I suppose in some ways I did, but it did little to affect my feelings toward Sid. When people would patronizingly suggest this as a foregone conclusion of me being me and her being her, I would direct any negative feelings at them, not at my sister.

Through it all, Sid and I were always best friends. We laughed over nonsense and had deep conversations about life. We fantasized about the future—what kind of men we'd marry, how many kids we'd have, where we'd live (next door to each other, with a circular connecting driveway). More accurately, I fantasized about the future for both of us, narrating detailed plans while she humored me, occasionally interjecting that she didn't want a blueprint for her life, that she hoped her future held things that couldn't possibly be imagined by a thirteen-year-old.

"Okay," I said to her. "I'll write to you," and then I rested my head against the back of the couch and closed my eyes.

CHAPTER THREE

B y the time I got back to New York, I already had a letter. It stuck out like a sore thumb among the catalogs and junk waiting for me in my little mailbox. I tore it open immediately, thinking, *So we're really doing this.* And that's exactly what the letter said:

We're Really Doing This!! No backing out!! xoxo

—Sid

My guess was that she had penned it Christmas Eve night after I'd passed out on the couch, since it was written in a faded purple Magic Marker on a torn-out page of notebook paper, both items easily found in Mom and Dad's basement.

Sid's loopy and childlike writing always made me feel tender toward her. Soft and wide and squishy, it evoked Mylar balloons, cookie cakes, and boy-band crushes. Dumb girl handwriting. It's okay; I can say this because Sid is not dumb. She was a National

Merit Scholar and has never in her life been on the losing team in a game of Trivial Pursuit. She does possess a certain innocence that no amount of intelligence or hard knocks will erode; that is what I see when I look at her bubbly scrawl.

That's all it took to catapult me from lukewarm to enthusiastic about our experiment in communication. I wanted to run inside and write to her that, yes, I was on board. We *were* really doing this. But I knew it would be hours before I could grab a second alone. Instead, I wrangled the twins up the stairs to our second-floor walk-up while Leo returned the rental car to the lot around the corner. Our mountain of luggage sat inside the foyer of our building. Leo would take the car seats to our basement storage locker and bring the luggage up after he returned the car. Our neighborhood and building were relatively safe, but leaving all of this loot in the hallway was still a risk and just one of the many inconveniences we suffered for the privilege of living in Manhattan's West Village.

When I found out I was having twins, one of my first instincts was to panic about whether we'd have to move from our beloved apartment. Leo thought yes. I convinced him that we could stay. "Much larger families live in much smaller spaces in other parts of the world," I remember saying, feeling smugly proud of my worldly outlook—picturing families of seven on the African plain huddled in a grass hut and how we'd be more like them than a family of four living in a McMansion in, say, suburban Houston. Or how every story I can remember reading in this Immigrant Women's literature course in college seemed to mention there being only one bed for the entire family. We weren't like ordinary Americans, needing their ridiculously large houses, raping the earth with fertilized lawns and central air. No, we would take only what we needed. We were New

Yorkers, I told him; we could handle this. How evolved, how drunk on my own superior lifestyle I felt.

I regret it at least four or five times a day. Say, for example, when I'm coming home with the boys and the dinner and the dry cleaning, and Quinn has a stage-five meltdown on the front stoop because I again refused to patronize the Mister Softee ice cream truck that followed us home from the park like a fucking stalker. (I'm sorry, but that Mister Softee driver has caused more family strife than a Vegas bachelor party.) And then I forget I'd promised Joey that he'd be the one to stick the magnetic key fob into the sensor on the outside door, and *his* meltdown begins. It wouldn't be out of the ordinary for the general angst of the moment to be escalated by one of the boys pooping in their pants or falling down and beginning to bleed. In these situations, I think about how I've made my life so much more difficult than it needs to be. I surmise that I'd be a happier, calmer, and better-groomed person if I lived in one of those suburban McMansions where the boys had space to run around and I had a kitchen with room for more than two days' worth of food and the counter space and appliances required to prepare it.

Add to that the publicness of it all. Can no moment of childhood ugliness happen in private? Why is it that some meticulously dressed gay man who lives in my building—one of the same guys I used to chat with about politics and restaurants while doing laundry or sorting recycling—seems to appear at the most shameful mommy moments, wincing past me, no doubt silently congratulating himself on the bullet he dodged by not having easy access to an ovary, and making me feel like a pox on our perfect neighborhood. *Don't you remember? I'm one of you!* I want to yell. Or, *I almost didn't have kids! I didn't know it was going to be so hard!*

But there's no "almost" about twin three-year-old boys, no blending in or quick and quiet entries. My only chance at getting them into the building smoothly is if one of Mrs. Tannenbaum's white pugs— the friendly one, hopefully—is hanging around the first-floor hallway. If the boys made enough noise, Mrs. T. would appear with a small dog biscuit and break it in two for them to give to Mitzi. "Thank you," I'd say to her as if she'd just fortified me for the long journey ahead. It's one flight—eighteen steps with a landing halfway—and we're home. It's not unusual for it to take fifteen minutes.

The apartment itself is lovely. The perfect place if you are childless, or maybe if you have anything other than twin boys who are between the ages of zero and three. It's technically a one-bedroom with a study, which was our combination closet and office until we turned it into the boys' room. The whole place is eight hundred square feet—about the size of the back porch in the house I grew up in.

During my pregnancy, I nested like some kind of crazed Martha Stewart protégée, intent on delivering on the promises made in my hard-fought campaign to keep the apartment. Determined to be right about how easy and wonderful life in our little apartment would be, I transformed our abode into the ultimate small but cleverly designed family home. It was even featured on ApartmentTherapy. com as "Cassie & Leo's Dreamy Oasis." Our dovel gray walls and white Eames rocker, the chandelier and half-sized travel cribs we painted the same midnight blue, handsomely awaited the arrival of their tenants, who were markedly less impressed than the dozens of ApartmentTherapy readers, who commented on our brilliant storage solutions and sophisticated color palette.

There are some upsides to living in our tiny apartment, including needing only twenty minutes and five or six baby wipes to clean it. But when I see my boys slithering off our supertall bed, running four steps to the sofa, jumping on that, then repeating the loop over and over, I can't help but think of a pair of puppies forced to live in a small pen.

Leo grew up with a bunch of brothers, but I only had my sister. My earliest memories of playing include coloring and dressing up dolls, and I guess I pictured the boys doing slightly more masculine versions of that. I did not foresee constant wrestling or the compulsion to run and jump and knock things over that is programmed into their DNA.

When I was pregnant, the market was booming and we could have sold our place for a nice profit. Now we'd have to take a loss to sell it, so I didn't feel like it was worth it to admit to Leo I was wrong about staying, to let on how frustrating I found my day-to-day life and that I held the apartment responsible.

Still, I loved our street. Someone once told me that Morton Street is the most photographed street in New York. I have no idea if that's true, but at certain times of day, it is breathtaking. In a city of straight lines and rectangles, Morton is one of the few with a bend, which allows the street to reveal itself slowly. With its low trees and stately town houses, it's quintessential West Village. Also, it's magically quiet. The crowds of *Sex and the City* tourists that can ruin Charles or Perry streets on a Saturday morning seem worlds away, though they are only a few blocks over.

It seemed unfair—impossible, even—that these two things I loved so much—my kids and my apartment—didn't go together at all. I wanted to sit them all down and say, "Can't you all just try to get along, for my sake?"

Upstairs, I stuck Sid's letter into a book under my bed and

helped the boys negotiate the bathroom. I didn't need to open my refrigerator to know that we had nothing to eat. Still, I was poking through its contents in search of the source of an awful stench when Leo returned from his second trip up the stairs with our luggage.

"Blech. This has got to go," I said, plunking the loosely wrapped morsel of soft stinky cheese into the trash and tying it up.

"Fair enough," he said, grabbing the trash from me. "Hudson?"

"Yeah, let's go. I'm starved," I said, and began herding the boys back out the door.

The Hudson Diner wasn't known for its food, but it was right around the corner and never crowded, so we could usually get a big booth by the window. There was something about that place that had a calming effect on the boys. Maybe it was the smell of gravy, the dim orange fluorescent lighting, the geriatric crowd, or the giant pile of individually wrapped saltine crackers the humorless waitress always plunked in front of them as soon as we arrived, but this was the only restaurant where we could eat an entire meal and not have to apologize to a half-dozen different people on the way out.

While the boys munched on saltines, I took out a pack of baby wipes and asked Joey if I could give his car a wash. He never went anywhere without clutching a little matchbox car. Sometimes I worried that his left hand would be permanently deformed into a little claw, and at night while he slept I'd pry his sweet little fingers away from the silver vehicle and massage his palm.

With the car scrubbed, I reached across the table and wiped the boys' hands clean one by one while Leo set up a windy sugar packet racetrack on the table. I cleaned my phone with a new wipe and then scrolled through Christmas pictures. "Hey, Joey, nice camera work," I said when I got to the million shots he'd snapped at Joe and Margie's. "Oh, bud, I love this one!" It was a shot of Sid and me sitting on the sofa, my head resting on her shoulder and both of us beaming in the completely unguarded way you do when a child asks you to smile. I posted it to Facebook and captioned it, "Good to be home but missing this gorgeous gal already."

It was such a nice shot that I cropped it and brightened it and made it my profile picture. By the time the food arrived, I'd accumulated forty-some likes and nearly as many comments from old friends who hadn't seen Sid in many years—virtually or otherwise.

I had to put my phone away when Joey spilled his water, and I spent the rest of dinner preoccupied by the logistics of getting letters from here to Singapore. How long would it take? What kind of stamps would I need? Oh crap, would I have to go to the post office? That in itself could be a deal breaker.

That night, after the boys were in bed, I got out the stepladder and rifled through the tiny cupboard above the refrigerator. Behind a ziplock bag containing our tax returns from the last five years, I found the dust-coated shoe box of old postcards, thank-you notes, and the set of yellowing monogrammed stationery Mom gave me when I graduated college.

Leo turned on the TV and lay on the floor groaning about his back being sore from sitting in the car all day. As the IT director for a chain of gyms, he spends his days crisscrossing Manhattan on his bike to fix one computer issue or another at the gym's eight different locations, so sitting for long periods was unusual for him.

I halfheartedly offered a back rub and surveyed the dozen or so dull pencils and freebie pens jammed into the jar on the desk in the foyer. The pencil jar was like a microcosm of my wardrobe, I thought: overstuffed with uninspiring items, most of them with no shot of being chosen.

Selfishly relieved that Leo responded, "That's all right," to my offer, I settled in on the sofa, using a fat September *Vogue* as my lap desk, a clicker pen from a Realtor in Pennsylvania in hand, and froze. I couldn't think of how to begin. I'd withdrawn only a single sheet of stationery and an envelope from the box, so I had to get this right if I didn't want to get out the stepladder again. But even without the logistical concerns, I just didn't know what to *say*. If asked, I would definitely have described Sid and me as close, but that moment of paralysis brought home the reality that many years had passed since we'd exchanged real intimacies. She was right, I thought, with a wave of sadness: I did know more about those people on Facebook than I did about her.

I promised myself that that was going to change this year. My letter had to be a good kickoff. I didn't want to set the tone for a year of vague updates and pleasantries. I wanted this thing to be real and meaningful.

But first, an important thing to know about Sid: She was nineteen and single when she had River. I'll tell you the story because having an unplanned baby at that age really changes a person.

It was the summer of 1994, and I had just graduated from high school. Sid was home from her first year at Ohio University, where I was to join her in the fall. She had declared a perfectly Sid-like double major in biology and poetry and thrown herself wholeheartedly into the pervasive counterculture in Athens, Ohio: that of the latter-day hippie.

In mid-June, Gretchen Steele and I tagged along with Sid and her boyfriend, Kenny Fisher, to a Grateful Dead show at Buckeye Lake in Columbus. Gretchen and I were not Dead fans—we listened to 311 and Sublime and the Red Hot Chili Peppers. But it sounded like a fun way to spend a summer weekend, and I'd do anything to hang out with Sid.

To people in Sid's old crowd, you just have to say Buckeye Lake '94, and they know that it was pouring rain and that the band did a whole set of rain songs and an unending jam that made me wish I had split that tab of LSD with Sid, so I didn't have to stand there swaying like a moron for twenty minutes while everyone around me went into some kind of reverential trance. At some point during the nine-hour preshow party in the fields around the stage, Sid and Kenny disappeared into his tent and accidentally made a baby.

Kenny sold marijuana and nitrous oxide balloons out of the back of his van. This makes him sound like a real loser, but forget everything you may have heard about drug dealers or single guys with conversion vans. Kenny was kind and funny and smart—at least that's how he seemed to my seventeen-year-old self. He was huge— six foot four and muscular except for his soft beer belly. He wore loose-fitting tank tops and board shorts, and had an animal skull tattooed on his tanned biceps. With his wraparound reflective sunglasses, fanny pack (essentially a drug dealer's briefcase), and New Balance running shoes, he affected a sort of trend-resistant, devil-may-care attitude. Again, he sounds awful on paper, but in the alternate universe of the jam-band circuit, he was definitely the "cool guy." Something about his scratchy deep voice, bright blue eyes, sunburned face, dazzling smile, and infectious laugh drew people to him. Sid and Kenny were kind of this power couple in that whole world. Gorgeous and uninhibited, their non-dreadlocked hair and pleasant smell set them apart from many of their peers.

Have I mentioned yet that Sid is a beauty? I know that's what everyone wants to know: what we look like. We look a lot alike— thin, average height, honey-colored hair, olive skin, dark eyes, big bright smiles—except she is strikingly beautiful in the way of movie stars and wealthy socialites and I am just barely above average in the way of plain girls everywhere. Our mom is part Native American and our dad is half Greek, so we looked vaguely exotic among the blondes and redheads of our childhood. And while our features are mostly the same, Sid's were put together just right. It's like she was carefully molded by an artist and I was the knockoff, hastily put together in a sweatshop to look like her. At certain angles and in some pictures, we look nearly identical. But on second glance, you notice that my eyebrows hover where hers lift, my nose hooks where hers dips, my skin blotches where hers glows, and my teeth suffice where hers dazzle.

On the upside, I am extremely photogenic. But every time someone tells me this, what I hear is, "You look much better in photos." Or, "It's disappointing that you don't look more like your sister." It's probably for the best I'd never tried online dating. If I'm being honest, it's part of the reason I was such a big Facebooker. As long as I never actually run into any of my ex-boyfriends, they are going to think they really missed out.

Being the less attractive sister, and I suppose a tad superficial, I spent a lot of time in my formative years thinking about physical beauty—what constitutes it, what it makes possible, how it influences one's personality. I've determined that the hair-skin-teeth trifecta is the most important of all. If you have that covered, you can have a big nose or a weak chin or small eyes (but not all of those, obviously!) and still be considered beautiful. This is the kind of deep stuff I thought about endlessly between the ages of about fifteen and nineteen.

At any rate, despite Sid's considerable charms, a baby turned out to be Kenny's deal breaker, and shortly after she declared she was going to have it, Kenny was gone. I probably don't need to tell you that Sid had never been rejected on any level prior to this point, so this was new territory for her. She went from golden child with the world as her oyster to heartbroken virtually overnight.

Seeing Sid in this new light came as a blow to everyone. I was as surprised as anyone when she decided to go through with the pregnancy. I guess those annual baby funerals that our favorite teacher in elementary school held on the anniversary of *Roe v. Wade* had an effect on her. Looking back, I cannot believe that my liberal-voting parents let us sit through that macabre production. Or that they let me wear that "tiny footprints" pin that I bought from Mrs. H for twelve dollars. Or that I had an eighth-grade teacher who sold dead-baby-themed jewelry to her students.

After the initial shock wore off, Mom and Dad did their best to act supportive and positive, but it was hard not to detect their disappointment that Sid's promising future appeared to be caving in. To be honest, I was devastated at first. *What about my plans for us?* I selfishly wondered. She was supposed to take me under her wing, to help me make friends, to be my roommate when I moved off campus, to backpack across Europe with me after college. I wanted to scream at my parents: "This is what you get for sending us to twelve years of Catholic school. Some of that stuff stuck!"

I went off to college while Sid was in her first trimester, barfing and crying all day. Her pregnancy continued in much the same way; she was basically a puffy and weepy mess for nine months. I came home a few weekends to spend time with her, and nobody in our open-minded family quite knew how to talk about it—or how to interact with a Sid who wasn't the shining sun around which we all orbited.

Eventually, I came to find comfort in Sid's lot. I'd read too many novels in which the only truly good character, the one who is beloved and respected by everyone, dies. Based on this, at some point during our preteen years, I'd developed an irrational fear that my sister would perish in a car accident or at the hands of a serial killer or of a rare disease or natural disaster. As it was, conversations about her could be downright eulogistic: *Kind to everyone. A beautiful person—inside and out. And so humble!* I harbored this secret fear for years, and in church, after Communion, I would actually kneel down and pray to God to keep my sister alive.

But her pregnancy was a major setback, and one that made her less mythical in my eyes. I stopped worrying so much about her then.

As soon as River was born, Mom and Dad and Joe and Margie promptly turned to mush, found their words, and couldn't stop talking about it, which was now a *him*. Sid, too, took one look at her new son and knew in her hippie heart that becoming River's mom at this moment in her life was her destiny. She went at mothering him with her trademark gusto. He had a charmed baby- and toddlerhood with an incredible support system, even if Kenny was never heard from again. Sid went back to school—premed—at the state school a half mile from our parents' house, where she and River lived until she became a certified nurse-midwife five years later.

New York
Jan 2

Dear Sid,

Happy New Year! I hope you guys had a smooth flight back and the jet lag isn't too bad. It was great to spend Christmas with you. I've been fantasizing about coming to visit you in Singapore. Alas, I don't think it's in the budget for us anytime soon.

But maybe if I start saving now, we can do Christmas there next year. Hey, you were right about this letter-writing thing. It is going to be fun. I can't tell you how thrilled I was to see something from you in my mailbox. What a treat!

I want to kick off these letters in the spirit of openness. I want us to really know each other again—like when we were teenagers. I've been racking my brain for a fitting way to begin, and the only thing I can think of is a truly embarrassing confession. It's really stupid, but I want to make a gesture of honesty to nudge us a little closer to the time in our lives when there were no secrets. Right about the time River was born, I got arrested for shoplifting in Athens. It had become a habit of mine. I started with books. Incensed that my Psychology 101 book cost $125, I slipped it into my bag and walked out. I couldn't believe how easy it was, and found it perversely thrilling. I moved on to the odd shirt or candle, becoming bolder and bolder with each success. A few times, I reached behind counters for sunglasses or jewelry. After about six months, I was caught. As I was leaving the bookstore, a security guard stopped me and asked to check my bag. Well, there were two textbooks, a planner, some pens, and a T-shirt in there. Oh my God, it was so humiliating. There were like a dozen people there who saw what was going on. It hurts me— physically hurts me—to think of it now. I called home from the police station, and Dad drove down and bailed me out. I went to court and had to pay thousands of dollars (borrowed from Mom and Dad) and do community service for a year and join this support group. I still have no idea what I was thinking. I may have been depressed . . . This is going to sound like

I'm blaming you, but please know that I'm not: When you got pregnant, it was like you suddenly dropped out of my life. I was so sad. I think the whole klepto thing was some sort of coping technique or distraction or simply a sign that I was going a bit crazy without you. What I should have done was made an effort to maintain our relationship then, instead of escaping into my ridiculous little crime spree, but good choices have never been my forte.

Okay, there. I did it. I'm mortified (even Leo doesn't know about this!) but I wanted to reveal something real and honest and hard to get things rolling. I promise to lighten up from here on out, and try to bring you rainbows and sunshine more often than not.

Love,
Cassie

The next day when I went to mail it, I got to the mailbox and something stopped me. When I send an even vaguely important e-mail, I'll go back and read it two or three times to make sure I didn't say anything stupid. Yet here I was about to send this massively personal letter, and I'd never be able to see it again. What if it got lost in the mail?

Instead of dropping it in the box, I put it back in my bag. I considered typing it out and saving it, but that seemed silly. Plus, that would tempt me to then send it by e-mail, and the thought sullied the delicious vision I had of the piles of handwritten letters accumulating over the year. I thought about taking a picture of it, but a bunch of photos of partial letters on my phone didn't appeal.

So I walked with the boys to the OfficeMax on Sixth Avenue and bought a scanner. The project, from making the purchase to getting the thing set up, took most of the day and all of my patience. But in the end I had a system to assure every letter Sid and I exchanged would be saved for posterity.

That night after bath time—letter scanned, saved, and re-enveloped—I let Quinn come downstairs with me while Joey played with Leo. There was a mailbox right on the corner outside of the Henrietta Hudson, our neighborhood lesbian bar. Its proprietor, Kim, was our downstairs neighbor. We had an unspoken agreement that I wouldn't complain about the noise from her bar or the patrons we sometimes found canoodling in the building's foyer, and she wouldn't complain about the running and stomping and screaming coming from our apartment at what must seem to a bar owner ungodly hours of the morning. I'd heard horror stories about angry downstairs neighbors from my apartment-dwelling friends with kids—heavy carpet; no running or jumping indoors; eviction threats from co-op boards—so Kim was basically the perfect neighbor for us.

"Would you like to drop the letter in?" I asked.

He held out his hand. "Yes."

I hesitated for a second. *Maybe I shouldn't send it. Maybe I should run upstairs and write a regular letter containing no shocking confessions. Maybe I should rewrite it. If it were an e-mail, I would have surely rewritten it several times.*

"Mama? Come on," Quinn said.

I brushed the dark hair away from his big brown eyes and kissed him on the forehead before handing him the letter. He pulled the box open and stood on his tiptoes to peek inside. To give him a better view, I hoisted him onto my knee.

"Huh?" he said, clearly disappointed that the envelope was just sitting there on a tray—I think he imagined peering down into a pile of letters and packages. I explained how the box works and he slowly pushed the handle shut, pressing the bridge of his nose to the lid so he could watch the letter as long as possible. As soon as he closed the lid, he quickly opened it again and gasped at the empty tray.

He looked at me, wide-eyed.

"I know, right! That letter is going to go on a truck to the post office and then on an airplane to the post office in Singapore, and then to Aunt Sid's house."

Singapore
January 2

Cass—

I'm sitting here in what has to be Singapore's oldest and saddest shopping mall FOR YOU. You have convinced me to get over my moral opposition to hiring a helper and to let you live vicariously through me. What was it you said at Christmas? That me not taking advantage of this perk of expat living was a slap in the face to people like you, who would kill for that chance? Well, far be it from me to slap you in the face—literally or figuratively. Plus, I wouldn't mind another adult in the house to talk to. (Adrian's in Bangkok again.)

So I'm at this mothball-smelling storefront office looking through a pile of résumés—each with a grainy black-and-white photo, which is weird because the women whose résumés I have are all just milling around in the hallway. It's like a Pantene casting call in here. The hair on these women! It's jet-black and thick and so shiny. Oh, here comes my first interview. To be continued. . . .

Okay, I just met the one I want to hire, and now I'm waiting while Mrs. Lee finishes up the paperwork. I couldn't get anyone to say anything other than "Yes, ma'am," or "No, ma'am," in response to every single question, which means each interview lasted only five minutes. So I gave up on getting an actual answer from anyone and went with my gut. Her name is Rose and she had me at "Good morning, ma'am," because of her dazzling smile. They have all seemed so nervous and afraid, but Rose's nervousness came across in smiles and giggles, and since she's going to be living with us, I figure the more smiles, the better.

She has three children back in the Philippines, and she's been in Singapore only two years. Can you imagine leaving your kids? But that's what they all do. She worked the last two years for a Chinese family. Almost every woman I interviewed is with a Chinese family and hoping to land a Western one. From the sounds of it, the Chinese don't treat their helpers very well. One girl told me that she was given a single chicken a week plus a ration of rice, and that's all she got to eat! I tried to foist a granola bar from my purse on her, but she refused it.

Another welled up with tears. "To work for you would be a dream come true," she said, holding my hand. I almost hired her just to rescue her. Her "sir" requires her to massage him every night, and her cell phone was confiscated for talking on it during "work hours," which are six a.m. till ten p.m. Today was her one day off for the month, so this is her only shot at landing a new job until next month. Can you believe that?

This is all so weird. I feel like I'm adopting a forty-three-year-old. I had to watch a video and take a quiz to make sure I understood that I'm not allowed to beat her or make her climb out of high windows to wash them. It's sickening, and part of me wants nothing to do with it. But once I started on this path I felt like I had to continue. I don't know, maybe I can help in some way. Here comes Rose with all of her worldly possessions in a roller carry-on bag. I think some of them are living in a back room in Mrs. Lee's office.

Love,
Sid

I couldn't enjoy this letter as much as I wanted to. According to the postmark, she'd sent it the day after I sent my letter, so while it would have been impossible for her to have read what I wrote to her, it stung a bit to get no acknowledgment of my confession. It took a while to get used to waiting weeks to hear back from her on something I'd written. Often I'd forget that I'd asked her about something and puzzle over her weeks-later response and have to open the scanned letter to figure out what she was talking about.

When the letter I was waiting for did come, it gave me great relief.

Singapore
January 12

Cassie,

WOW. I was not expecting that. You always were the rebel of the family. But really, it's not so horrifying a crime. I'm more concerned that you mentioned you were depressed and felt like you couldn't come to me anymore. That makes ME sad. I'm sorry you went through that rough patch alone. I would give anything to go back in time and be there for you. Thank you for that honest and real kickoff. I have a good feeling about this year. I feel like I should reciprocate, but alas—or maybe thank goodness—I have no major confessions to offer. When I really think about it, I realize we haven't talked about much else other than the kids or Mom and Dad or Joe and Margie in the past, oh, seventeen years, so there probably is a lot you don't know. But none of it seems important now. You rest easy, little sister. My admiration for you only grows.

—Sid

New York
January 24

Sid,

Thanks for that last letter. I feel good now that you know.

Now, moving along. A helper!!! Woot-woot! (Or is it whoot-whoot?? That's the first time in my life I've written that, but I think it's warranted here.) I want details. This is like mommy porn for me. Send me a letter telling me—slowly—about everything she does for you and also what you are doing while she's doing it (napping? reading a magazine? drinking your own beverage that doesn't contain toddler backwash?). I'm not joking.

Also, that is so messed up re. the way they are treated. I don't get how that's even allowed. Isn't there some kind of union?

I just remembered something. When the boys were about four months old and I had been back at work for a month, I used to watch TV during their two a.m. feed. I got into that show on Showtime with Chloë Sevigny about the Mormon polygamists, and I remember thinking, these people are genius! A few extra wives really come in handy with a house full of kids. It's just good sense. We could have used an extra wife right about then (still could, actually). I would have gladly let her sleep with Leo. God knows I wasn't. I fantasized about it for weeks—not the sex part, but the wife part, the extra set of hands to take care of the babies, cook, clean, all that. Now you have that, minus the husband sharing.

xoxo,
Cassie

———

Singapore
Feb 3

Cassie,

I can't get used to having a person here all the time. Her English is good, but there's still something of a language barrier. I was telling Lulu that I saw a frog earlier, and Rose said, "You like the frog?" And Lulu clapped and smiled. And Rose looked at me and said, "You like I prepare for you, ma'am?"

What? What was she thinking? That I wanted her to go spear a frog from around the koi pond and fry it up for dinner?

And she mops the floor every single day. Which would have been great back before our furniture arrived and Lulu was eating off the floor like a puppy, but now it seems a bit excessive. I tell her to relax, but she's totally uncomfortable unless she's scrubbing or cooking something.

She also keeps propping up Lulu's dolls and teddy bears around the house, which I have mixed feelings about. On one hand, it's funny to walk into the living room and have three teddy bears staring at you from the base of a lamp (and it's sweet that she's taking such care), but on the other hand, no, thanks! I mean, grown-ups live here, too. And just because I don't have the refined New York tastes that you do doesn't mean I'm cool with being surrounded by stuffed animals.

The best part is that sometimes it feels like we live at a hotel—Lulu and I go to the pool, and when we come back, our beds are made and the bathrooms are spotless. Actually, scratch that—the best part is the on-call babysitting. I can go for a run or to a yoga class with no advance planning. I just tell Rose I'm going, and I go. I almost feel awful telling you this, but I even go grocery shopping alone.

I've been letting her cook dinner for us every night, because I'm still so in awe of this whole thing. But I do want to reclaim the cooking at least partially at some point—which is going to be necessary if I don't want my heart to explode. The woman has never met a food she can't drown in vegetable oil. She went through a huge jug of it in one week! Everything—a chicken breast, broccoli, whatever—is basically deep-fried. Last night I showed her how to sauté vegetables without so much oil, but I can tell she feels awkward with me in the kitchen. If I do even the tiniest bit of tidying up, she seems mortified. And you should see her go pale when Adrian goes for the sponge or tries to put his plate in the dishwasher. She will drop what she's doing and sprint toward him, practically yelling, "Sir! I do it, sir!"

We have a guest room in our condo, and I figured she would sleep there. I even got it all ready for her. But she prefers the maid's room in the back of the house. It has its own very small, very basic bathroom (a spigot on the wall and a toilet). Her room does have a window, but the room is so tiny that I had to buy a toddler's bed at Ikea so that it could also fit a dresser. (The toddler bed isn't so bad actually. I curled up on it in the store. Still, it just seems wrong.)

On the bright side, our guest room is now ready for visitors.

Okay—I feel completely obnoxious about this whole thing. But you asked for details. I'm going straight to oxfam.org to set up a regular donation to alleviate my white guilt.

XO,

Sid

I did this only once, but I read that letter aloud to Leo, who hung on my every word.

"And how much do they pay her?"

"Six hundred a month I think is what she told me at Christmas."

"Holy crap. That's less than what we paid our nanny in a week." He was right. When I was working, we paid Wanda, a lovely Dominican woman who doted on the boys and never complained about lugging them up and down the stairs every day, $850 cash every Friday, wiping out almost all of my paycheck.

We spent most of the rest of our evening fantasizing about having a person living in the back of our house, swooping in to help with the kids when we needed her. Since there was no back of our apartment, though, we supposed we could fit a small mattress on the platform we erected for storage that spanned the ceiling from the front door to the bathroom. She (or he!) would have to be a gymnast, we decided, tiny and limber so as to not require anything more than a rope or a little springboard to launch him- or herself back up to their tiny platform. We could ring a bell when we wanted our helper to come down to do some laundry or dishes. She'd cook exotic and nutritious meals on which we would dine with joy and civility around our family table. For the next few days, when one of us was doing the dishes, in what we imagined a Filipino accent to be, the other would start yelling, "Sir! I do it, sir!"

Both of us did Internet searches for jobs in Singapore, e-mailing the other links. It was all we talked about.

Leo came home one night and said, "Let's leave the kids with the helper tonight and go out to dinner."

"Great idea. Now, where is that bell?" I said, looking around in jest. And then we both sighed and stared off into space, imagining the possibility.

"In the old days families would just help each other. According to my mom, her parents never went outside of the family for help," said Leo.

"What are you saying? That we should call your uncle Sal and have him come watch the boys tonight?"

"Yeah, right." Leo laughed. "But seriously, it's kind of sad that families don't do that anymore—don't you think? I mean, everyone trusts total strangers to practically raise their kids. Wanda spent fifty hours a week with these guys, and we found her on Craigslist."

"Wanda rules," I interjected. "Don't knock Wanda." And then I teased Leo about turning into an old man who'd hold up his finger and trill, *In my day* . . . But in the back of my mind, privately, I returned to my old fantasy—now picturing Sid and me living in a huge house with our families, helping each other with the kids and the housework.

It was a fun week for Leo and me, having a playful inside joke. But later, I felt a bit guilty for reading Sid's letter to him. I doubt she would have minded, but I promised myself I wouldn't violate her trust again. There was already something sacred about these missives. They couldn't be forwarded or copied and pasted. I was the owner of a bespoke object, and I held that dear.

CHAPTER FOUR

◈

L eo's mom was coming over, so even though it was freezing, I sent Leo out with the boys to tire them out and pick up bagels and lox. I stayed home to clean the apartment and do some deep breathing exercises while trying to focus on my husband's positive attributes. I had a good enough relationship with my mother-in-law, as long as I wasn't irritated with Leo at the time. But if I was even mildly annoyed with him, a visit from Mary Costa was all it took to send me over the edge.

Of her four boys, Leo was Mary's favorite. I'm not just saying that. She freely admits it; it's even a running joke among the Costa brothers. He'd had some health problems as a child, which cemented their special bond and made him a quiet mama's boy. She doted on him and he on her. At first, his close relationship with his mother was endearing and led me to think of him as a good egg. Of course I'd heard the jokes about watching out for men who had an extra-close relationship with their mother, but I've never trusted people who claimed to hate their parents or not be on speaking terms with a family member. Leo was the opposite, which made him seem extra trustworthy.

Once, when the boys were just a few months old and I was deeply resentful of the amount of time he felt he was entitled to spend on the toilet, we'd had a silly fight about it minutes before Mary arrived. I complained that one bathroom session for him was more time than I'd spent using the toilet, showering, and grooming over the course of a week. His reply was, "I'm not stopping you. Go ahead. The bathroom's right there." I threw up my hands and continued to pick up the apartment. Twenty minutes later, Mary came in carrying a six-pack of Leo's favorite beer, and even though it was only one in the afternoon, he opened one and started drinking it. I was nursing Joey in the chair, and Quinn was on the ground gnawing at his own feet when he began to cry. So Leo, bowels empty, showered, dressed, and rested, put down his Samuel Smith Oatmeal Stout and picked up his own crying infant. Mary nearly threw him a parade.

Meanwhile there's me, still wearing yesterday's clothes, slumped in the corner with a baby at my breast, empty water glass beside me, my irritation building by the second.

I was parched but too proud to ask one of them to refill my glass, so I walked over to the fridge with Joey still attached to my breast and poured myself some water. My passive-aggressive water retrieval went completely unnoticed, and Mary used her baby-talk voice to say to Quinn, "Do you know how lucky you are that this guy is your dad?" Technically, I didn't disagree, but to hear it from Mary at that moment filled me with contempt for my husband. I looked at his freshly shaven face and remembered that I'd always preferred scruffier guys, glanced at his RUN-DMC shirt, and thought, *You haven't listened to them in ten years, you poseur.*

Mary did have a sense of humor, so I could get away with saying, "The man picked up his own baby. Let's not canonize him just yet." She laughed and called me a riot and we moved on. I think she was as confrontation-averse as I was, and while the two of us did genuinely like each other, I believe we could have loved each other, had I been married to any of her sons except the anointed one.

When Mary arrived that day, the boys were, as usual, thrilled. And rightfully so: She always brought candy or gifts—sometimes both, even though she saw them every other week. Today it was candy hearts and Spider-Man chocolates, in honor of Valentine's Day. She also brought a tray of vegetable lasagna, which she set on the countertop right beside my suddenly conspicuously not-home-made (but still delicious) bagel-and-lox spread.

Filling her in on what I regarded as Sid's great fortune at having a helper proved to be a nonstarter conversation-wise. I gushed on and on while she made a feeble attempt to disguise her disapproval for someone who would require full-time help with matters of the home.

New York
Feb 13

Sid—

I love it!! Rose sounds like a hoot! I'm so jealous. I want to move to Singapore now. Not only would I not have to spend every other Saturday morning frantically cleaning my apartment in anticipation of Mary Costa's biweekly visit, but those visits would be MUCH less frequent. A girl can dream . . . Sometimes I think she wishes Leo never met me. I'm sure she would love nothing more than for him to be a bachelor forever, living at home with Mom. She is entertaining, I will say that—almost a caricature of an overbearing mother-in-law. I shouldn't complain—no one gets along with her mother-in-law, right?

What really annoys me is that she always makes me feel like an inferior homemaker (something I don't, in fact, care about being a superior version of until she shows up). She raised four boys with a husband who—from what I've gathered—sat in his chair, watching sports and drinking beer. I imagine her racing about like an enthusiastic hotel manager, aiming to make everyone's stay as pleasant as possible. Leo says the only time he remembers seeing her sit down was in the car.

No chance Joey and Quinn will ever say that about me. Spending all day in the kitchen sounds awful to me. I've never felt as if I were wired for domestic pursuits. I get no satisfaction from cooking, cleaning, or organizing things. I blame the apartment for this—specifically, my kitchen, which is really more of a wet bar.

Eyes closing—must sleep.

Love you.

—Cass

Singapore
Feb 28

Hi, Cassie,

I've never had a mother-in-law, so I couldn't tell you. Adrian doesn't speak to his mother; I'm not entirely sure why. His dad seems like a nice guy, though I've only met him twice.

Remember how close I was with Greg King's family when we dated in high school? His mom would have been a great mother-in-law. We still meet for coffee every once in a while back in Ohio.

Actually, Kenny's mom was cool, too. I didn't know her as well, but she was very sweet. I've often wondered if I should have gotten in touch with her about River. She probably doesn't even know she has a grandson, but it seems wrong since Kenny cut off all ties before he even had a chance to meet River. Thank goodness Joe and Margie were such amazing grandparents. Hopefully he's never missed having two sets.

Meanwhile, having a helper has really shaken up my social calendar. For one, now I've got all these new mom friends inviting me to coffees and teas and lunches and tennis and bunco. (Bunco! What are we, retired?) This is such a different world. I can't keep up, and I don't really care to. So I'm finding myself playing matchmaker with the moms in my orbit. I'll meet a Kiwi who lived in India and I'll introduce her to the British-Indian woman who is planning a summer trip to New Zealand, and make my exit graciously. I'm almost ashamed to admit this, but the more international my friends become, the more I find myself lapsing into stereotypes. The British and the American women are the fanciest—wearing overly thought-out outfits, strategically highlighted hair, and perfect mani-pedis. The Aussies and the Kiwis are mostly unadorned and straightforward. French women, as expected, are chicly dressed, often smoking, and cool in demeanor. I haven't quite figured out the rest. As for me, being the American gal that I am—pedicures have become an every-other-week ritual. I'm afraid I'm turning into a bit of a Stepford

Wife. Needless to say, I'm itching to get up to a little mischief. Let me know if you have any ideas.

When I go to someone's home for a playdate or a coffee or dinner or whatever, we actually sit there across from each other and have a conversation, like in old movies and novels! I'm used to chatting while chopping vegetables or washing dishes, so it's a little strange sitting across from someone you hardly know— more intimate in some ways, but in other ways, less. There's a bond that forms over a sink, where the silences seem natural and the conversation is broken up with practical exchanges about where dishes go or what kind of detergent works best.

A lot of the talk is gossip and salacious stories. Some of them are real doozies. Here's the worst one: Claire Linden's family (Dutch, if you're keeping track) was going to Phuket for a long weekend. Her husband, Stefan, planned to meet them two days later. Claire and the kids go to the airport only to find that their seven p.m. flight is canceled. After booking a flight for the next morning, they return home and find Stefan and two of his colleagues having what she described as a "pool party with seven or eight Thai hookers"!!!!!! (Who knows if they were actually hookers, but that's how the story goes!)

Turns out Stefan is a real piece of work. And by "work" I mean "shit." Do you know what he said to her? He told her, what does she expect—it's like a smorgasbord out here. It sounds made-up, I know. Oh, here's another one. An American family moved to Singapore, into the house of an outgoing American family, and the first family's helper stayed on to work for the next family. The wife and kids were out for the day and the husband is home. The helper finishes her morning cleaning and asks the husband, "What would you like me to do now, sir?" And he says, "Whatever you used to do for Bill, I guess." So what does she do? Takes off her clothes and climbs into his bed! Apparently, he was mortified and shooed her out and made her get dressed. I have no idea if he told his wife or what became of the helper. There are dozens of stories that the old-timers seem to delight in telling newbies like me, just to watch our eyes pop, probably. Everything about this place is bizarre. I've vowed not to become one of those women who sits around and gossips, but with stories like these, it can be hard to resist. Most of the time I find it's easier to hang out with the Filipinas, who are likely having the same conversations, only I can't understand what they're saying, so to me, they're innocent.

Anyway, Rose has four other helpers and their charges over for a playdate. I've got zucchini bread in the oven, so it smells divine right now—reminds me of Joe and Margie's house. (All I need is *Wheel of Fortune* or *Murder, She Wrote* on the TV.) You should see the looks on the helpers' faces when I offer them tea or coffee. But I've gotten a few of them to loosen up around me, and our place is becoming the go-to spot for rainy-day playdates, which is fine by me. I love having a full and busy house. I'm hoping to pick up a little Tagalog. I swear "Burt Bacharach" is a commonly used expression. I will let you know when I figure out what it means.

Gotta go. Love you.

—Sid

PS—Here are a bunch of preposted airmail envelopes. Aren't they cool-looking? I know you're just trying to avoid the post office, but I don't think you need a dozen stamps for every letter.

The airmail envelopes were a godsend. I had been buying books of stamps from the postal truck that occasionally parks itself on Sixth Avenue and University. This sounds idiotic in retrospect, but I would put about ten stamps on every letter and cross my fingers that they were enough to get my letter to Singapore. Eventually, I would have Googled it and figured out the correct postage, but this was working for me, and the boys loved it. I'd let them each affix three stamps, guiding their hands with mine to get them on straight. I always went for the exotic ones: dinosaurs, superheroes, butterflies, whatever they had other than the standard American flag. After their six were on, I added three to five more, depending on how many were left, and then we'd walk to the mailbox. It was a ritual that we all enjoyed, and the boys kept track of whose turn it was to drop the letter in the box. Some nights I quickly wrote a letter to Sid just so the boys and I would have this small errand to accomplish in the morning.

Once in a while we'd run into the postal worker collecting the mail from the box. This was less interesting than you'd think it would be for a couple of three-year-olds, who were invariably disappointed to have someone messing with their routine. I, too, was disconcerted by the lack of care she displayed when ushering the letters from the mailbox into her bin and then to the back of her truck. It was always the same woman, wearing shorts and worker boots with her unbuttoned, too-big uniform shirt over a tight white tank top. Earbuds in and wires dangling, phone clipped to her arm on one of those Nike running accessories, she was often deep in conversation. If things were getting interesting, she'd stop midchore and make an emphatic point, or listen intently, head nodding side to side while humming deeply, the box of letters just sitting there on the sidewalk. It was like seeing your diary lying there for anyone to scoop up and read. So we would wait vigilantly until the bin was in the truck and she was driving away. I silently congratulated myself for buying that scanner every time we stood guard over the mail transfer. At least I would have a copy if one of my letters got lost. They were becoming increasingly precious to me, and I loved reading back through them. I'd cringe to reread an awkward turn of phrase and delight over the clever bits. I also loved the sight of our writing on my screen, which felt artsy and retro in a way that comforted me. Sid would often draw little pictures in the margins, use all caps for emphasis, or write my name in puffy balloon letters. Many of her letters looked like the notes we'd exchanged in high school, a touching reminder that her youthful exuberance and inhibitions were alive and well.

Two weeks later, when Quinn spilled chocolate milk on my open laptop, I felt the way I'd imagined I would if that postal worker ever really did let the mail fall victim to oncoming traffic, vomiting vagrants, runaway dogs, the wind, or any other destructive force that might show up at the corner of Hudson and Morton streets. I decided then that I needed another layer of protection. So that night I went to fishfood.com, the same host we'd used at the magazine for our private internal blog, and selected the basic template. I uploaded the scanned letters, organized them by date, locked the privacy settings, and patted myself on the back for having a plan B for my aging MacBook's hard drive. I thought about how fun it would be to e-mail Sid a link at the end of the year, and spent an hour changing the background color, header fonts, and page organization. I wanted it to look just right—for the sight of it to give me as much joy as the letters themselves did.

I felt important with my computer and my scanner and my process—a frivolous replacement for the career I missed so much. I had control over something, which was incredibly therapeutic. Listening to myself now, it kind of begs the question, why didn't I become a mommy blogger like everyone else? The ironic answer is that I was way too private a person for that.

CHAPTER FIVE

New York
March 12

Sid,

That story about your friend's cheating husband is crazy. If karma is real, that guy is in for some serious trouble of the genital sort.

Oh, I think River is fine with the one set of grandparents—it's pretty common, isn't it? I mean, we hardly knew Mom's parents. At any rate, he turned out fantastic, so you did something right.

Out of the blue I got a message from my old nanny, Wanda, asking if I knew anyone who needed help on Tuesdays because she has that day free. Well, as it turns out, I do. I need help! So I made a financially reckless but mentally essential decision on the spot and promised her four hours every Tuesday morning.

I barely slept on Monday night, imagining what I would do with that free time. Visions of a clean and organized home, pedicured toes, an exercise-toned body, a fridge full of premade meals danced in my head. When she showed up at eight thirty, I practically ran out the door and went and had a coffee by myself and then wandered around the neighborhood. It was one of those perfect New York early-spring days that has people walking around smiling at one another like a bunch of cruise passengers. So when Wanda texted to say they were going to the park, I bolted home and did what most New Yorkers do when the weather changes; I switched out the winter with the summer clothes in storage. I still have half of March and all of April to get through, so this ~~might be~~ is certainly premature (I mean, it could still snow). But I was in the mood, so when it gets cold again, I'll have to make do without my winter layers. I got all of the summer clothes up from my storage locker and realized that my summer wardrobe was either pretwins and too small, unwisely worn through my pregnancy and all stretched out, or just plain ugly. I couldn't find a single item I was excited to wear. So I called Leo and perhaps a tad overdramatically stated my case, and he told me to go ahead and buy some new clothes. (God, I hate having to ask for permission to buy myself clothes.)

Two hours later, the boys and Wanda came home to find me on the floor with my laptop, my ShopBop.com shopping bag overfilled, and surrounded by heaps of unwanted summer clothes. I told Wanda to take as much as she wanted. She took almost all of it, so I had to buy more stuff. I'm a bit sick over putting $3,900 on the credit card—and then I couldn't send poor Wanda on the subway with two hefty bags of clothes, so I gave her $40 extra for cab fare, so there goes our pizza money for tonight!

You'd think I'd be excited about the new wardrobe, but I just feel sad that the most exciting thing that's happened to me in weeks has involved online shopping. I never felt this way when I was working. I was busy and productive, *and* I managed to use the toilet when I needed to and ate a respectable lunch every day. Here, I'm busyish and hardly productive, but the toilet and the lunch things seem like absolute luxuries to me now. At my job, stuff happened. Here, it never feels as if anything happens. I'm just trying to survive each day, and before I know it, a whole season has passed and nothing has changed. And then, of course, I look back at pictures of the boys from just a few months ago and tear up at how much they've grown. (What is it they say . . . kids make the years fly and the days drag?) And then I hate myself for not treasuring these fleeting moments. If being a mom is my job now, I'm not a very good employee. I mean well, but I'm always screwing it up. The other day I caught myself looking at Quinn doing something asinine and thinking, I'm trying to enjoy you. Now be enjoyable, damn it! The thing is, I felt differently about the boys when I was working. I was good at being a working mom. I was efficient and decisive at work (way more so than I was before having kids) and at home, I was present and just "on," you know? At least that's how I remember it, but maybe I'm romanticizing.

Some mornings I lie in bed thinking, I need a change. I can't do this all-day every-day mommy thing anymore. I'll psych myself up to schedule a coffee or a drink with an old work contact, to get around to freelancing, but I never do.

Is it too pathetic to wish for something just a bit thrilling to happen to me? I'm so flipping bored all the time. Do you ever feel like that? Some days I wonder if I'm ever going to feel excited again at the sound of Leo's voice at the end of the day. Honestly, it's hard to imagine a scenario in which I feel anything close to "in love" with my husband. I mean, I am glad to see him, but mostly because as soon as he walks in, I go out for my run (confession: I don't run so much as walk around the neighborhood and look into people's windows at dusk. There's a house on Morton and two on Charles that I've developed a serious obsession with. You should see these chandeliers!).

It's getting late. I should sleep.

Love ya.

—Cassie

⚬⊰⊱⚬

Singapore
March 13

Dear Cassie,

Well, Adrian's job contract extended . . . It was supposed to be two years, but they said they wanted him here indefinitely. I'm not sure how I feel about it. I mean, I do enjoy living here, but part of the reason I like it is because it's temporary. It's like a break from reality . . . My helper, my superrich friends, my weekends in Bali—what's not to love, right? Only it's not home. And I don't know that it ever could be. I don't want Lulu to grow up seeing Mom and Dad only once a year. And River will go to college next year, someplace in the US. I don't want to be on the other side of the world from him. I've asked A. if they might change their mind. But he wants to stay. We're supposed to go to dinner tonight and talk about it. I'll let you know how it goes.

XO,
Sid

⸻⧜⸻

New York
March 24

Sid—

I only have a minute, but re. staying in Singapore indefinitely? No!!! Come back!!! I miss you too much. What happened with your talk??

xoxo, Cassie

⸻⧜⸻

Singapore
March 26

Cassandra Marie—

Are you okay? Tell me you were just having a bad day when you sent that last letter. You do a lot. It just doesn't feel that way when you're with little kids all day. You are their world— don't forget that. It's no small thing. As for the new clothes, just enjoy them! What are you supposed to do, walk around in maternity gear for the rest of your life? Your kids are three.

BTW, I saw those stretched-out old undies of yours in your pile of clothes at Christmas. I really hope at least four hundred of those dollars went toward lingerie, or at least some suitable knickers. (Another perk of my expat life: I get to co-opt all the words I like from the Brits and the Aussies. Coming soon: "keen" for interested in and "pissed" for drunk.)

Sex is a great cure for boredom, you know. Don't tell me that you and Leo are all set in that department because I can tell that you're not. This is something that men understand and a lot of women don't: It's not about quality; it's about quantity. In the spirit of our letter-writing challenge, you should do a sex challenge. Every night for a week, and then see what happens. And if that doesn't cure your boredom and perk up your marriage, join a book club or something. Or write me more letters. Seriously, Cass—the ripple effect is real. One thing changes for the better, and soon everything is looking up.

Big, big hug,
Sid

⸺⟨∞⟩⸺

New York
April 4

Sid,

This may be what rock bottom looks like. The boys are on their second hour of TV, and I have collapsed on the floor in a quietly maniacal cry-laugh at your sex challenge suggestion. I'm sure this isn't what you intended, but God, did it make me feel depressed. Every night for a week? It takes us nearly three months to have sex seven times!

I blame several factors.

1. You. You who got the entire skin-elasticity allotment for our family. Maybe if I didn't have the midsection of a ninety-year-old, I could let my husband see me naked. But I will not! Leo knows something horrible is going on under my clothes and he used to respect that, but now I swear he keeps trying to catch me off guard in the buff.

2. Honestly, I don't even look forward to it. Sex between Leo and me these days seems like more of a hassle than it's worth. There are other factors, of course—but they are totally predictable, and I can't bear to spend the time to write down a bunch of stale-marriage clichés.

Xo,
Cass

———— ⋘⊃∞⊂⋙ ————

Singapore
April 21

Cassie!!!

You're nuts! I hope you are joking. Every time I saw you in a bikini, I would think, damn, why did I quit ballet? Remember Evan Rogers, the football captain and my junior-prom date? He once told me that he thought you had the best body in the whole school. If he hadn't been such a meathead, I might have told you at the time. You are beautiful. And seriously? Your husband hasn't seen you naked in more than three years? Get over yourself! He'll just be happy to see boobs. Trust me. Sorry this is so short. I am running out and just wanted to get this note to you as soon as I read your last one. Will fill you in next time!

Love,

Sid

I'm embarrassed to admit it, but that story about Evan Rogers did give me a little thrill. And the same day the letter arrived, my big box of new clothes finally showed up after two failed delivery attempts, and so did a notice from Little Oaks Preschool: The boys had made their way up the wait list and were being offered two mornings a week, immediately. It was like my birthday and Christmas all rolled into one: a twenty-year-old compliment, a letter from Sid, two spots in a great preschool, and the largest wardrobe upgrade to which I had ever in my whole life treated myself.

The timing was perfect because I'd spent the morning being annoyed with Leo, who had reminded me he would be spending most of the coming weekend in a "boot camp" for turophiles at Murray's Cheese, which meant the boys and I would be on our own, just like every other day. Plus, I knew he'd be bringing home the world's rankest cheese to sit in our refrigerator and smell up the entire apartment. I'd blown up at him about it that morning, so to get those letters and the ShopBop box that day was a welcome distraction. I called Leo right away about the preschool. When we'd put them on the waiting list, I was still working. Leo seemed surprised, but the cheese-boot-camp episode worked in my favor after all, because he didn't dare suggest that since I was at home now, perhaps the boys didn't need to be in school just yet. (In fact, that's exactly what I was thinking, but I was so overjoyed at landing the two spots that I pushed on through those doubts.) Nor did he balk at the astronomical deposit we'd need to pay in the next seventy-two hours, bless him. Instead he commented that it was strange that the school still sent notices via mail, especially with such a tight deadline. But in my world important things came in the mail all the time, so to me it made perfect sense.

"So we can do it, right?" I asked him.

"Do they really need to start now? There are only two months until summer break. Couldn't they just start in September?"

"It's now or never. There are hundreds of people waiting for these two spots."

I told him I'd let Wanda go as soon as she found another family for Tuesdays.

"All right." He sighed. "We might have to eat beans and rice for the rest of the month, but you can drop off a check today."

"Yes! Thanks, hon. Love you."

"Love you, too. Bye, Cass."

But my hands shook as I dropped off the pile of paperwork and the check that afternoon. And I cried like a baby when their first day of school arrived. I waited until I was home, but once there, I curled up on Joey's bed and sobbed into his pillow for a good twenty minutes. Leo, who could tell I was barely holding it together when we'd said our goodbyes to the boys that morning in the light-filled welcome zone, called to check on me.

"They're just growing up so fast," I choked out, the way every mother must on her child's first day of school.

CHAPTER SIX

❦

Every Wednesday my closest mommy friend, Monica Jones, and I take our kids to a playground or a museum or a free music class or something like that. I met Monica in a twins baby group. Hers are Ana and Jonny. We bonded because neither of us was superexcited about being there, and it showed. Our eyes caught each other on a roll after another mom got all verklempt at the "incredible bond she feels with all of us." I was still working at the time, and my need to be out of the house and around other adults wasn't as fierce as it is now. Still, I had forced myself to go since I'd already taken the morning off for the twins' checkup, and it was in the basement of a church that was on my way home from the doctor's office.

I pinned Monica as a potential friend from the second I laid eyes on her. She was beautiful and stylish; her jet-black hair and intricate eye makeup made her seem like some exotic creature among the other haggard, no-time-for-makeup moms. (Never mind that I more closely resembled them than I did Monica, despite the fact I was headed into the office after the playgroup.)

Leo grew up in a big, extended, tight-knit family, so he's most comfortable when he's surrounded by a bunch of people. Me, I'm in my element around beautiful and fabulous people. I think that's why I love New York. Being Sid's sister, I'd grown comfortable in my role as the plain sidekick. So while the others drifted toward their fellow messy and mousy moms, regarding Monica from afar as some freak of motherhood, I went right up to her and introduced myself. *Silly slobs*, I thought. *Don't they know that they should latch onto someone like this any chance they get?* Life is just easier for good-looking people, and if you can align with one, good on you, as Grandma Margie would say. Monica turned out to be warmer and more open than her eye roll suggested. Within minutes, I learned that her husband is an artist who is at home a lot (so that's why she has time for makeup). She lived around the corner from me on Leroy Street, on the first floor of a brownstone next door to the house that served as the facade for *The Cosby Show*. I was immediately eager to see her apartment, and told her as much—as one can do without shame upon learning a fellow New Yorker's address. She invited me and the kids for a playdate that weekend.

We turned out to be kindred spirits, potty-mouthed foils to the overearnest moms around us. Don't get me wrong—we love our kids as much as the next gal, and we want them to have a magical childhood and grow into balanced, kind, and productive members of society. We just think that this is achievable without all the hand-wringing and obsessing over their every transgression.

Monica grew up way up on 116th Street in Spanish Harlem, and then studied fashion design at Parsons, where she met TJ, a painter. They'd lived with three roommates in a sixth-floor walk-up on Avenue D, and then through a friend of a friend of a friend, TJ ended up painting a mural for Liv Tyler's kid's room, and it got into *domino* magazine. Now every parent on UrbanBaby wants one of his murals, which he now charges a fortune for. Monica helps TJ run his business and is also a mommy blogger. About 70 percent of all full-time moms in New York have a blog. Monica's is my favorite. Her posts have titles like "Show Me a Mom Who Brings Sugar-Free Brownies to the Halloween Party, and I'll Show You a Real Asshole." She hosts a weekly caption contest for photos she takes at playgrounds around the city, eyes blacked out like in *Glamour* Don'ts and sends the winner goodies from swag she's always getting. California Baby sent her an enormous basket of products to review. And LeapFrog sent two of those LeapPad things that no one could get two Christmases ago. She is positively wicked when it comes to the more sanctimonious mommy bloggers like my neighbor Jenna, who I'll get to later.

I love Monica because she reminds me of Sid in her confidence and quick laughter and always-on-ness. But where Sid looks first for the good in someone, Monica looks first for the ridiculous or pathetic, and then homes in on it for her own amusement.

Monica's posts were often picked up by *Babble, The Huffington Post,* and other mainstream websites. She even had a following among the hipster, baby-opposed crowd. *Gawker* profiled her with the headline "Our Favorite Breeder." Once, we went to hand-deliver the prize to her photo caption winner and it was this fifty-year-old unshaven guy in a bathrobe, and I'm pretty sure he didn't have kids. His prize was a My Breast Friend nursing pillow, and we roared with laughter, imagining the uses he might find for it. (In fact, I had used my own as a snack tray as often as I'd used it as a nursing aid.)

When I rounded the corner onto Hudson, Monica was already there waiting for us, which was a first. I'm perpetually punctual and she is always late. It felt nice to have someone waiting for me for a change. *So this is how the other half lives,* I thought. In addition, I was feeling refreshed to be out of my black leggings, Frye boots, and oversized V-neck T-shirt combo, and upbeat because of the sunshine and determined daffodils promising warmer days to come. Café tables dotted Hudson Street for the first time since October, and my new striped maxi dress was comfortable and casual and magically skimmed my breasts and hips but not my stomach. If I'd had any money left, I would have ordered three more. I'd even taken forty-five seconds to apply mascara and lip gloss. I felt like making the most of this day.

Monica was always put together. She was never without makeup and a bona fide outfit—and usually overdressed for a day at the playground, if you ask me. Today it was skinny jeans with an expensive-looking sheer white oversized tank through which you could see her salmon-colored lacy bra when her ikat-print scarf moved around. The brown leather moccasin booties were an unusually practical footwear choice for her. Layers of thin gold bangles and intricate eye makeup in shades of peach and gold pulled the whole thing together.

I do always look forward to her outfits. She's one of those people who dresses to reflect her mood, making her fashion choices all the more fun to observe, especially for someone like me, who tends to wear the exact same thing every day. Last week she wore one of those NEW YORK FUCKING CITY T-shirts you see in all the schlocky stores on Bleecker Street and totally pulled it off. And she wore it to the playground—under a jacket, but still. Maybe it's because she can accessorize like nobody's business, or maybe it's because she has a unique brand confidence mixed with defiance that comes with having been born and raised on the island of Manhattan. For the first time ever, I didn't feel like her sloppy sidekick.

We were walking the long way to the park to take advantage of the streets with wider and smoother sidewalks. The kids ate their lunch while we pushed along and did our best to have a conversation. We were on West Eleventh, two blocks from the river, when we were approached by a sheepish young guy in a faded black T-shirt and ripped jeans.

"Hi there. I'm so sorry," he said. "Could I get you to cross the street? We're just doing a photo shoot here."

"No," said Monica. "That's not happening."

I was typically accommodating in these situations—there were always film crews around, and they had the nicest border patrol people—but with our double strollers and the street lined with parked cars, there was no way to get across without backtracking to the corner. I stood beside Monica and shrugged at the guy apologetically.

"Okay, um, maybe you could just wait here a second," he said, looking over his shoulder. "Sorry. I'll just check and see . . ."

I bent down to pick up a sippy cup that had been flung from my stroller and heard a familiar voice calling my name.

Walking toward me was Jake Brunner, the guy I'd dated on and off for three years before I met Leo. (When I replay this scene in my head, I'm equal parts flattered and weirded out that he must have recognized me by my ass.) He wore blue jeans and a chef's coat, and as he got closer, I could swear he was wearing mascara. His new restaurant, the Pig, had recently opened in a narrow two-story spot on West Eleventh. With three-hour waits and an effusive *New Yorker* review, everyone was talking about it.

"Jake. Hi. Congratulations—I keep hearing about you," I said.

He leaned in for a peck on the cheek, and I surprised myself by going weak at his scent: vetiver cologne tinged with bacony kitchen smells. The combination of his nascent star power, my new clothes, and the lovely spring day turned me into a nervous schoolgirl. I stammered and tittered my way through some chitchat, and then he said, "Hey. Have you guys eaten?"

Monica, still in bold and brassy mode, stuck her hand out. "Actually, we're starved. Hi. I'm Monica."

I apologized for having failed to introduce them, and then, when I floundered awkwardly to give Jake a designation—I think I went with "old friend"—he interrupted. "Listen, we're about finished here, and I just made all this food for the photo shoot, so why don't you come in and eat?"

"Oh, that's very tempting," I said, regaining some level of coherence. "But we can't. Got to get these kids to the park before they combust."

Out of the corner of my eye, I saw Monica's head snap back in what I guessed was objection.

"At least let me send some with you," he said, glancing down at my kids for an uneasy second but not really acknowledging them. "Come on. I've got Brussels sprouts," he said, drawing out the words playfully.

He had wooed me with those Brussels sprouts, and he knew it. On our second date, he made me a sexual bet—which he'd won—that he could make me (a proclaimed Brussels sprouts hater) love the tiny cabbages. With an excitingly foreign tingle in my stomach, I realized that he was flirting.

Jake went inside, and Monica, the kids, and I stood out there while the photographer and his awkward assistant waited impatiently. I was nervous and buzzy while he was away, and I could feel Monica's eyes on me, but I refused to look at her. Instead I busied myself with the kids, wiping their peanut-butter-smeared faces and hands until Jake returned with a large white shopping bag.

"Here you go. I threw in a couple of invitations to this opening party we're having next month. You guys should come."

"Oh, thank you. Sounds fun," I said.

He pecked me on the cheek again and gave my arm a light squeeze, then told Monica it was nice meeting her.

Monica and I walked the three remaining blocks to the West Side Highway in silence. Waiting for the traffic light, I could feel her eyes on me, but I kept looking straight ahead, trying to hide the smile that was creeping onto my lips.

Finally, Monica blurted out, "Well?"

The noise of the traffic meant that the kids probably couldn't hear us.

"He's cute, right?" I said, still refusing to look at her head-on.

"Yeah," she said, still staring at me expectantly.

"My ex. Serious. Right before Leo. Didn't want kids."

"We're going to that party, right?" said Monica.

"No."

"Yes! Please!"

"Maybe," I whispered. I normally would have said, *Sure, why not?*, but the butterflies in my stomach were a red flag.

"You already have the perfect outfit in that ShopBop box, don't you?"

Actually, I had two possible outfits in mind. "We'll see, okay? I don't know," I said.

Leo and Monica's husband, TJ, had never met. We rarely got together without the kids, but when we did, it was always just the two of us. So it went without saying that if we did go, the guys were not coming.

We arrived at the playground, found an empty bench, and set the kids loose before tucking into our bag from Jake. It contained a heaping box of the famous Brussels sprouts braised in beer and bacon fat, six grilled lamb chops, and a box of short ribs in a thick and gooey sauce. He'd also included two bottles of sparkling water, which he knew I regarded as a special treat.

Besides being mothers of twins, Monica and I are also both married to vegetarians. My dinners this week so far had consisted of cereal and milk, an Amy's frozen pizza, and vegetable lo mein from the Chinese takeout.

At first I'd admired Leo's vegetarianism. He had stopped eating meat for ethical reasons when he studied land management at Ithaca College. I was in awe of his commitment and didn't disagree with anything about it, but I also couldn't imagine my life without the prospect of a great burger. Leo never made me feel bad or judged for that. I'm not sure he'd say the same about me. In fact, there were times when I found his vegetarianism annoying—like when I was pregnant and starving and just wanted to pop into any old restaurant but had to study the menu first to make sure there was something he could eat. He always insisted he could find something to eat any-where. But I hated to see him order a side of rice and steamed vegeta-bles while I enjoyed a nice club sandwich.

A giddiness took hold of me and Monica as we beheld the spread before us. "Beats the granola bar I planned for lunch today," I said, selecting a rib.

Monica let out a deep and gurgling laugh as she tore into a lamb chop. She had tucked a spare T-shirt of Jonny's into her shirt to act as a bib. Our feast was attracting the attention of the other parents and nannies. One mom actually stood and watched us like a specta-tor as we feasted on the piles of beef like a couple of Vikings home from battle. Monica held out a lamb chop and beckoned her over with it. "Do you want one? There's plenty!" When the woman looked away, embarrassed, Monica chirped, "It's okay! It's organic, grass-fed, local, all that!"

I nudged her and hissed, "Shut up!"

She just cackled, drunk on meat. "You're right. More for us." Then she yelled over to the other mom, "Never mind!"

I normally felt embarrassed or annoyed when Monica was needlessly confrontational, but I was as gaga as she was. When we made eye contact, our faces and hands covered in whatever heavenly sauce the short ribs were in, we dissolved into a giggling fit. Though it only deepened our hysterics, we kept looking at each other through sobs of laughter, gasping for air and trying not to choke. I'd finally worked myself down to a groaning giggle and grabbed a pack of baby wipes from the bottom of my stroller, but the crime-scene handprint I made on the package only set us off again. My stomach and face hurt for an hour afterward.

<hr/>

I got home that day and had a letter from Sid. My heart did a little dance the way it does every time I see her writing on the envelope. I've got a thing with handwriting. Leo's was nearly a deal breaker. If he weren't such an exquisite eater, it would have been. This will sound incredibly shallow, but the way someone writes and the way they eat are as important to me as how they vote and how they kiss.

We had been together six months. On Valentine's Day, he surprised me with a weekend at the Royalton on Forty-fourth Street. It was all very romantic, with nothing but eating, drinking, and hotel sex for two days. I woke up late on Sunday morning and found a note on the pillow. *Wake up! I miss you! Went to get bagels. —Leo.* I recoiled in disgust. *Who was this from? Surely not the man I love! He's not a lefty! Why is everything leaning backward? Did he recently have hand surgery? I thought I knew him. How is it possible that this is the first time I'm seeing his handwriting?*

Then he came back with the bagels and we sat on the bed eating them. It was those bagels that saved him. He was a great eater. You know how Brad Pitt eats in every movie, and there's something so sensual and enchanting about it? Well, that's how Leo eats. With his mouth closed and eyes twinkling, he chews fast and with purpose, but miraculously silently. He'll raise his eyebrows and give little grunts of approval or interest while he's chewing, but he waits until he's finished to speak. It's the perfect combination of gentlemanly and rugged. I focused on the bagels and coffee and my lover's eating and tried to put the shock of five minutes ago out of my head.

"I got something else while I was out," he said.

"The paper?" I asked.

"Already here." He motioned to the fat Sunday *Times* on the floor in the corner.

"What else is there?" I said. As far as I was concerned, everything I needed for a perfect Sunday morning was in that room. If only that wretched note would disappear.

He reached down and produced a small red box from the pocket of his jacket on the floor next to the bed. I stopped chewing. He was looking down, seeming to focus on getting the box opened just right. Both of us were staring at the box when it finally opened to reveal a sparkly circle-cut diamond ring. We looked up at each other at the same time, and he said, "Will you marry me, Cassie?"

I forced myself to finish chewing the huge bite of salt bagel and cream cheese before I said anything, but tears were already coming to my eyes and I was nodding my head affirmatively.

We cried and giggled and hugged and kissed for about fifteen minutes, and then I suddenly had the urge to call everyone I knew and go buy a pile of *Brides* magazines. I phoned my parents first. They already knew. Leo had called and asked for their blessing. When

I heard about other people doing that, I thought it was a bit stupid and sexist, but at that moment it made me feel like I had landed the sweetest, most thoughtful guy in the whole world. Sid was there, and we shrieked on the phone together. She made me put Leo on, and I could hear her cooing at him and telling him how happy she was. My family had always approved of Leo. I think at first they were merely relieved at how normal and stable he seemed after my two previous serious boyfriends, Spencer, the trust-fund brat for whom I'd moved to California right after college, and of course, Jake, the on-again, off-again heartthrob who seemed to be constantly reevaluating my worthiness as a girlfriend. Leo's big Italian Catholic family of brothers gave him immediate credibility, and his even-tempered and affable nature signaled a low-drama future.

A more sentimental person might have saved that note for a scrapbook or to stick in the side of a picture frame. But when we checked out of the hotel at two in the afternoon, I chucked it in the trash and tried to forget about this gross shortcoming of my future husband.

CHAPTER SEVEN

My big box of pretentious and embarrassing "Cassandra Marie" stationery that Mom gave me when I graduated college had finally run out. So had the thank-you cards left over from my baby shower. To reward myself for my thrift, I went on a spree at Greenwich Letterpress on Christopher Street. I had stopped in with the boys last week and gotten just past the welcome mat when I knew I was going to need to come back without them. I came straight from school drop-off, knowing I might spend the bulk of my three hours of freedom at that store.

Walking among the thick card stock, the thin rice paper, the carefully edited selection of pens, I was transported back to my childhood, when I would often visit a neighborhood shop called the Depot, which sold greeting cards and candles and had an entire wonderful wall of Mrs. Grossman's stickers. I spent every cent of my allowance on that wall for the whole of my eleventh year. We stopped every week on the way home from ballet. Occasionally, Mom would wander off in search of a greeting card or even pop over to the pharmacy next door, and I remember being scandalously thrilled by the row of "adult" cards, only their tops visible behind the plain white card placed in front of them to hide what debauchery lay beneath. This being the eighties, it meant we saw only teased blond bangs on the women or feathered dark brown hair on the men.

Once, Sid climbed up on a stool and quickly grabbed two cards. She foisted one on me, and I beheld a close-up of a red-lace-clad bosom, a single lit candle peeking out from the heaving cleavage. I stifled a giggle and traded cards with Sid. The next one was an oily naked muscleman holding a strategically placed white box with a red bow on it. When Mom and the clerk had returned from the back of the store, Sid grabbed both cards and shoved them in with the birthday cards.

That night, Sid and I lay in our beds wondering out loud if our boobs would ever be big enough to hold a candle. "Do you think Mom's can do that?" I asked.

"No way."

"I heard that you know you need a bra when a pencil stays between your boobs without falling to the floor," I said.

"I don't think so. Tricia Peterson wears a bra and hers are nowhere near big enough to hold on to a pencil or a candle—or even a roll of paper towels," she said.

"Oh. Well, maybe you need a bra if you can smush them together and hold something."

"Maybe."

The memory made me wistful. There was no such adult shelf at Kate's Paperie—or even any Mrs. Grossman's stickers—but it smelled exactly like the Depot, and I wished I could find that cleavage card and send it to Sid to see if she remembered. Instead, I settled for a "Brandon and Dylan" card, which I knew would deliver a similar brand of nostalgic giggles.

After spending way too much time trying to calculate how different pens would perform on various papers and seriously considering a quill and ink pot, I finally settled on a set of thick notecards embossed with a lone and lovely zebra that came with ornately lined envelopes, a handful of funny postcards for short notes, and a stack of thick and mottled cream-colored sheets for longer letters, along with a mix of gray, pale purple, and orange envelopes.

I started my next letter on one of the zebra notecards, and about midway through I regretted it. Something this lowbrow didn't belong on special paper. So I tossed it and started over on my trusty notebook of Japanese graph paper.

New York
May 1

Hey, Sis,

Guess who is becoming quite the celebrity chef. Jake! I ran into him a few weeks ago doing a photo shoot in front of his new restaurant (which is about six blocks from me), and he seems really good. I haven't seen him in years—since the last time we broke up, I guess. Now I see him everywhere—in the *Times*, on the Food Network, or just walking down the street. His Brussels sprouts are the talk of the town.

I have to admit that I felt a few pangs of jealousy for the exciting turn his life has taken. Mine must seem so monotonous and boring to him. And part of me feels ripped off for those unglamorous years I spent with him when he was the sous chef at Public. I'm comforting myself with the idea that maybe now he has a raging ego, but when I saw him, he seemed to be as normal as ever, and I'd be lying if I said I didn't find myself fantasizing about what my life might be like now if we'd stayed together. I know it's beyond blasphemous for a mother of two incredible little boys to say such a thing. I mean, obviously I wouldn't give them up for the world. They *are* my world. But some days, just for fun, I wonder about other worlds.

Be honest: Do you ever think about what your life might have been like if you hadn't gotten pregnant that summer? I know I do for you. I hope that doesn't make you feel bad, because it's only because of the timing of it all. It doesn't mean that we'd trade in River (or Quinn or Joey) for a second, but you must have thought about it, too. Or—what about ending up with Kenny?! Would you guys be following Phish around in a camper van, River selling grilled cheese alongside Kenny's kind buds? ☺

Love you, and I never think about what life would be like without you!

—Cassie

PS—Remember the Depot?

—❧❀❧—

Singapore
May 15

Oh, Cass, my darling—

The grass is always greener, isn't it? Re. Jake, I'm happy that his Brussels sprouts are finally getting the attention they deserve. But for all the sprouts in the world, I don't for a second think you should have stayed with him. He is a good guy, but not a great guy. And he was kind of always messing with your head, wasn't he? Or were you the bad guy? I can't remember. Either way, Leo is a good egg, and I had a good feeling about him from the first time I met him. And you know, there's an excellent chance Jake was looking at you and thinking that your life looks fantastic and full and perfect.

All is well here. Adrian's job gave him a car, which smells to me like a bribe to get us to stay longer. He uses it when he's in town, but it mostly just sits there because I stick to taxis. The drivers are a hoot! No one tips for anything here, but I usually round up, which sends some of them over the moon. My driver today was struggling to put into words how grateful he was for my seventy-cent tip, and finally came up with, "You are a nice, sporting lady!" How do you like that? I was wearing yoga clothes, so maybe that explains his comment. Either way, it made me smile for hours.

I'm still enjoying my role as den mother to all of these helpers. I started a Monday-night personal finance workshop to help them budget their money and start savings accounts. The stress these women are under to send money back to their families is unreal. Most of them make $500 or $600 a month, and with a few exceptions, every cent goes back to their families. Still, it never seems to be enough, and there are a lot of tear-filled phone calls telling sons, no, you can't go on the class trip, or brothers, no, you can't buy any extra seeds for this season's planting, or mothers, no, you can't get the hip-replacement surgery. It's all pretty gut-wrenching.

I even started a backroom savings and loan here, where I keep envelopes for them to put away $5 here and $10 there, so they can save up the $400 minimum to start a real bank account.

I've started paying them interest—$5 for every month they go without withdrawing any money. It sounds silly, but I'm finding it so fulfilling.

I'm also coaching them on how to ask for a raise. A few of them are making way under the going rate. Unfortunately, it's created a bit of a fissure between some of the other "ma'ams" and me, which is a shame because most of them are really nice people—they're just a bit, oh, I don't know, unsure how to "have help" in a way that's anything other than this master-servant thing.

I realize now that I'm as big a cliché as the rest of the expat wives here. So many of them—of us!—gave up a career to move here. And those who didn't were busy with their kids and housework, but now we have all this time on our hands, so we develop projects. When I meet someone new, I can usually suss out her project within minutes. Either it's fitness (honestly, the bodies on these moms! Most of them have the ass of a twenty-year-old), or it's obsessing over their kids' schooling and extracurriculars, or they've started a small fashion business, or they volunteer or blog or whatever—certainly no one will admit to not having a project. That would just be lazy. Oh, the tyranny of having help!

Mwah!
—Sid

In fact, I was in the midst of a little project of my own: a rich and ongoing fantasy in which I was Jake's wife instead of Leo's. I imagined serving ten-dollar tacos on his trendy new food truck, tending his rooftop garden, hanging around at TV show tapings, having romantic candlelit dinners, feeding each other chocolate cake before steamy lovemaking sessions . . . that kind of thing. I had just enough self-awareness to laugh at myself over the whole thing. But I stopped short of an actual reality check, which would be that I'd still be working long hours while Jake worked the opposite hours at his restaurant. I'd still be watching friends and colleagues have babies and vacillating between convincing myself that I didn't want kids and panicking that my window on becoming a mother was closing. Because the truth was that I'd longed for an unoriginal life, as Jake called the well-tread path of parenthood. I'd wanted to get fat and have cravings for pickles and ice cream in the middle of the night, to scream at my long-suffering husband during labor, to smilingly complain about sleepless nights, to wear my baby in one of those slings that looked like a big Ace bandage, to be out on the streets of New York in the early-morning hours when only dog owners and parents were awake. That's what I always wanted, and here I was punishing the great guy to come along and give all of that to me by longing for the good but not great guy who wouldn't. Leo, who wanted what I wanted, who'd spent his life savings on the IVF treatments that made me pregnant with twins—"a two-for," we'd called it—was getting the short end of the stick. At least in my fantasies. I was conscious of my bad behavior but somehow also removed from it because I wasn't acting on it. But, in fact—of course—I was. You can't think about something that much and not have it show up in your actions.

An unfortunate side effect was that when I wasn't feeling annoyed with Leo for some small transgression involving cheese or whose turn it was to wake up first, I started to pity him for having an ungrateful wife like me who doesn't appreciate him. And pity is not an emotion conducive to romance. The guiltier I felt, the less into Leo I was. And the more into Jake I became.

My restless legs syndrome—a maddening affliction I'd not been able to shake since the end of my pregnancy—had reached an all-time high right around this time. And many of these fantastical escapes from reality took place as I paced the living room floor in the middle of the night, shaking out my legs and scrolling through Facebook on my phone, increasingly cruising Jake's new "public figure" page.

Soon I was following his food truck on Twitter and picking up tacos from it every week when it was parked on West Fourth Street. I'd walk the boys past the sex shops and tattoo parlors, brushing off their questions about the crotchless leather bodysuits or the Day-Glo water bongs and trying to distract them with questions about what kind of tacos they wanted. Once, I surreptitiously took a picture of Quinn in front of one of the seedier adult shops and tagged it #citykid. It didn't get as many likes or comments as I thought it would, and we walked the long way from then on, avoiding the tawdriest section of the street. Jake was never there at the truck, but we kept going anyway because the boys loved those tacos, and so did Leo. I didn't tell him who was behind them.

Meanwhile, Monica and I took to strolling past the Pig on our way to Chelsea Piers each week. That was actually Monica's idea. She was hoping for more free meat.

All these things—which amounted to vague stalking—soon became part of my routine.

My routine had become precious to me this year. When I found something that worked, I created a little ritual around it and we'd do it every day or every week. The experts say that regimens are important for kids, but I think I benefited more than the boys did. Before I got it all figured out, I would look into the abyss of a fourteen-hour day with them and despair at the bleakness of it all. There is nothing more dismal than waking up to a cold and rainy day with two toddlers in a small apartment and nothing planned for the day. The key, I've found, is to have something slated every morning, to force you out of the house early, and to stay out as long as you can. Our Friday mornings from spring through September met those requirements handily, for it was when we walked across town to the Lower East Side, where my friend Mandy was in charge of the community garden's chickens in the Sara D. Roosevelt Park.

Mandy is one of the few single friends with whom I've been able to maintain a friendship since having the twins. She is great with the boys, and they adore her, so the Friday mornings we spend with her are a real treat. She holds a lease on a dozen apartments on the Lower East Side and in SoHo and is able to make a living renting them out by the week to European tourists. (It's not altogether legal.) She's always got this big set of keys with her, and she spends her days zipping around downtown on her red Vespa.

Mandy has a Chihuahua named Chato. Chato is a rescue dog with some emotional issues and has bitten Quinn no less than four times (just nips, he's never broken the skin) yet the boys remain undeterred and lavish him with affection. The chickens arrived in March on loan from a farm upstate. We bring them Greek yogurt and worms, which we buy at the bait shop around the corner from the Chinatown fish market.

Occasionally one of the chickens—who were supposedly menopausal—would lay an egg. Discovering one was pure magic for the boys, and we'd always get to keep it. I'd wrap it in a T-shirt and put it in my bag, and we'd have scrambled eggs from Regina or Hattie or Daisy for lunch.

After chicken duty, we'd visit Mandy's vegetable plot. The boys had planted tomato seeds with her, and while I'm 80 percent sure what they dutifully watered every week was a weed, they loved checking its progress and seeing the chickens and being the only kids ever allowed in the coop. Other children would watch with envy as Mandy invited them in to check for eggs. Mandy called Joey the chicken whisperer because the birds always went right up to him. He spoke to them low and soft. "Hi, girls. Good girls. Good chickens." Quinn was a bit jumpier and was known to scream at their approach, causing them to flap their wings and cluck in reaction, but Joey would set them right in a matter of seconds while Quinn hovered nervously behind Mandy's leg.

On those mornings, if we managed to get to the garden without incident, if we bought the worms without anyone having a tantrum for a candy bar in the bait store, if I hadn't yelled, if they were both in the coop and no one was crying, I would stand there holding Chato by the leash, watching my boys with Mandy and the chickens and feel genuinely satisfied. I was proud that those were my adorable boys in there with the chickens and that I was able to give my city-dwelling kids this experience. At these moments, I loved my life.

CHAPTER EIGHT

New York
June 1

Sid,

You are the coolest. A backroom bank—I love it. But is it legal?
Just be careful—don't they cane people for less over there?

Remember our "office" in the garage attic? We had that
box of index cards where we'd keep files on the neighborhood
boys? God, I'd love to have a look at those cards now.

I've come around to your sex challenge idea, by the way.
Leo doesn't know it, but I'm aiming for three times this week.
Boy, is he in for a shock. I'll report back with results. In fact,
do you know what's really depressing? We had a new mattress
delivered last week, and neither of us made the inevitable
jokey-but-not-really comment about "christening it." (Nor
have we "christened it," I probably don't need to tell you.) And
you know what's even weirder? We literally (and I do mean

literally) have not spoken one word about the mattress, despite the fact that it was a heavily researched decision. Over months, we e-mailed and texted links to articles on mattresses and went separately to Sleepy's and reported to the other on our preferences via e-mail. When it arrived, I texted him, and when he came home that night, the boys and I were already asleep on it.

Anyway, I'm off to my first yoga class. I hope it will make me a calmer, nicer, sexier version of myself—which would make me you, I guess! Wish me luck.

—Cassie

PS—In case you were wondering, the mattress is amazing—a long-overdue upgrade from the pile of coat hangers and cotton balls that I was sure comprised our old mattress. I haven't slept better in years! If only my restless legs would cease and my kids would stop climbing on top of me in the middle of the night . . .

When Leo arrived home at six forty, I had the boys in the tub. Ten minutes later, I walked the four blocks to Up-Dog Studio above the juice bar on Hudson Street (which Monica and I are convinced is a cover for a major drug trade). The narrow stairway was lined with votive candles, and soft music played while incense burned from above. I paid my thirty dollars, removed my shoes, and grabbed a towel from the pile atop the shoe shelf. A bit nervous, I pulled my phone out of my bag and pretended to be busy on it while entering the studio. Had I been paying attention, I might have made a quick retreat, but by the time I silenced my phone and dropped it back into my bag, it was too late.

"Hey, neighbor!" My heart sank. It was Jenna, who lived across the hall from me. And as if that weren't bad enough, *Jake* was there, too.

"Cass," he said with a nod of his head and what might have been a wink, but I wasn't sure

"Hey, guys," I said softly, looking around, and then accepting my predicament and taking the last open spot, right between them.

Jenna Newman and I had a complicated relationship best summed up by the term "frenemy." She's just the kind of person Sid would have had no complaint with and might have even befriended, but whom I couldn't stand. Her daughter, Valentina, was six months older than the twins and light-years ahead of them developmentally. Jenna was, naturally, a mommy blogger and seemed to think that this made her a sought-after parenting expert. We've been neighbors for years and were always sort of friends, but motherhood changed everything about our relationship. When she found out I was pregnant, it was the beginning of the end, only I didn't know it at the time. With her placid and perfect newborn daughter, whom she had delivered in her bathtub, Jenna was quick to offer advice. Advice that I gladly accepted at first. I was so busy at work that I didn't have time to read the stack of books she loaned me: *So That's What They're For, Ina May's Guide to Childbirth,* and *Birthing from Within.* Luckily, she was ready with a CliffsNotes version each time I passed her in the hall. And I ate it up. In fact, between her and Sid, I didn't *need* any books or childbirth classes. I felt fortunate to have them both.

Jenna is a single mom, and I've got a real soft spot—and a lot of respect—for single moms, which made me hate myself for hating her.

When the twins were first born, I was still grateful for her counsel and neighborly hot meals. It was kind of her to check on me and sit with the babies while I showered, and she does make a delicious cauliflower quinoa pilaf. Technically speaking, she may be a better person than I am, and if Grandma Margie's version of heaven exists, there's a good chance she's in and I'm out. But at a certain point, her offers of help and handy tips seemed mere excuses for her to show off. With great annoyance, I came to realize that Jenna had appointed herself my mentor when I'd only wanted a friend. I started to resent her pride in her skills and felt I deserved a little credit—a handicap— for having two babies at once. By the time the twins were eating solids and I was three months back at work, I'd reached my limit with her.

It was the BÉABA baby-food maker that did it. She'd bullied me into buying it in the first place, telling me all about it no less than seven times. I would nod and say, "Yes, sounds fab. I should get one." And then she just picked one up for me at Babies "R" Us and told me I owed her $120. And what could I do? Refusing it was as good as signing my kids up for cancer. Baby food out of a jar, with its chemicals and preservatives (and ease and convenience) was so vilified that to even buy it in my neighborhood was a secretive, shameful act, and one that I engaged in every week while that cheerful green-and-orange machine sat occupying more counter space than I could afford.

The thing was, I did love my kids and I didn't make them food. So as it turns out, it is possible. Because I'm still insecure about it, let me present my case. I'd get home from work at six fifteen on the dot, send my nanny home, and immediately nurse the boys, feed the boys (from a jar), bathe the boys, cuddle and coo with the boys, read *Is Your Momma a Llama?* with the boys, nurse them again, read *Goodnight Moon* with them, and then attempt to put them to sleep. All the while, the pristine appliance loomed like a judgmental beacon, its very presence actually lessening the quality of my time with my babies. Leo usually came in around seven thirty with takeout and we'd pass Joey and Quinn around until they fell asleep, scarf down the Thai or Chinese or Mexican, and then one of the boys would be up. I'd crawl into bed at some point, where I would sleep for an hour or two at a time, awakened intermittently by my restless legs or my restless babies, until I woke for the day at five or six a.m.

The organic kale and cauliflower and sweet potatoes turned browner by the day, and each night before I slinked off to bed, I'd think, *I've got to make that baby food before the veggies go bad.* To this day, the sight of a CSA box tugs at a dark little part of me that wonders whether my difficulties at getting pregnant in the first place were a sign that I wasn't meant to be a mother.

Once the boys entered toddlerhood, Jenna would see me, wild-eyed, coming up the stairs with the boys, who were often covered in sand or ice cream or both and crying, refusing to budge from the landing, roaring like T. rexes, barking like dogs, fighting like ninjas—anything other than calmly and quietly walking beside me, in the style of Valentina. In these moments, she would cock her head to the side and say, "Oh dear, let me help you." Sometimes she would take my bags, but other times she would go all Supernanny, and in a treacly voice, say something like, "Hey, kiddos, do you know how to play the quiet game?"

When we had playdates on rainy days, Jenna was known to say things like, "Don't worry, Valentina; I'm sure Joey's mom is going to have a talk with him about sharing," and then look at me expectantly. When she put out a tray of crudités for snack time and Quinn asked, "What's that?" referring, I assume, to the jumbo white asparagus nestled among the carrots, celery, and cucumbers, she said, "Oh, honey, these are organic vegetables with pesto Greek yogurt dip," her voice dripping with pity, as if the boys had never before seen a vegetable. "This is Valentina's favorite snack."

Then, in a fake effort to alleviate what she assumed was my great mortification, she stage-whispered to me, "Actually, she doesn't have a choice."

I felt like she was trying to lure me into some mommy competition. But instead of giving her that pleasure, I retreated further into my slacker-mom persona. If anyone was keeping score, Jenna was surely crushing me, so why not just accept my booby prize? But acknowledging this only further aggravated me: I felt like I should have been a great mom. All the prerequisites had been met: a happy childhood; an affinity for children in general; positive role models in my mother, grandmother, and sister; a supportive spouse; a strong desire to become a mother in the first place. So what was the problem? All signs pointed to some defect of my personality. Still, I preferred to assign little bits of blame here and there, a good chunk going to the complicated feelings churned up by Jenna.

Her blog was called *My Funny Valentine,* and it was a record of everything Valentina ever did or said. It had a cool, spare design and ethereal photos. Each post would wrap up with a bit of parenting wisdom from the mother of this amazing child who did and said only altruistic and hilarious and precious things. The way I saw it, she'd lucked into having a girl with an extremely easygoing temperament and a taste for broccoli, and was going around taking credit for something she actually had very little to do with.

She had one post about how she had planned out Valentina's gradual exposure to screens. Valentina had not touched an iPad and never watched TV, and Jenna claimed to use her phone for emergencies only while she was in Valentina's presence. Jenna planned to start introducing television in ten-minute increments, slowly building to her first feature film, which would be *The Wizard of Oz* when she was seven. I love *The Wizard of Oz,* but I would never admit it to Jenna.

It bothered me that our neighbors tended to group us together, assuming we were close friends. There weren't many kids in our building, which was made up of mostly gay men and elderly people hanging on to their rent-controlled apartments from before the building went co-op. I worked hard to distance myself from her in every way I could. Unfortunately, we have similar tastes in furniture, music, and children's clothes. And even more maddeningly, I agreed with a lot of what she said about children and parenting in general, but her superiority was so sickening that I fought every instinct to side with her, even if that meant not doing the best thing for my kids. For instance, every time she blathered on about "screen time," I went home and sat the boys in front of the TV for a healthy dose of it, a prophylactic against ever being in the position to tell some poor beleaguered mother that *my* children hardly ever watched TV. When she "discovered" Elizabeth Mitchell's children's music, I had also recently been playing it for the boys every night while we got ready for bed. When she told me, complete with a smug explanation as to why this was the perfect bedtime music for Valentina, that Valentina sang along so sweetly and that it was their special thing, I pretended like I thought it was fine, but that we usually listened to lullaby versions of Ramones songs. I immediately went inside and downloaded that *Rockabye Baby!* Ramones album, so it wasn't really a lie.

Monica and Jenna have never met and I don't plan to introduce them, because I couldn't bear to watch the carnage that would ensue if Monica got ahold of her. Despite being terribly annoying, Jenna wasn't a bad person, and I felt slightly—perversely—protective of her.

When we were dating, Jake had tried to get me to go to yoga classes with him, but I was a Pilates girl and we became jokingly exclusive to our chosen exercise regime, never crossing the line. Aside from one or two prenatal classes I took four years ago, this was my first real yoga class. Needless to say, Jake and Jenna were the last two people I'd want witnessing a potentially vulnerable or embarrassing moment—let alone hour. I considered staging an emergency with the help of my phone, but I naively thought my years of Pilates and ballet would help me fake my way through the class.

As I sat down, Jenna looked impressed that Jake and I knew each other. He was becoming quite famous, and with his sleeve of tattoos, scruffy face, and perfect teeth, he looked the part.

"I've never seen you here before," said Jenna.

"Yeah, I haven't taken a yoga class in years," I said, making an effort to speak slowly and softly.

A wiry and kind-faced woman who looked to be some exotic mix of South Asian races approached me and quietly asked, "Is this your first time here?"

"Yep," I said quickly, a bit uncomfortable with her eye contact.

"Not your first time to yoga, though?" she said, making a face as if this possibility would be unfathomable.

"No, no," I assured her with a wave of my hand.

"Okay, then, we'll get started," she said to everyone.

I shot the instructor a look that I hoped said, *Cover for me—my ex-boyfriend and my archnemesis are here, and I need to look good, okay?*

Any meaning my look imparted was quickly diminished when she said, "My name is Yiren and this is Flow One. Welcome."

Maybe it's spending my days with a couple of three-year-old boys, but at the combination of her name, which sounded exactly like "urine," and the word "flow," my eyes bulged and I stifled a giggle. A quick scan of the faces in the mirror that spanned the front of the room revealed that I was among mature adults. I wished Monica were there. We would have dissolved into a giggling fit and had to leave the class, embarrassing ourselves, yes, but that would have been preferable to what I endured for the next hour.

I had to watch Jenna and Jake to know what to do next, my shoulders weren't opening the way everyone else's were, and I kept defaulting to ballet-style turned-out feet and pointed toes, which repeatedly drew Yiren over to correct my stance. My faded Detroit Tigers T-shirt and Old Navy brand yoga pants weren't helping. Jake and a few of the model types looked straight off the ashram in some loose-fitting linen-hemp blend pants and tight ribbed tank tops, while Jenna and the rest were all wearing the same brand of extremely flattering yoga outfits. I made a mental note to find out where to buy a pair of those pants that made Jenna's butt look ten times better than it actually was without having to ask her.

I muddled my way through the next hour and then rushed out at "Namaste," without even a glance in Jake's or Jenna's direction. To put some extra distance between Jenna and me, I jogged home, dreading the annoying yoga tips she was probably already planning to work into our next hallway encounter.

Needless to say, I was not feeling like the goddess I wanted to feel like in order to kick off the sex challenge—plus I needed a dose of Jenna antivenom, so I was relieved to get a "yes" in response to my text to Monica: *Need a drink. Wine bar in 1 hour?? Please!*

I took the stairs two at a time, hoping to catch the boys before they fell asleep and get Leo's blessing to go back out for a drink. Leo had the boys in pajamas and was reading *The Circus Ship* on our bed when I came in. I climbed aboard and nuzzled the boys while Leo finished the book, and things were already better. We each took a boy and lay in bed with them, singing, "If I Had a Hammer." They were asleep before the final verse.

I didn't stop singing until we had crept out of the bedroom.

"Hon. Would you mind if I grabbed a quick drink with Monica?"

"No. Go ahead. Have fun."

I kissed him on the lips, lingering a bit longer than our typical goodbye peck, as if to signal forthcoming intimacy and as a "thanks" for always being so cool when I needed to escape. I showered quickly, put on a non-cotton bra and undies, jeans, and a brown knit cowl-neck top, blasted my hair half dry, and ran downstairs.

I grabbed a stool at the oval-shaped bar and ordered two of the second-least-expensive glasses of red zinfandel and a cheese and olive plate. With no sign of Monica, I fished my notebook out of my purse and began a letter to Sid, my second that day. Monica showed up just as I had stopped to apply a Spider-Man Band-Aid (also found in my purse) to the writing callus on my middle finger. Looking and smelling fabulous, she planted kisses on my cheeks while I crumpled the Band-Aid wrapper and slid my notebook back into my bag. Monica had been a party girl about town before the twins, so she's in her element in a bar.

"I need your help," she said, settling into her barstool. She took a sip of the wine I had ordered for her. "Mmm. Thanks." Then she opened up her laptop and we hovered over her draft post: "The Racist's Guide to Child Care." We snickered our way through a completely offensive and simplistic nationality-by-nationality guide to selecting a nanny. It was all based on actual comments we'd heard from other moms. "You've got to get a Tibetan; they're so gentle and calm." Or, "Jamaicans can cook, and nothing fazes them," or, "An Eastern European will never complain."

A group of banker types hovered nearby, and a few of them

approached Monica at different points during our two hours there. She was ruthless. I felt so bad for them.

Sid, who was approached just as frequently, would talk to anyone, which often annoyed me. I'd try to shoot the guys a sympathetic yet firm look that conveyed that they had no shot, despite the confidence they felt in the warm glow of Sid's smile and eye contact. But they seldom got the hint. I've never been one to suffer fools gladly, and so in addition to being the plain sister, I was often also the rude sister. With Monica, I was the plain, but kind, friend, often finding myself stuck talking to some guy she'd just heartlessly rebuffed.

I like to think I played each of these roles to equal effect. I've never minded being the "friend" or the "sister" of the person of most interest in any given social setting where men are present. But I do fear it's made me a bit superficial. I don't mean to, but I catch myself judging people based on their appearance all the time. It's ironic, really, considering I do things like go to a bar with damp hair.

New York
June 1

Dear Sid,

It took me thirty-six years, but I have finally accepted that I need to put more of an effort into my appearance. I'm sitting in a bar surrounded by people looking lovely and put together in the flickering candlelight and feeling like a bit of a slob. The truth is that I grew up sort of letting that whole area slide because I was always intimidated by you. I guess I was hoping people would assume that I actually looked just like you but I just didn't try. I didn't want people to see me in an outfit with my hair just right and makeup on and think, "That's the best she can do?"

It sounds so silly and it's embarrassing to write it down, but I sometimes have that thought when I see a person who has clearly put a lot of effort into their appearance and the result is kind of meh. I'll think, Oh, how sad. That is the best they can do. I'm not a nice person, I know, but it's what has kept me in sweatpants all these years, so maybe that has been my punishment! I guess I wanted to create the illusion that I had potential. At the same time, I took pride in what I felt to be a certain authenticity that comes with not trying too hard. Of course, now I see that authenticity and putting effort into your appearance are not mutually exclusive. The clothes were a start, and this week I have a hair appointment and may just stop by Sephora on the way home.

And that's what's up with me. Your turn.

xoxo,
Cass

PS—How would you sum up the Filipino people as a whole in regards to child care?

When I arrived home, Leo was snoring on the sofa with a bowl of popcorn on the floor next to him. I disappointed myself by feeling a tad relieved that I wouldn't have to seduce my husband, and after checking on the boys, I climbed into bed with my novel.

In the next scene in my book, the main character, a married woman, begins a steamy affair with a sexy drug addict she meets at an art gallery. I put the book down, got out of bed, and went back to regard Leo. His face was a little weathered, but he still looked as handsome as ever—the main difference being that instead of wild and wavy, he wore his dark brown hair shaved close to his head, a preemptive strike against male-pattern baldness.

I went to the fridge to pour myself a glass of water and found half of a brownie on the countertop. I knew immediately he had saved it for me. He was always saving me halves of things. If someone at work brought cupcakes, he'd eat half and wrap up the rest for me, keeping it in his bag until after the boys were in bed. He was the first good guy—okay, great guy—I'd ever fallen for. I was always more into the bad boys, and I wondered for a minute where I would be now If I'd married a guy who didn't save me half of his brownie. *Probably in bed with him*, I thought, sighing, and went back to my book.

———✦———

I knew it was Jenna by her knock.

"Hi, Jenna. What's up?" I said, hoping to convey with my voice that I didn't have time for chitchat.

"Great yoga class last night, right?"

"Eh." I shrugged.

"Where do you normally practice?"

I noticed an envelope in her hand. Ignoring her attempt to get me to ask her for yoga advice, I said, "Is that my mail?"

"Oh, yeah. I found it in my box."

"Thanks," I said, holding out my hand.

"It looks like fu-un," she said, looking down at the envelope, annoyingly still in her clutches. I could see that it was from Sid and that indeed it did look fun, with my name in big bubble letters and sparkly rainbow stickers festooning the edges (Lulu's contribution, no doubt). "You're lucky I checked. I rarely check my mail."

I gave her a *that's weird* look and said, "Okay, thanks, then . . ." But she went on.

"I get all my important mail in my PO box. I set it up when I was going through the divorce and I didn't know where I'd be living."

Damn her. Defeated, I said, "Do you want to come in, Jenna?"

"Sure—Valentina's at school, and I'm stuck on this blog post. I could really use a coffee, if you have any."

Leo was home for the morning, a rare occurrence. Having just finished a wrestling session with the boys, he was sprawled out in the middle of the floor, groaning and stretching while they all watched cartoons together. He'd been working late the night before, so he stayed home until ten to spend some time with the boys. Leo was good like that; he made a point to see them every day, even if it meant dashing home for twenty minutes in the middle of the afternoon.

"Leo, are you okay?" Jenna asked.

"Oh, hi, Jenna. It's just my back. I'm not used to our new mattress."

"Here, let me show you something," she said, sitting down on the carpet beside him and then proceeding to guide him through a few yoga poses, much to the annoyance of Quinn and Joey, whose view of the television was now obscured by Jenna's and Leo's butts. *That didn't take long*, I thought.

I started washing the breakfast dishes, my back to the room, as much to demonstrate my indifference as anything else.

Done with Leo, she made her way back over to the table. I poured her a cup of coffee and continued to tidy up while she prattled on about the post she was working on—something about how she talks to Valentina about the "bad nannies" they encounter out at the playgrounds. At some point I joined her at the table. As irritating as I found her, I was glad to sit and drink coffee with an adult for a few minutes while the boys were occupied with Leo.

Singapore
June 5
Cassie,

Adrian was in town all week—a rare occurrence. This is terrible to say, but we've gotten so used to him being away that his being here was as disruptive as it was nice. He messed up my whole routine. I eat dinner every night with the kids, and with Rose doing all the cleanup, my evenings are so relaxed. I love playing music and rocking Lu to sleep, then watching *Mad Men* with River. It's become my idea of a perfect evening.

When Adrian's here, he comes flying in the door, usually on the phone, just as I'm about to take Lulu to bed, adding this whole frantic energy to our night. He'll try to read her a story, but a client or his boss will call and he'll have to excuse himself, leaving me to take over. And then I find myself eating two dinners—one with the kids at six and then one with him at nine, which is not an ideal schedule when it's swimsuit season year-round. Poor Rose was a wreck about what "sir" was going to have for dinner every night. She hardly knows him, so she's all nervous when he's around.

And now I have a request for you: more talk about the weather, please. I want to remember what it feels like not to be hot. I miss the seasons so much. It's actually hard to remember important events, because when you look back on the day, it was hot and you went to the pool. In real life, you can rely on what you were wearing or whether you had to shovel the driveway or buy more sunscreen to set things in time, but here, every day is kind of the same. Did you know that we're eighty miles from the equator? Lulu and I practically live at the swimming pool, and you should see her go. She loves the water. Speaking of swimsuits, I took Rose shopping for one today. She doesn't know how to swim, so I'm enrolling her in lessons.

Kisses!

—Sid

PS—If you know anybody at John Deere or Toro, you might let them in on this hot tip: A wealthy nation in Southeast Asia has never heard of you. I'm watching the elderly Chinese gardener cut the grass on the hill outside my condo with scissors. Scissors! Maybe too many people complained about the noise, and since this guy is making only a few bucks a day, they can afford a half-dozen more of them to spend all day snipping the blades of grass like they were bangs.

CHAPTER NINE

O ut of the blue, my old boss from the magazine e-mailed and offered us tickets to an Alvin Ailey dance performance at Lincoln Center. When I called Wanda to see if she was available, she said we had already booked her for that night. I checked my calendar and discovered it was Leo's brother Stevie's fortieth birthday party in Hoboken. Irritated because I really wanted to go to the dance performance, I begrudgingly got to work on an eighties costume for the theme.

On the bright side, I would get to hang out with my sister-in-law Emma. Emma, Stevie's wife, is British, which makes her more of an outsider than me. She's giggly and mischievous and hands down the best thing about spending time with the Costas. She keeps a stack of British celebrity gossip magazines in her purse and drinks sparkling wine almost exclusively. No matter what else is going on, we manage to sit down and drink and flip through magazines. Forty-five minutes with her is like a mini vacation.

I came into the family only a few months after she did, and we bonded quickly, probably because she clung to me like a life raft in icy shark-infested waters. Which isn't far from the reality of, say, a lunch with Becky and Alyssa, who, as the wives of Rob and Tony Costa, had formed an early alliance, both being Jersey girls and— either actually or pretending to be—at ease with what Emma and I saw as an unusual family dynamic.

Rob Costa the first was killed in a truck accident when Leo was in high school, and Mary had received a large insurance settlement. The trucking company also provided a big payout, which she'd used to buy a house on the Jersey Shore. I have a feeling it was always this way, but Rob Sr.'s absence likely ramped up Mary's intimate involvement in each of her sons' lives, perhaps best summed up by this anecdote: A week before our wedding, she pulled me aside and suggested I "powder *down there* to keep things fresh for the wedding night." I was unable to look Mary in the eye for weeks afterward.

While I eventually surrendered to Mary's lack of boundaries and built a friendly relationship with her, Emma hadn't made much progress since those early days. To make matters worse, I think Mary enjoyed keeping her on edge. She made a lot of xenophobic comments, which were mostly based on Wimbledon or the royal family or crumpets, to which Emma would guffaw and say things to only further alienate herself, like, "But I'm from Hounslow!" as if it were proof against the snootiness that Mary couldn't separate from her accent, which did sound more Dick Van Dyke than Julie Andrews. For all Mary knew, she may as well have been from Timbuktu. Mary had never been out of the tristate area and was wary of anything unfamiliar.

Long ago, Emma learned to stop mentioning the summer she'd

spent working in Italy, because Mary's lack of interest could seem downright hostile—especially if the topic was authentic Italian food. I used to think she was intimidated by Emma's worldliness, but what I think it mostly boils down to is a fear that Emma would take Stevie to live in some far-off land, which, I have to admit, I get.

The fact that I'd delivered Mary's only two grandsons—her prized princes among a gaggle of granddaughters—is the chief reason for our improved relationship. I did suffer some major setbacks, including my decision to keep my own last name when Leo and I married and the awful Easter lunch—late in my pregnancy, at the height of my blood-sugar problem, when I had dared to help myself to a plate of food before fixing one for Leo. I hadn't eaten since breakfast and was feeling light-headed when we arrived at Mary's house just as she had finished setting out the food. With Leo still in the yard catching up with his brothers, I went straight to the table and filled my plate greedily. When I slumped into the closest chair I could find, and balanced the paper plate of lasagna on my belly, poised to slice into that red-and-white rectangle of goodness, I felt a pair of cold eyes on me. One look at Mary told me that I had broken the natural order of things: Women never eat before all of the men and children are fed. But with my mouth watering and my blood sugar dropping, I felt I had no choice but to continue with plan A.

"Leo, sweetheart," she yelled out of the kitchen window, her eyes still on me. "You must be starved. What can I get for you?" as if he were incapable of figuring out a standard buffet line.

There is a unique brand of vulnerability associated with eating food you are not welcome to, especially if you are a woman and currently weigh something in the neighborhood of 170 pounds, and my cheeks burned with shame as I chewed. Slowly, my dizziness subsided, and as I ate, I cycled through the embarrassment all the way to anger, which eventually dulled to annoyance. I was annoyed that Leo wasn't in the room to defend me, to tell his mom that I hadn't eaten since seven a.m. and that the doctor said I should be vigilant about my blood-sugar swings. Annoyed at Mary for reducing me to the meek little wife sitting in the corner and annoyed at myself for allowing it to happen.

By the time I got up from that chair, I had decided that this whole dynamic was not going to work for me. I wasn't going to let her push me around, yet I had no interest in bucking her firmly established system. Swimming upstream when it's not absolutely necessary is a fool's errand, if you ask me. I vowed to stop behaving like a watered-down version of myself, ramped up my mirror neurons, and found a way to be the most Mary-complementary version of myself I could be. I embraced my role as prep cook in her kitchen, and she even had me over to learn to make sauce. She also taught me lasagna and stuffed shells—"with meat, for when Leo grows out of the vegetarian thing and you can cook nice family meals."

New York
June 15

Sidney Sue—

It's Saturday night, we have a babysitter coming later, and Leo and I are headed out to—what else?—spend time with his mother and his brothers. Bleh. What we need is to spend time together, but every second is filled with his obnoxious family. I mean, it's fine when the kids are involved. I like them to spend time with their cousins. But when they encroach on our kid-free time—ugh.

I should go get ready for this party—the theme is eighties, and I have to try to repierce one of my ears (remember how you did it with a needle and a potato the first time—in the eighties!!) so I can wear these awesome plastic earrings I bought for $4 in Union Square. My look is very *Desperately Seeking Susan*. To be continued . . .

Hi again—well, I looked like a prostitute at the party. Seems everyone else went with a preppy tennis-court look. Popped collars, turtlenecks, and argyle, and there I am in my black miniskirt, garish jewelry, bra straps, and black panty hose complete with a run. Needless to say, I drank more than was advisable. I don't know why Leo didn't stop me from dressing like that. Of course, he was wearing a bolero tie and puffy pleated pants, so he looked almost as ridiculous as me. Emma, bless her heart, tried to make me feel better and got drunk with me while giggling about the awkward way their friend Carl kept steering his eighteen-month-old daughter away from me.

Yes, there was a toddler at the party. They have these friends, Carl and Michelle, nice people, but they bring their kid EVERYWHERE. The rest of us are putting down good money to leave the kids behind, dress like harlots, and say "fuck" with abandon. And there's Carl, behaving as if we're at the after-Mass doughnut reception. He does this thing where he narrates his kid's every move, in a faux-clever, overrehearsed monologue. "Yep, there she goes for the doorknob. Fascinating contraptions, aren't they?" His poor wife must endure his ridiculous routine every time they go out. It has got to be hard to have sex with someone like that.

Speaking of sex, I am having a slow start to the challenge (although compared to Carl, Leo's looking pretty damn good). But on the way home from the party, Leo and I held hands, which led to kissing, and I think we both assumed we'd pick things up when we got home, but honestly, I wasn't sure I'd still be in the mood by the time we got home, and—emboldened by my outfit and seven or eight champagnes—I was very much in the mood right there, so I climbed on top of him. Oh Lordy, our livery-cab driver completely freaked. He flipped on the interior lights in the car and yelled, "No sex in my car! No sex!" My miniskirt was pulled up high around my waist and my Pillsbury Doughboy tummy was bulging out of my control-top panty hose. It was about the least sexy sight you can imagine. We played the part of the loudmouth bad kids getting busted. "All right! All right!" I yelled, in my best eighties Madonna voice, shielding my eyes and dismounting Leo. Leo rested his head on the back of the seat and said, "We're not doing anything, man. Can you turn off the lights?"

By the time we got home, as I had predicted, the mood had passed. Leo was asleep by the time I returned from the long session in the bathroom required to rinse off four coats of black eyeliner and mascara. So I'm sitting up writing to you so I can make the morning mail.

But wait—I haven't even covered the evening's low point. Leo's sister-in-law Becky, that bitch, suggested (in front of a bunch of people) that I have Joey "tested." Leo and I were telling some story about him, and she interrupted to say, "Have you thought about having him tested?"

Me: For what?

Her: Well, perhaps to see if he might be on the spectrum?

Me: What spectrum?

Her: Autism?

Us: Blank stares.

Her: It's just that some of the things you are describing sound a little spectrumy.

I mean, don't get me wrong; sometimes I think I could be more patient with Joey if he had some sort of label or diagnosis. I could tell people that he has "special needs" or whatever you're supposed to say, and then, instead of looking like a shitty mom who can't control her kids, I'd get nods of respect or smiles of empathy. But he's three! I don't want to dive down a rabbit hole of coping strategies and therapy for kids "on the spectrum" unless we really need to. My pediatrician says he's probably fine, and I'm going with that.

Love you.

—Cass

That wasn't my only letter written under the influence, but I really should have had a rule about writing after drinking. It hurts to read that one. I can think of a hundred more diplomatic ways to have said all of that, but the things you say when you think no one is listening are a lot different from the things you would say otherwise.

CHAPTER TEN

The week of Jake's restaurant party had arrived, and after the embarrassment of the yoga class, I was determined to redeem myself. I had worked more running into my nightly walk-runs, a strategy that was supposed to help both my restless legs syndrome and my overall physique. A free makeover at Sephora and three hundred dollars' worth of products had me looking a bit more put together, and I had the perfect outfit from my ShopBop splurge. It wasn't only about being seen by Jake, I told myself. This was going to be the way I always dressed and looked from now on.

The night of the party, as I was headed out the door to meet her, I got a text from Monica. "Covered in barf! A+J both sick. Can't come. So sorry! xM." I texted Mandy, but she was on a date. I thought about going home, but it was a gorgeous June night, and I was all dressed and the party was only a few blocks away. I figured I'd go, congratulate Jake, have a bite, and leave after one or two drinks.

I wonder how differently the night would have gone had Mandy been available. Mandy is the one who introduced Leo and me. They were neighbors, and she had mentioned him to me a few times—the cute guy who always helped her move stuff. Mandy doesn't like labels, but she dates women. So when she learned that Leo was single, she immediately thought of me, fresh off my latest breakup with Jake. She invited both of us and a handful of other friends over for one of her game nights. After several rounds of Balderdash and red wine, we started on Encore, a game where your team wins by being able to sing a song with the word on the card. Leo and I were on opposite teams, but we were unquestionably the MVPs. He seemed to know every pop song ever recorded from the mideighties through the early nineties, while I specialized in nineties alt-rock and show tunes, thanks to my high school devotion to the local college radio station and Grandma Margie's love of musical theater. He had a terrible voice but could carry a tune, so everyone recognized his songs. My voice wasn't as bad as his, but I couldn't carry a tune to save my life. In all, we sounded awful and had everyone in hysterics over the obscure songs we'd recall. We went back and forth for what seemed like an hour on "rain" songs. By the time we petered out, everyone else had lost interest in the game, which left Leo and me drunkenly serenading each other, gray toothed and purple lipped from the red wine.

The party moved from Mandy's to the Spring Lounge, where Leo and I huddled at the jukebox and flirtatiously argued about what to play. When a group of twentysomethings vacated a booth near us, we nabbed it and sat across from each other, until last call, yelling to be heard above the noise. I remember thinking that it would be easier to continue our conversation if we sat beside each other, but I was afraid to make any small change for fear things would be less perfect if any single variable was shifted. For the same reason, I held my pee for the last hour.

My heart beat faster when I realized why he seemed so familiar to me. With his kind eyes, longish face, perfect smile, and wavy, wiry hair—he looks an awful lot like Jimmy Stewart. I had seen both *It's a Wonderful Life* and *Rear Window* at least a dozen times and had always had a strange crush on Jimmy Stewart. Of course, it was 2006 and not 1947, but still, I couldn't believe my luck that this guy was single and, it seemed, interested. We sat in that booth until last call, when Mandy and the rest left without saying goodbye. We clearly didn't want to be interrupted.

While he walked me home at four in the morning, I stopped myself from busting into "Buffalo Gals," but I did allow myself to imagine me as Mary and him as George. That night I learned that he'd spent most of his childhood and adolescence in the back of a Volkswagen Vanogan listening to Top 40 radio. He was one of four boys and had some kind of bone disorder and had to wear leg braces until he was thirteen, so while the rest of his brothers were shuttled around to their various sports activities, he sat and listened to music, memorizing lyrics.

The next day I slept until two in the afternoon, and he called me at six and asked me to join him in a five-mile run in Central Park later that week. It was called the Run Hit Wonder, and every mile there was a one-hit-wonder band from the eighties or nineties playing their famous song.

<hr />

After we passed Tone Lōc performing "Funky Cold Medina," he said, "This is a cool first date, isn't it?"

When I didn't answer right away, he nudged me with his elbow.

"Hey, don't pretend you didn't know this was a date."

"I wasn't!" I panted.

"I mean, I did pay your entrance fee, which includes all-you-can drink Vitaminwater and a banana. Plus, we are going to, like, five concerts in one. I mean, did you ever imagine you'd be this close to Tone Lōc?"

"Okay, you're right. It's an awesome first date."

We exchanged a smile that remained on both of our faces for an embarrassingly long time.

Afterward we took the subway back to my stop and he walked me to my door. It was a strange time of day to end a date—about eight o'clock at night—but we said good night and I let him kiss me. Then I went upstairs with my race swag, took a shower, ordered Thai food, and fell asleep on the couch, watching *It's a Wonderful Life*.

Things progressed quickly between us from there. Within two weeks, we were sleeping at each other's place nearly every night. Jake's predictable call a few weeks after that went unreturned. Leo and I had settled into our own routine. We went to a new restaurant every Thursday and the same little Chinese place around the corner from his apartment every Friday. Saturdays we'd stay in and watch a movie, and we'd spend Sundays—my favorite days— lounging around reading the *New York Times*, eating bagels, having afternoon sex, and occasionally going to the park or a museum. We'd retreat to our own apartments for a night or two on Monday, when I'd catch up on doing laundry, paying bills, and other mundane tasks that tend to fall through the cracks when one is in love.

But I wasn't replaying the early days of our romance when I walked alone to the party. I was psyching myself up for a solo entrance and hoping I would be able to find some non-mom things to talk about with a bunch of hip strangers.

New York
June 20

Sid,

I'm sitting at the bar at the Pig, trying to pretend I'm not really here. I can't leave. So I'm sipping my ~~third~~ fourth Stoli and soda and scribbling this to you because apparently I've forgotten how to talk to adult people. I might not actually send this to you, but I'm just relieved that my hands and eyes and brain have something to do. Jesus. Bono is here. Fucking Bono. And so is Emilio Estevez! This is too funny—remember how many times we watched *The Breakfast Club*? He is so small! Honestly, I could hold him in the palm of my hand. He's not talking to anyone. Maybe I'll go tell him about our *Breakfast Club* obsession—I'm sure he never gets that from drunk thirtysomething women! Never mind. Now he's talking to Jake. Jaaaake. He looks so good, Sid. I'll try to snap a picture for you. This is bad, but I can't stop wishing Jake would pull me into that tiny bathroom and push me up against the wall. I'm starting to think that's why I came here, actually. I didn't admit it to myself at first. I mean, of course I wouldn't have come with that as my mission. But now that I'm here and with a few drinks under my belt and all this candlelight and no one to talk to, it's all I've been able to think about.

I'm so embarrassed. When I first arrived I was all giggly and touchy and he was all "Where's your husband?" And then he introduced me to his beautiful girlfriend, who looked really familiar and is possibly famous. But I can't leave NOW. I don't want him to think I was thinking what I was thinking, so my brilliant strategy is to stay and prove to him that I'm not in the least bit interested in him. That I'm just here as his mature, happily married ex to offer support and congratulations. And that I'm so secure that I don't mind hanging out all by myself. And that I'm some sort of reporter or poet or songwriter who needs to be scribbling away at the bar in the middle of this party. (Sorry that I'm writing this really, really small—it's so no one can see it.) Even though I've spent most of the evening alone, it is fun to be out. I miss this. No one here is in any way connected to my kids or me as a mom. I haven't felt this free in years.

Okay, I need to stop now and make another attempt at small talk. I think I was a bit unkind to these tiny, pretty twenty-five-year-olds who were actually being nice by talking to me, but they kept misusing "random" and "literally" and I just couldn't go along with it. One of them was doing this bit about how much she loved bacon and kind of tittering about it, like a hot, skinny girl with an interest in bacon was the most hilariously adorable thing ever. Clearly this bacon-loving shtick has worked in the past, but God, was it painful to watch. Did I ever act like that when I was single? I don't remember anyone ever behaving like that. Lord help me if I get stuck with those two again.

Xoxox,
Cass

I carefully tucked my letter into the zipper inside my clutch, climbed down from my barstool, and noticed that a small dance party had broken out in the opposite corner of the restaurant.

I'd like to point out here that I was always a good dancer. The reason I know this is that good dancers were always coming and dancing with me. So, welcoming the opportunity to do something other than make more awkward small talk, I made my way into the fray. Within forty-five seconds, two realizations set in: One, I hadn't been dancing since before the twins were born, and two, prebaby dancing is a whole different animal from postbaby dancing. It was as if my hips and core were in no way connected to my arms and legs. My inebriated state and the lack of recent practice I'd had in four-inch heels couldn't have helped. I knew that things were off, even without the added assurance of my seeming invisibility to the better dancers in the crowd. Nonetheless, I plugged away for several songs, thinking—hoping—it would all come back to me. And then it was, *Maybe this shot of tequila will loosen me up.* I remember feeling indignant: I mean, I used to be somebody on the dance floor. Now I was clearly somebody's *mom* on the dance floor. When I finally decided it was time to go, I was having difficulty walking, let alone dancing. I found Jake and made an attempt at a classy goodbye.

I must have slurred my words, because he laughed at me and took me by the arm. "I'll get you a cab," he said, leading me to the door.

"Don't be crazy—it's, like, four blocks!"

"Maybe I should walk you home," he said.

"Oh my God, stop it!" I said, playfully pushing him away. "Listen, thanks for the invite. Great party. Congratulations on all of this. I'm so happy for you." The hand I was using to push him off was still on his chest. He ushered me out the front door, and I said, "Okay, take care, Jake," and we both leaned in for the perfunctory cheek peck.

One of us leaned the wrong way or something. I'm not sure

what happened, but the sides of our lips grazed, and then, instead of correcting themselves to their rightful place in the air on his outer cheek, my lips—his too, I think—were pulled back to the center, where they met and lingered for three or four seconds before I pulled away and then went back in, my hands at the back of his neck. For a few frantic seconds, the kiss deepened, his hands seized my ass, and we walked backward until I was pushed against the side of his restaurant. Suddenly we both pulled away at the same time.

He didn't apologize or act as if anything strange had happened, and neither did I. Without another word, I turned and left. Walking home, I convinced myself that nothing had happened—not really. Before going upstairs, I picked up an egg-and-cheese sandwich and a Gatorade from the bodega, an effort to get in front of a hangover as well as erase the taste of Jake's lips. I carefully entered my dark apartment and sat at the tiny desk in the entryway, then took the letter out of my bag and added,

PS—Oh shit!!! Jake and I made out!!!

Then, because I was already sitting there at my desk eating my sandwich, I scanned the letter and saved it before finishing the Gatorade with two Advil, washing my face, brushing my teeth, and climbing into bed.

—————⟡⟡⟡—————

You know that terrible feeling when you realize you sent an e-mail to the wrong person? Say you're making fun of your boss and instead of forwarding your zinger to your best friend, you hit reply and it goes to your boss. And then you fumble around trying to unsend it, to no avail. And then you sit there with a stomachache until you get a response? Well, that's how I felt times ten when, moments after I watched Quinn drop my letter from the Pig into the mailbox, I opened this:

Singapore
June 23

Hey, Cassie,

I have a bad feeling about Adrian's business trips to Bangkok. I can't put my finger on it, but every time he comes home, something is off. His smell, his mood, everything is just different. It's nothing concrete, and I might be paranoid from the "smorgasbord" type stories I've heard. I can't believe I'm saying this, but I can feel myself looking the other way. Me! Looking the other way! Who am I?? Honestly, I just don't want to deal with this right now.

Love,
Sid

I immediately knew it was true. Adrian. That ass. Who was *he* to cheat on Sid? A hundred guys would have given their left arm to be with her. She chose him. He should have spent his life proving himself worthy.

There was always something a little off about him. He was supercharismatic yet somehow removed. He'd be all chummy with you, making jokes and elbowing you in the ribs like you were old pals, and then the next time he saw you, you'd expect to pick up where you left off, but he would be distant and quiet. Also, at his only Christmas at Joe and Margie's, he'd found an excuse to leave the room during "The Twelve Days of Christmas," which didn't sit right with anyone.

Next, deep shame and panic set in. I believe my exact thoughts were, *fuck, fuck, fuck, shit, shit, shit.* I considered waiting for the mail lady to come, but I knew there was no way she'd give me my letter back. My chances were better of having the boys create a diversion and stealing it myself, but involving my children in what is likely a federal offense was just a bit further than I was willing to go.

I couldn't wallow in misery over the letter for long because I had a nasty hangover to contend with and a full day ahead with the boys. Before I had kids, I actually enjoyed the occasional hangover— that is, if I hadn't done anything too stupid the night before. Because if there's one way to ruin a perfectly good hangover, it's by being the kind of person who is sure she embarrassed herself a thousand times over. The other way is to have twin three-year-old boys to care for. I still remember my first real postbaby hangover when the boys were nearly one. Leo and I had gone to a friend's holiday party and I had what I thought was a modest amount of champagne, but it had been nearly two years since I'd had more than one glass of anything. The next day, I updated my Facebook status to say, "Add hangovers to the long list of things my kids have ruined." My mom friends added things like, "Museums!" "Bookstores," "Sex," and "My tits" in the comments. We all had a good giggle over it, and Monica turned it into a funny poem and one of her highest-rated blog posts ever.

Around noon, while I sipped my fourth Vitaminwater at Bleecker Playground, Monica called.

"Details!!" she shouted when I answered with a flat, "Hey."

"Oh, Lord, no. Can't do it."

"Well, I know there was dancing. What else?"

"How do you know there was dancing?" For a horrifying moment I pictured myself as a YouTube sensation: Drunk mom on a dance floor thinks she's still got it.

"You texted me, 'Add to the list: dancing.' I take it Cassie didn't get her groove back."

"Oh God, oh God, don't make me relive it. No. No groove back. And why can't someone tell Rhonda to clean the goddamn bathroom?"

"Hand your phone to Rhonda. I'll talk to her," Monica said.

"You're sweet. But she's gone now."

I'd had to visit the playground's toilet more than once that morning. Rhonda was the maintenance woman at the park responsible for emptying the garbage and cleaning the bathroom. She was cheerful and always singing, knew Quinn and Joey by name (and could tell them apart), and was generally difficult not to love. She disappeared into the bathroom with a bucket of cleaning supplies once a day, but I have no idea what she did in there because the bathroom is always so hideously disgusting that I often let my boys just pee through the fence into the landscaping surrounding the playground rather than enter that snuff-film set. Some days—today not being one of them—I thought about asking Rhonda to watch my kids and give me ten minutes with her mop and bleach.

"Wait, how are the kids?" I thought to ask.

"Not great. We're headed to the doctor in ten. Do you want me to bring you something on the way? Advil? A milk shake, maybe?"

"That's all right, hon. I'll call you tomorrow," I said, opting not to tell her about Jake.

After the boys were in bed that night, I forced myself to open the computer and reread my last letter. It was as bad as I remembered and probably on a truck to JFK right now. I'd write her an apology letter tomorrow, I decided. Maybe it could get there the same day as my other letter, or the day after.

It didn't help my guilt over the whole matter that if it weren't for me, Sid would never have even met Adrian. It all happened when she came to visit after the twins were born. Her plan was to be there for the main event—she'd helped me develop a birth plan and had even walked me through several hypnobirthing sessions over the phone. I wanted her by my side, coaching me to envision myself floating on a strawberry cloud or whatever it was. But I went into labor six weeks early, and by the time Sid made the drive in from Ohio, we were a family of four. Quinn came out first, but Joey did some kind of flip at the last minute, requiring an emergency C-section. There was no hypno anything, but there were plenty of drugs.

Sid lived on our couch for those first two crazy, beautiful, terrifying weeks of the boys' lives. One evening, Leo's good friend Grant Eshel stopped by with a gift for the babies and a bottle of champagne. He had a friend with him—Adrian—which was weird. It's kind of an intimate moment, visiting new babies, not one you bring a stranger to. But Grant is no Ann Landers, and apparently he'd just run into Adrian on our block and had dragged him up. Adrian handled it well, politely congratulating us and hanging back while Grant met the babies.

They invited Leo to join them for dinner. He looked at me, unsure. "Go, go. Please," I said. Then, to my surprise, Adrian spoke up and said, "And what about you, Sidney? Are you hungry?"

"Oh, Cassie and I will just order in," she said. "But it was nice meeting you."

And then he turned to me. "Does your nursemaid ever get out?"

I laughed uncomfortably. Sid was busy cooing at one of the

boys, and we both stopped to look at her. He looked back at me with a questioning smile, and I said, "Actually, I wouldn't mind some alone time with the babies. If you're hungry, why don't you go, Sid? Bring me something, okay?"

She looked even more unsure than Leo did.

"Really—I want you guys to go. Have fun."

When Adrian tells the story, he fell in love with her at first sight and worked like hell to get her to fall in love with him. In other words, the standard narrative as far as Sid's relationships go. He said she was the most beautiful girl he'd ever seen and she wasn't even trying. To be honest, I'd questioned whether he'd ever been around a girl who wasn't "trying" and wondered if that in itself was a red flag. He said that when he saw her holding the baby, he felt for the first time that he wanted to be a father. It sounded sweet enough, if not completely original.

Sid admitted to liking him and was glad to have him visit her in Ohio, but stopped short of calling him her boyfriend. Meanwhile, Adrian courted the whole family, which no doubt helped his cause. When he sent me flowers and a charming note congratulating us on the twins and apologizing for intruding, I called Sid and gushed about how thoughtful he seemed. He made an ally in River, too, taking him to basketball games and the scary movies that Sid refused to see. His persistence eventually paid off, and she fell for him. Right around the time the twins turned one, he proposed and transferred to his bank's Columbus office.

Moving to Columbus meant he'd had to travel once or twice a quarter to meet with colleagues and clients in Chicago and New York, but Sid never seemed to mind. She was used to being on her own, and she'd mentioned time apart being good for their relationship. His comings and goings played nicely into his penchant for romantic gestures, and he was often surprising her with lavish gifts and expensive jewelry purchased on his business trips.

After the proposal, I made Leo invite Grant over so we could pump him for intel on Adrian. Grant had bland answers for us: "A great guy," and, "Rich as hell." He did tell us that Adrian had described Sid as the perfect girl next door: simple and beautiful and kind—the type you can't find in New York anymore. I'd felt that was nice, but something about it made her seem like a commodity. His use of "simple" made me think that he either got her perfectly, or not at all, and Grant was less than helpful at discerning any nuance in Adrian's assessment.

CHAPTER ELEVEN

We all overslept on the boys' last day of preschool before summer. It was eight fifteen when Joey placed his warm little hand on my cheek and yelled, "Mommy! Gotta go poop!" I went from deep sleep to full-on mania, which at least spared me that guilty prerousing moment of *I need to write Sid that apology letter today*. It had been almost two weeks, so chances were she'd read my embarrassing letter already. Coincidentally, I hadn't received any letters from her during that time, so even though it wasn't possible that those two letterless weeks had anything to do with my transgressions, it was hard not to feel like I was being punished.

"Go, go, go," I whispered to him as I chased him into the bathroom. The vaguely sore throat that had been building for the last few days had crossed over to the kind where your whole body shudders with each swallow. I brushed my teeth and did a few extra gargles while he sat on the toilet, singing "The Wheels on the Bus."

Leo poked his head in. "Are you done, bud? Your brother has to poop, too."

"Mmmm. No," Joey said.

"Okay, try to hurry, my man. He's really gotta go." Then, frowning at me, "You all right, Cass?"

"Throat's killing me," I whispered before going in for another gargle.

I splashed some warm water on my face and leaned into the shower for a pump of face wash. I was rubbing it into my skin when I felt Quinn's head butting my hip.

"Poop, poop, poop, poop, poooooop!" he hollered.

I rinsed and dried my face and mustered the will to use my voice again. "All done, Joey?"

"Nope! Still pooping!"

"Try to finish up," I said in a whisper.

But it was too late; in one fell swoop, Quinn pulled down his Spider-Man pajama bottoms, crammed his fingers under Joey's thigh, and held on to the toilet bowl while he squatted down.

"Shit! Leo!" I yelled, pain ripping through my throat.

"Quinn, what are you doing? Hold it! Joey, hurry up!" I begged. I put my hands under Joey's arms, planning to move him off of the toilet and into the tub and replace him with Quinn, but my nose told me that it was too late. Indeed, a rather large brown pile of (blessedly solid) feces had appeared on the black-and-white-tiled floor between Quinn's chubby feet.

When I let out an exasperated sigh, Quinn's lower lip curled and he started to sob. I grabbed him under the arms and lifted him over Joey and into the bathtub.

"Look, Mom! It's like a snake!" yelled Joey.

"Sorry, Mommy," Quinn bawled.

"You're fine. You're fine," was all I could mutter. I felt bad for him, but despite what he'd once seen a grown man do into a pizza box on the C train platform, it's not okay to defecate on the floor, and I wasn't going to tell him it was. I carefully took his clothes off, set them in the narrow space between the toilet and the tub, and started to hose him down.

"Hands!" I barked, holding the bottle of Burt's Bees shower gel.

"No!" Quinn screamed, and shoved his hands under his arms.

I lathered my own hands and slid them into his armpits, managing to cover most of his fingers and palms.

"All done, Mommy!" yelled Joey from the toilet, as if nothing unusual were happening.

"Stay," I said, and aimed the water flow at Quinn's butt crack. He was screaming about the water being too cold, but I was almost done and I knew if I moved the temperature a hair in the other direction, it would turn scalding hot, so I'd have to err on the side of freezing.

"Leo!" I yelled. My throat was on fire.

"Daddy!!!" hollered Joey as he moved to get down from the toilet.

"Hang on, Joey, please," I said. I didn't want him to make a move before I cleaned up the pile of shit that he would step right into should he attempt to exit the area, which I probably don't have to tell you is only slightly larger than an airplane bathroom.

I wondered if Leo had just up and left. I recalled him mentioning he had to be in Long Island City by nine to do something to a server. Or maybe he had the same sore throat as me and went back to bed. Either scenario made him a jerk, and my resentment was building.

Another squealing sound coming from the other room now competed with Quinn's sobs and Joey's entreaties. I bundled Quinn in a towel and carried him like a baby into the living room, yelling at Joey to hang tight. From the stove, the teapot rattled angrily and shot white steam onto the wall. Quinn was crying even louder and covering his ears. I dumped him on the couch and ran over to turn off the stove and move the teapot.

Quinn calmed down a bit, but Leo was still nowhere to be seen. I silently cursed him and went back to help Joey, who was now standing backward on the toilet seat—one foot on either side of the bowl—straining to see his butt in the mirror above the sink.

I grabbed him and placed him in the bathtub, safely isolated from the poo pile, despite his pleas to let him see if there was a red mark on the back of his legs from sitting on the toilet for so long. I wiped him, helped him wash his hands, and then lifted him over the mess and set him down in the hall, asking him if he thought he was fast enough and big enough to get dressed all by himself before I finished cleaning up the bathroom. "How about we race?" I said.

"I'm gonna win! I'm gonna win!" he yelled, running toward the bedroom.

I took a moment to close my eyes and sigh. The pain was spreading to my ears, and a dull headache was building. I grabbed a wad of toilet paper and went to scoop the poop from the floor but was dismayed to see a little toe-shaped indent on the side of the otherwise symmetrical brown coil.

I grabbed a pack of baby wipes from the shelf over the toilet and took off to find the toe in question. Quinn was still lying down wrapped in his towel on the sofa, rolling from side to side and muttering something about the gingerbread man.

Joey stood on our bed, struggling to pull his T-shirt over his head—backward and inside out—when I yelled, "Joey! Stop! Sit! Sit down! Let me see your feet!" His feet checked out. Then, with horror, I realized that, of course, it was my toe that had brushed the poop. I was the only one who hadn't been carried out of the bathroom. I ordered the boys to stay where they were, walked on my heel to the bathroom, washed my foot in the tub, grabbed two towels and threw them over the spots I'd just tracked on the living room rug, and Swiffered the other parts of the floor.

Leo came home as I was replacing the Swiffer on its back-of-the-door hook, so the door whacked me in the forehead when he opened it. "What the hell!" I hissed.

"'Hell' is a not-nice word!" the naked Quinn chirped from the couch.

"Oh, sorry about that," Leo said, rubbing my head. "I just ran down to get you a lemon for your throat. Is the water done?"

It was a thoughtful thing to do, I admit, but I had been shooting mental daggers at him for the past ten minutes and was not quite ready to switch gears. I also knew that under the guise of a good deed, he had shot the breeze with Amir, scanned the front pages of the *Post* and the *Times*, and smoked half a cigarette. In other words, he'd enjoyed a nice little grown-up moment while I endured a literal shit storm.

Leo needed to be out the door in five minutes if he was going to make it to Long Island City on time, so I couldn't ask him to drop the boys off. He took a two-minute shower, grabbed his travel coffee mug, hugged the boys, and kissed me on the forehead. "I'll probably stop by to take a dump before my meeting at Varick Street," he said.

That did it. "What is wrong with you?" I said, incredulously. "Your wife does not ever need to hear you say 'take a dump.' And neither do the boys. This isn't a flipping frat house. I feel like dying, and my entire morning has centered around poop. I don't want to hear it!"

"I was just telling you in case you were going to be here!" he said, looking at me like I was crazy.

"Actually, I will be here," I said, scrapping my plans to go grocery shopping and to Pilates in favor of a nap. "And I'd rather you didn't come here to stink up the place."

"Okay, bye," he said, and left.

I walked into the bedroom to grab clothes for Quinn. Joey was fully dressed, in a backward and inside-out T-shirt and a way-too-small pair of sweatpants the exact same shade of gray as his T-shirt. He was pulling a pair of Leo's socks onto his hands.

"Mommy, do you want to die?" he asked me gravely.

"What? What? No!" I snapped. Then I vaguely recalled having spat something along those lines to Leo just ten seconds ago, in addition to a few other ill-advised comments. I sat on the floor next to Joey and pulled him into my lap. "It's just an expression grown-ups use sometimes when we're very frustrated. But it was a dumb thing to say. I made a mistake. I don't want to die and I'm not going to die. Okay?"

"What's an expression?"

Ugh. Why is every situation this morning requiring me to speak? "Just words people say when they don't have the energy to explain how they're really feeling. Sometimes they sound silly."

"Huh?" he said, lip curling up on one side.

"Come on, honey. Take Daddy's socks off your hands and let's go eat breakfast."

Normally, when we're running late, I give them a granola bar for the road, but I couldn't make myself hurry today. I poured the boys Cheerios and the last of the milk and sliced up a banana and an apple before squeezing the lemon and some honey into my hot water. We sat at our small square table, which was pushed up against the window. The rain fell hard, making *plink, plink, plink* sounds on the fire escape.

I calculated that circle time was well over by that time and they'd be lucky to make it for snack. Walking fast, I hunched over the stroller in an effort to grasp the umbrella and steer the double-wide, which required both hands on a slippery morning at the tail end of rush hour. My umbrella made a perfect dome over my head and shoulders but not much else, so my entire backside was soaked within minutes. I loved that umbrella. It was totally transparent except for a red "Gensler" printed on it, the name of an architecture firm that had sponsored an event I'd attended years ago. The little spokes pointed toward the ground and not out to the sides. With it, I felt superior to the other umbrella-wielding commuters, unable to see properly and unwittingly poking other people in the side of the head, or, worse, taking up way too much space with their planet-sized golf umbrellas, which are my least favorite thing about rainy days in Manhattan. People who use them must think that their absolute dryness is more important than anyone else being able to walk down the same side of the street as them. If everyone had an umbrella like mine, rainy days would be much more civil.

On my way into school, another mom was coming out, perfectly coiffed and made-up, in a silk blouse and pencil skirt. I fixated on her spotless four-inch heels as she trotted into a waiting town car. If I'd kept working, that could have been me, I thought. But in my cutoff jeans shorts, marled gray ARMY T-shirt that had belonged to the roommate of my college boyfriend, and a yellow childlike rain-coat, it was hard to imagine ever attaining that level of sartorial sophistication. On the bright side, I always felt chic in my black Hunter Wellingtons, although three out of every five women on the street were wearing the exact same pair.

After drop-off, I headed north out of habit. Within a few blocks I remembered that I'd meant to go home and nap, not do my weekly Whole Foods and Trader Joe's run. But our cupboards were nearly bare, so I kept walking, planning to skip Whole Foods and get a couple bags' worth at Trader Joe's, then hopefully catch a cab home in time for a hot shower and a quick nap before pickup at noon.

I was pushing my little red cart around the meager produce section when my phone in my back pocket started buzzing. *Oh shit,* I thought. My entire rear end was soaking wet, which meant the phone was, too. I withdrew it and saw the photo of my mother, Rita Sunday, beaming and balancing a boy on each hip. I didn't want to answer, given the state of my throat, but I was curious to see if my wet phone still worked and was also alarmed that Mom was calling at nine thirty on a Thursday morning. Our weekly Skype sessions, eight a.m. on Saturdays, supplemented by her call to me Sunday nights in the hour after the kids went to bed, were immutable. I couldn't recall a single time she or I had called each other off schedule. I wondered if she and Sid kept to a similar schedule. With only the teensiest pang of not jealousy so much as sorrow, it struck me that they probably talked on the phone several times a week and didn't need a rigid schedule to keep in touch.

"Mom? What's wrong?" I answered.

"Oh, hi, honey! No, no, nothing's wrong. I was thinking of you and thought I'd call to check in." But her voice sounded strained.

"Oh, okay. Well, I'm at the store, so . . ."

"Are you all right? You don't sound good."

"Sore throat," I said, economizing my words.

But instead of the expected instructions to make some tea and go to bed, she soldiered on. "So what's new with you and Leo?"

"Uuuh, not much," I said, girding myself against the pain that erupted each time I spoke or swallowed.

"Are you finding time to be together as husband and wife?"

"What?"

"I mean, it's important to remember that you aren't just parents. You are also man and wife."

"Man and wife? What are you talking about?" I said while attempting to steer my cart into the fray at the free-sample counter. I was chilled and starving, and the steaming plastic ramekins of Roasted Corn Tortilla Soup were beckoning me. But the cluster of senior citizens leisurely sipping their soup right there at the sample counter made things difficult. I was not in the mood for this. To check out, I found the end of the line, which snaked around the entire perimeter of the store, and did the rest of my shopping by grabbing whatever I could reach from my place in line.

I half listened and tried to do as little talking as possible while reaching for the odd loaf of bread, canister of coffee, and bag of flax chips. Mom yammered on about "date nights" and "keeping him interested," and then it hit me: Sid must have told her about my letter from the Pig.

"Mom, I'm sorry. I've got to go. I'm in line at the store. I'll talk to you Sunday, okay?" I wanted to get off the phone before she confronted me about the kiss—or worse, talked about her own affair.

Mom had had an affair when I was in the sixth grade. I found out on a Sunday afternoon when Sid was at a friend's house. I had been napping on the family room couch and awoke when I heard the phone ringing. Dad answered and called to Mom in a clipped voice that her boss was on the phone. She got on the phone and said that yes, she could come in early tomorrow to assist with a root canal. Then Mom and Dad had a brief and barely audible argument about why she was still working for Dr. Shapiro. Apparently, Mom had given her notice but still had a week to go. This was surprising information for a few reasons. I hadn't known that she had any intention of quitting her job. She liked being a dental hygienist, as far as I knew. She used to come into our classrooms with her giant toothbrush and a set of model teeth and teach proper oral hygiene (brush up and down, not side to side; don't neglect the gums and tongue; soft bristles, not hard; eat an apple or some cheese before bed if you forget your toothbrush on a sleepover).

Furthermore, she needed that job—we were a two-job, one-(used)-car, clearance-rack-shopping family. Then Dad wondered out loud if her boss really needed her help in the morning or if it was just an excuse to see her alone, before the receptionist arrived. I got the shock of my young life when Mom said sharply, "I told you it was over with him." It's a line I'd heard dozens of times on *Santa Barbara*—the soap opera Sid and I faithfully watched, in which the wealthy Capwell family navigated an endless storm of lust and betrayal from their picturesque town on the sea—but not one I ever imagined hearing in my own home. "I told you it was over with him," was something Gina the slutty villainess said, not my mom. My parents walked out the back door to finish the yard work, and I heard no more.

For an hour I remained in the fetal position on the couch, under the crocheted afghan. I remember desperately needing to talk to Sid. But in the time that passed between my shocking discovery and Sid's arrival home, something shifted in me. I couldn't tell her what I knew. I didn't want my sister to hate Mom the way that I did now. I think this was the moment I started to become my own person, to grow away from my sister a bit. I felt very grown-up, protecting Sid from something that would hurt her.

This secret became my dark superpower: a source of strength, but also the saddest and most uncomfortable thing I'd ever encountered. I both relished my ownership of it and deplored its very existence. The whole thing was downright Capwell-esque, and I envisioned myself as a character: the strong and stoic sister, my eyes flickering knowingly each time I caught Dad gazing at Mom with those pathetic puppy-dog eyes. It was a defining phase for me: I was not a frivolous blabbermouth. I was a shrewd and serious player who knew when to keep her mouth shut. I felt that I understood darkness and pain.

I got my first period a week later, and instead of telling Mom, I told Sid, who set me up with Kotex and Tampax and a hug. Mom, of course, found out and came to me in a jubilation I could hardly share in. "You're a woman now!" she said, hugging me. And I thought, *Indeed I am.*

I may not have been (definitely was not) a woman, but it was by keeping that secret that I stopped being a little girl who modeled herself after her big sister. I still admired Sid as much as ever, but now that I'd made a conscious decision to protect her, I was a force in the world, distinct and separate. I became wry and sarcastic. A shade bitter, even. I grew to own my new outlook, taking pride in not seeing the world through rose-colored glasses. I was the Rizzo to Sid's Sandy, the Laverne to her Shirley.

Meanwhile, I daydreamed about sitting Dad down in front of the TV so that he could see how these things work. A woman who says, "I told you it was over with him," is, in fact, receiving long-stemmed red roses by the dozen that cause her to gaze longingly into space while she replays in her mind the sultry evening they'd spent in a bubble bath only the night before. I wanted him to storm out, to give her an ultimatum, maybe go to her office and threaten to rough up Dr. Shapiro.

But the irritation I felt with my father's meek nature paled in comparison to the indignity of having to think of my parents in a sexual way. The horrifying flashes I'd get of Mom mounting Dr. Shapiro on the very chair in which my family had our teeth cleaned were deeply troubling to me at this tender point in my development. Dr. Shapiro was older—or at least seemed older, with silver hair and deep crow's-feet. The pictures in his waiting room were all of him partaking in bike races and marathons and rock-climbing adventures. He had perfect sparkly white tombstone teeth, and I wondered which came first, the teeth or the interest in dentistry. Was he so vain that he built a career around his best feature? Or had he had awful teeth his whole life and gone into dentistry to fix them? Either way, I thought he was totally lame.

After that Mom took a few months off and then got a part-time job working for another dentist, a female dentist. Dr. Shapiro must have been paying Mom pretty well, because right about this time, Sid and I were told we had been "chosen" to work one day a week each in the church rectory. I think it must have been some kind of work-study program to help pay our tuition. In the four-to-seven-thirty shift on Tuesdays, as a thirteen-year-old, I was tasked with answering the phone, taking money from people who came in to reserve a Mass for someone, and following the day cook's instructions for preparing dinner.

Since no one in our house ever cooked, both Sid and I were completely useless when it came to this last part. Each Wednesday, I'd read the cook's scrawly, old-fashioned cursive note instructing me to prepare something I'd never eaten. It was mostly a matter of heating a meat loaf or shepherd's pie, but I was also expected to mash potatoes or assemble a salad. Terms like "relish tray," and "gravlax" had me on the phone to friends' mothers every week. The whole thing only fueled my irritation with my own mother. *Why does everyone else in our town know what a Betty's Salad is? Why haven't we ever once eaten meat loaf?* Sid was perplexed when I lashed out about this, and I came close to telling her why we were working there in the first place, but my vision of myself as a *Santa Barbara* character steadied me, and I kept mum.

Eventually, it all came out. Mom and Dad sat us down at the kitchen table one night and explained that they were having trouble with their marriage. They sensed that we had noticed. They wanted to stay married because they loved each other, but marriage was hard and they were working on it. Sid cried and asked a series of invasive questions provoking Mom to confess her affair. I watched, stone-faced, wishing I could make it all stop, to go back to it being my secret.

Sid's emotional reaction and my non-reaction led my mother to sign us up for three sessions of family counseling.

No one I'd ever heard of went to therapy, which made the experience all the more strange and embarrassing. I suffered through those awkward meetings saying as little as possible, but Sid and my parents made up for my passivity with copious crying and hugging and sharing. I imagine our therapist felt like a real healer.

Despite—or perhaps because of—the early encounter with my parents' sexuality, I always clammed up like a fourteen-year-old when my mother broached subjects of a carnal nature (which she did quite a lot, unfortunately). She and Sid had teased me about it at Christmastime.

"Well, I'm just saying it's important, is all," she said after I rolled my eyes at some thinly veiled double entendre she made as we stood in the kitchen sipping wine and putting away dishes.

"All right, Mom, we got it," I said.

"Well, I think it's beautiful," said Sid.

"Thank you, Sid. It is beautiful. And sometimes it's fun and sometimes it's dirty and sometimes it's . . ."

"Jesus!" I yelled, cutting her off. "Listen, Mom, there's gotta be some kind of Internet chat room for frisky empty nesters. Go tell *them* about your conquests with my father."

"Oh, come on, Cass!" Sid said. "You know how many of our childhood friends' parents are still married? Not many. And how many of them are still enjoying a healthy sex life? Probably even less. I say, you go, Mom!"

"Thank you, Sid," Mom said, and then started doing an embarrassing dance around the kitchen, where she kind of rolled her fisted hands at waist level while rocking side to side. I groaned and closed my eyes, while Sid, just to make me squirm, started dancing with her and chanting, "Go, Rita! Go, Rita!"

Suffice it to say, I was not cool with my mom calling to talk about sex, and I was even less cool with Sid telling her about my note.

I managed to get home by eleven, and I could have taken a thirty- or forty-minute nap but was revved up from that phone call, mad at myself for being mean to Leo this morning, angry with Sid for presumably telling Mom about my kiss with Jake, and trying hard not to think that maybe infidelity is simply in my blood. I unloaded my groceries, washed the breakfast dishes, took a quick shower, spot cleaned and vacuumed the living room rug, forced myself to gargle with salt water, and went to pick up the boys. It was drizzling again, but my favorite umbrella was nowhere to be found. I must have left it in the cab. I purchased a four-dollar number at the bodega and walked with my unspecial black umbrella back to school.

As soon as I got there, I was accosted by one of the assistant teachers. "Oh, Cassie, hi. Do you have a minute?" She was a young woman named Breezy, who always seemed completely wonderful with the children but took an imperious tone with the parents. I stepped into the office with her before Joey and Quinn noticed me.

Apparently Quinn had a lot of questions about death and had told his friends that his mom wants to die, which forced me into a long explanation of the morning. Once she seemed assured that I was not having suicidal thoughts and sharing them with my three-year-olds, I sheepishly presented her with one of the Trader Joe's gift cards I'd picked up after seeing the pile of last-day gifts and apples and flowers on the windowsill when I'd dropped the boys off.

The rain had stopped, so I took the boys to the playground and let them get muddy with the goal of wearing them out before the movie I had planned for that afternoon. I hoped the huge bag of Pirate's Booty cheese puffs and sachets of dried mangoes combined with Buzz, Woody, and the gang would keep them content long enough for me to lie down and not speak or swallow for an hour or so. I was so intent on getting to that couch that I wasn't even going to check the mail, but it was Joey's day to be in charge of the keys and he insisted on stopping.

Singapore
June 29

Cassie,

Double whammy! I found a questionable text message on Adrian's phone from an "AP." It said, "Miss u. Come back to BKK soon, OK?" BKK is obviously Bangkok and I knew that, but for some reason I felt the need to Google it, on the off chance that it was, oh, I don't know, a bank or something with extremely personal service. So I opened River's laptop and when I typed "B," I hesitated for a second, and a scroll of terms starting with the letter "B" appeared, and "birth father locator" was the first one. That means River must have typed that into his computer recently, right? Shit!

I wonder if I did the right thing by never searching for Kenny—never even trying to connect him with River. I think he went to jail at some point for selling drugs, so who knows what became of him? I figured if he wanted to find us, he could.

But now I wonder, was I being too proud? Was that what was best for River? Or just for me? River and I have talked about his dad a few times over the years. He knows his first name, that he decided he wasn't ready to be a father and went to live his own life. I never once consulted a book or the Internet or even took him to a counselor. I guess I thought he was fine with it.

I still think he was mostly fine. He was so close with Mom and Dad and Joe and Margie growing up that I never felt like he had a typical single-mother childhood. I really never even thought of myself as a single mom. Someone was always at his baseball games. Dad taught him how to drive. I feel so stupid to have assumed that was enough. I thought if I could just make sure someone was always around for him, he'd never feel that hole. But maybe he did. Adrian certainly didn't make any attempt to fill it, which is a whole other story.

At any rate, I'm sad about all of this. My marriage—not even three years old—is going to end, and I'm not enough for my son.

Love you.

—Sid

Her sad and insecure feelings stuck with me through the night. By the next morning, I still felt sick as a dog, but that letter plus the burning question of whether she had told Mom about the kiss, added to this business with River, had me agitated. The kids were eating

Cheerios and watching *Sesame Street*, and I could think of nothing else but phoning Sid. I knew it was an okay time to call, because she was either twelve or thirteen hours ahead of me, or behind me. I could never remember, but I did know that if I was ever going to call her, it should be in the morning or the evening, and not in the middle of the day. So without overthinking it, I picked up the phone and dialed the fourteen digits I had taped to my refrigerator.

She answered on the second ring.

"Sid?"

"Cass? Is everything okay?"

"Yeah, yeah, yeah," I said, taking a sip of my honey-lemon tea and simultaneously fighting back tears. I hadn't heard her voice in months, and the sound of it grabbed my heart and squeezed.

"It's just . . . I just . . . I just wanted to see how you were doing . . ."

"You sound terrible. What's wrong?" she said.

"Oh, a nasty cold. But it's fine. I got your letter about the text message and the birth father Google yesterday."

Sid let out a soft sigh. "Oh, yeah. That's a doozy, right?"

"And, actually, I had a weird phone call from Mom yesterday, too," I continued. *Just do it*, I thought. *Rip off that Band-Aid.* "You didn't tell her about my letter from the Pig, did you? You know, the kiss?" I whispered that last part into the receiver.

"Hon, no," Sid said. "Shit. No. Noooo. I wouldn't do that. Of course not."

Of course not. I immediately felt bad for thinking she might have but also relieved that I knew for sure. She didn't sound mad. Surprised, but not mad.

"She does know about everything that's going down with Adrian, though. Why? What did she say?"

It was obvious to me then that, not unlike me all those years ago, Mom was in marriage-rescue mode, trying to shore up one daughter's union while the other's fell apart. I felt duty bound then to hold it together with Leo, if only for Mom's and Sid's sakes. I had to be the one who got it right, who had life go according to plan. Sid could be the different one—she was the free spirit, after all. It was kind of a relief that I could get on with my life. I didn't need a famous TV chef as my lover or husband. My husband was the IT director for a chain of gyms, and I was an ordinary stay-at-home mom. Now let me get it over with, move to the suburbs, and take my Pilates classes at the mall.

Sid and I ended up chatting for forty-five minutes. She was giddy, having just returned from a yoga retreat in Bali.

"Holy shit, it was beyond amazing, and it helped me put some of this craziness in perspective. I mean—suddenly my life is like . . . It's like I'm a fucking Capwell, with my baby daddies and my suspicions and my snooping and—so I just needed to clear my head. I hardly slept at all. I was kind of in this zone and didn't want to miss anything, but now I just need to crash. Sorry—excuse my language. When I'm sleep deprived, my vocab is the first thing to go."

"I was just thinking of the Capwells yesterday!" I told her.

And I did that same thing when I was tired. I had to laugh—"fuck" and "shit" can really fill in for any word, or add nuance to a thought when you don't have the mental wherewithal to make your point in a more sophisticated way. The mood on the phone lifted even higher, the iffy note the call had started on a distant memory. My whole body felt light and happy.

"Fucking shit, Sid. I miss you so much," I said, ignoring my boys, who were sitting four feet away. "But wait—is everything good with River? And what's up with Adrian? Do you need me to come out there? I will, you know."

"No, no, no. I mean, it sucks about Adrian. It really does. But you know what? I'm actually fine—or I'm going to be."

"Of course you are, sweetie. Hey, I felt really bad about sending that letter where I threw myself at Jake while you were in the middle of finding out about Adrian. You should hate me. I never would have said anything—actually, I don't even know if I would have kissed him if I'd known you were dealing with that. It was such an immature and selfish thing to do. I'm sorry."

"Don't apologize to *me*! You didn't know. God, Cass, it's great to talk to you. But it's kind of weird too, right? Like it doesn't fit in with this whole alternate-time continuum we're on. I'm not even sure what you know because I don't know what you've read yet."

"I know what you mean! It does feel like . . . I don't know . . . like I just accidentally saw a current episode of a TV show I've been watching reruns of or something, you know?"

"Totally! Okay! Fuck! Let's hang up!"

"Nooooo! Okay, fine! Shit! Bye! Love you!"

"Love you, too! Bye."

I put down my phone and let out a big sigh.

"Shit! Bye! Shit! Bye! Shit! Bye!" yelled the boys, who had miraculously been relatively quiet during that conversation.

Despite my miserable cold, my spirits were high and I wanted to reward the boys for a good morning.

"All right, you two, who wants to go visit the chickens?"

CHAPTER TWELVE

Ubud, Bali
July 7

Cassie,

I'm in Bali right now on a yoga retreat. It's so beautiful here, and my problems seem like a distant memory when I look out at the rice paddies built into the hillside across the way. The edges of green that make up each tier of the watery plateaus, sometimes intersecting or crossing, look kind of like a road map. The monkeys, meanwhile, are a menace! They keep stealing food and pooping on my patio. When I try to scare them off, they look at me like I'm the pest.

Cass, unless there's something I don't know, Leo is a good person. He is great with the kids and has always treated you well. And I see the way he looks at you. He loves you so much. If you are bored, please don't mistake boredom for a bad marriage. I know what an actual bad marriage looks like, and I know what actual single motherhood looks like. I'd take a boring marriage to a good guy over either one of those scenarios any day. So your heart doesn't sing when he walks in the door. So what? Did you expect to feel like a newlywed your whole life?

You've got to stop waiting for something to change and make something happen. You have all of the ingredients for an exciting life, but maybe you haven't figured out the recipe yet. (Oh Lord, that was corny—sorry—but true!) You know what our writing experiment has taught me? The power of having something to look forward to. Knowing every day that when I go to the mailbox there might be a letter from you—it's transformed my whole outlook. Let things transform you. Little things, even, can be magic. Be open to them. Create some rituals with Leo that you look forward to.

So that's my rescue effort. Please say you'll give it a try. I can't bear to see your marriage fall apart; you have one of the good ones.

Love,
Sid

The mail from Bali was obviously slower than from Singapore. I'd had to wait nearly two weeks from when we spoke on the phone until I received that letter. I know because I'd just finished a ten-day course of antibiotics for strep throat. Going so long without the letters was hard on me. And it wasn't just the letters I'd missed. The act of scanning, saving, and posting them had become an empowering and comforting ritual, an antidote to the impotency that comes with mothering three-year-olds. To compensate, I doubled down on my Facebook habit. But that's like replacing a nourishing breakfast with a glazed doughnut. It gives you momentary pleasure but ultimately leaves you empty, disappointed, and hungry for more.

Needless to say, her letter was a welcome delight, and one I devoured greedily. I nodded my head yes and teared up as I read. As soon as I finished, I read it again. And then I scanned it and read it yet again. She was not wrong about Leo. I bristled to see "fall apart" used in association with my marriage. I stopped short, though, of heeding her advice directly. But I promised myself I would—soon.

Meanwhile, my most recent letter, well on its way to Singapore, likely gave her little confidence in my ability to turn things around.

New York
July 10

Sid,

I've started acting—in secret—on my fantasy to move out of the city. There are several levels to it. The most guilt-inducing one is when I picture myself driving some sort of big, gas-guzzling vehicle while the boys watch cartoons from a screen in the back. I go to Target and Costco and buy giant containers of toilet paper and juice boxes. I pull into our garage and let the boys charge in, where they have their choice between a basement rec room full of plastic toys of unknown origin and our big backyard jungle gym. The more mild versions of this reverie involve Brooklyn.

So today I went to look at apartments with my secret broker, Wendy. Leo has no idea I'm thinking about moving. I fought him so hard to stay, but I am going insane here. Last night I told Leo I was going to dinner in Brooklyn with a friend, which was not really a lie—I did grab a burrito, and Wendy is like a friend. She showed me two apartments in Park Slope, which is kind of like the West Village but with gay women instead of gay men balancing out the families. One was amazing—the bottom two floors of a brownstone on Garfield Place. The seven quiet blocks to the subway seemed so strange. I'm going all the way to Westchester County next week, just to see if I can picture us living outside of the city. Tell anyone about this and I'll deny it, by the way.

What is going on with Adrian? Have you confronted him? Sid, you could always have any man in the world—and you still can. I know that's not the point, but it must be some small comfort to you. Or is this stuff just as hard on beautiful people as it is on us mere mortals? I'm thinking of you all the time and hoping for only good things.

Love you.
—Cassie

My fantasy of leaving the city felt almost as scandalous as the one about leaving Leo. My commitment to urban life—and more specifically to New York—was deep and well documented. As managing editor of *City Green* magazine, I'd carved out a public persona based on the firm belief that cities were the key to the world's environmental salvation. I'd moderated panels of urbanists and "futurists" who preached that developing existing cities—up and never out—was the only way to save the planet from certain ruin. How handy that where I live became the ultimate reflection of my values. My perfect-ten "walk score" delighted me and validated my lifestyle all the more. But now I see that I was simply (and often smugly) taking credit for the situation I found myself in. I was no better than Jenna, claiming to be a parenting expert because she has an easygoing child.

But beyond that, my address was as much a part of my identity as being a mom or having brown hair was. I arrived in ninety-nine and stayed after 9/11. It's how I bought my apartment for such a good price. It made me interesting to my friends and family back in Ohio. Sid is the beautiful one, the kind and charismatic one, the one who had the baby so young, the midwife, the one who married the dashing and rich man, the one who moved to Singapore. And I'm the plain one—but the one who lives in New York City. It was a vital differentiator.

When I got pregnant, it was like a three-way honeymoon between Leo, the city, and me. The first weeks after that plus sign finally appeared on the little stick were a combination of secretive celebrations, trying not to get our hopes up too far, and detoxing from a year of chore sex.

By the time my second trimester hit, we let ourselves believe that it was actually happening. When I started to show, I felt special and cute. Even though we didn't have a savings account, I spent an obscene amount of money on fashionable maternity clothes I could wear to work. I was in love. In love with my city, with my husband, with my life and my future. The hormones buzzed around inside of me, making me exceptionally agreeable to Leo's infatuation with my pregnancy-induced porn-star breasts. Instead of being hungover on Friday and Saturday mornings, I felt vibrant and healthy. While I walked around all glowy and sexed up, the city embraced me as never before. I reveled in the renewed attentiveness: seats offered on the subway; nods of respect from transit workers and police officers—family men and women, no doubt. As I waddled across Seventh Avenue sometime in my eighth month, a man yelled from his car, "You look beautiful!" Then, as if to explain himself, he added, "Sorry! I just love pregnant women!" Leo thought it was weird. I thought it was about par for the course. Neighbors carried things for me. The delivery guys from FreshDirect and UPS asked me how I was feeling. The manager at Health & Harmony— after having ignored me for years—suddenly knew my name and which brand of yogurt I preferred. Being pregnant turned the West Village into my own personal Mayberry.

I wonder if all of these kind strangers had known they were going to turn on me when the babies were no longer constrained to the safe haven of my gigantic womb, but out in the world and demanding to be reckoned with. I was crestfallen to learn that a mom with a stroller ranks nowhere near a pregnant woman in the city's hierarchy of acceptance. In fact, she is right down there with chubby Midwestern tourists puttering three abreast down Forty-eighth Street during rush hour.

My favorite cafés and shops became off-limits. My double-wide stroller fit through almost no doors, and when I did manage to jostle my way in, I always felt as if I were in breach of that unwritten contract among New Yorkers: Don't mess up the flow. I looked with envy at the mothers of one baby, casually going about their day with their little treasure strapped to them in a sling like a poetic accessory, while I might as well have been riding around Manhattan on a tricycle kitted out with a siren and a flag.

Had all those smiles and well-meaning chat sessions been good-byes? If it was assumed that we'd be leaving once the babies were out, I didn't get that memo. Looking back, I suppose it's what a lover who knows he's about to spurn you might do. Be a little more patient, a little more kind in those days and weeks leading up to the big letdown, knowing that the day was coming when he would turn to you and say, "You have too much baggage and you don't fit in my life anymore. I'm afraid you'll have to move out now. Also, you look like shit. Get some sleep and get out of those sweatpants."

In those early sleepless months, I wanted to cry sometimes when a counter person was impatient with me. It just no longer seemed crucial that I have my money out and ready, my order on the tip of my tongue, when I'm sixth in line at the bagel shop. But each time people behind me ordered and paid, with me still fishing for my wallet in my messy diaper bag and yelling out changes to my order, I proved to them that I no longer belonged. I made silent apologies to any slow-moving tourists or dreamy newly initiated New Yorkers I'd ever let feel my impatience. And although I couldn't remember ever heaving a heavy sigh at a discombobulated new mother, I'm sure I must have, God forgive me.

I no longer walked the streets with easy confidence. No one stopped me to ask for directions. I wondered if one less baby would have mattered, or if maybe I wasn't cut out to be a mom.

Three and a half years on, I've gotten over a lot of my insecurities about motherhood, but most days I still struggle to feel like a valuable part of the living, breathing, perfect mess that is New York. And depending on the day, the general mood in the air, and the behavior of my children, my attitude ranges from meek (I'm so sorry. Excuse me. I know we don't fit. We'll be out of your way in a minute. Sorry.) to defiant and brazen (We clog up the subway entrances, we spill things, and we're here to stay. Deal with it.).

When I started looking at other apartments, it felt slightly icky. I loved that Morton Street apartment like a family member. I considered the fact that I had purchased it (with a loan from my parents for half of the down payment) to be the crowning achievement of my life. Anyone with a working uterus can have babies, but a precious few can own a charming prewar apartment in Manhattan.

The first place Wendy showed me was truly dreadful and only reaffirmed my commitment to Morton Street. I was going through a phase where I thought I wanted a place that wasn't so old. Someplace where each night from September through April the creaking and clanging radiator didn't work itself into such a frenzy that you worried it would burst from the floor or, worse, wake the children. Someplace where when I scrubbed the floor, it would appear clean. Someplace perhaps with a second bathroom or, say, a broom closet. But the new construction in "Park Slope" was atrociously banal. Its location, on dodgy and treeless Fourth Avenue, between a parking lot and an auto-repair shop, across the street from a crumbling cement wall and a garishly signed chiropractor's office, deflated and depressed me. It was a far cry from the leafy brownstone-lined streets dotted with small cafés and bookstores I'd imagined when I'd schlepped out there. (Thank goodness Wendy later showed me the real Park Slope.) The apartment itself did feature the sleek and modern kitchen and baths it advertised, but the cheap drywall and fake little "balconies" half the size of my fire escape sent me running back into the loving arms of Morton Street.

And yet. It did get the wheels spinning. After the Fourth Avenue disaster, I needed to erase that bad taste from my mouth. If I was going to step out, I was at least going to do it with a handsome, large, well-dressed number, not some cheap and pretentious poseur. So I spent every spare minute scrolling though real estate listings on the *New York Times* website and StreetEasy, e-mailing links to Wendy. *Are these in your budget?* she'd ask, as the apartments became more and more generous in size. I intimated that there may have been a touch more wiggle room in the budget than I'd originally let on.

I just needed to see a place in the city in which I could envision being happy. Someplace with charm and character and convenience and space. It had to exist, I told myself. I didn't go so far out of the budget that it would be impossible to fathom—just enough that I'd have to go back to work at a 20 percent raise, or maybe win the Powerball, which I'd started playing every week. I quickly learned that the farther I went from my beloved neighborhood, the more I could get for my money. If I went to Red Hook, I could have closets in every room. To Westchester, a front porch and a backyard. To the Hudson Valley, a proper upstairs and a second bathroom.

Singapore
July 20

Cassie—

I haven't confronted Adrian because I barely see him. He works fifteen hours a day and travels constantly. I fall asleep with Lulu or am in the middle of a movie with River when he gets home. We haven't had a meal alone together in weeks and never go to bed at the same time. It's partially on purpose—I'm avoiding him because I want to delay the inevitable. I don't have a plan for the kids and me, and he's a nonfactor in our lives. I know that when we do talk, it will be over. I'm not going to stay with him. But I'm not anxious to throw everything into upheaval.

Cassie Sunday in the suburbs? Well, I never!

Xo,
Sid

CHAPTER THIRTEEN

By the second week in August, everyone who can afford to be is in the Hamptons or Connecticut or at the Jersey Shore. Apparently, Wendy can afford it, because she had hightailed it to Amagansett, instructing me to think through what I really want, neighborhood-wise, and to come up with a realistic budget. I think she was starting to sense that I was only half serious and possibly wasting her time on my housewife hobby.

In August, the pedicures in the city are sad and chipped, the flip-flops are dull and overworn, and all the children are pasty-white because their mothers have spent a good part of the last three months slathering organic sunscreen on their squirming, sticky bodies. The city loses its buzz when it empties out. Things don't run as smoothly. The heat is oppressive. The garbage rots quickly. In August, if the city so much as looks at me cross-eyed, I think, *This shithole rejects* me? *No, no, no, no. I reject it.*

Even the stamp truck wasn't immune to the August doldrums. It didn't bother to restock the interesting stamps, which left me with the standard-issue Statue of Liberty ones, the ones you have to lick. The boys became enthralled, though, asking how big she was and if she was made of metal or bricks and whether she could talk. When a stroll along the Hudson River to view her from a distance didn't satisfy them, I promised I'd get them closer.

The Staten Island ferry—which used to be my go-to tourist attraction when I had visitors—was the obvious choice: It was easy, free, only took up an hour or two, and offered fantastic views of Manhattan's skyline and the Statue of Liberty.

The outing turned out to be a series of small disasters—a broken fire alarm in the terminal was a sob-inducing stressor for Joey; my refusal to buy candy on the boat triggered a good ten minutes of whining and begging from both of them; and then I sat down in an unknown liquid, which didn't help my overall patience level. It was one irritation after another from then on—hardly the magical memory I'd envisioned. Still, I'd posted a selfie of the three of us smiling as we passed Lady Liberty, a brief happy moment bookended by threats (me) and tantrums (them).

During the taxi ride home, while the boys groused and bickered, I texted Leo and monitored the likes and comments on the photo. *Look, everything's amazing! Right?* it beseeched. And with every like, my Facebook friends assured me that indeed it was.

I had two choices every time I looked back on the photo of that day in my news feed: I could believe what my friends did, that everything was great. Or I could let it make me feel like a fraud.

I wished I'd written a letter that day instead. I would have admitted that it was a shitty day, and that I'd not handled it well. And I would have mostly forgotten about it until Sid's reply came and validated my honest and complicated feelings. I would have been forced to reflect, and probably to forgive myself. Those letters were like therapy, only better.

I loved the physical, sensory aspects of letter-writing, too. I loved that I had to use my hands, hands that often cramped up and bore a thick writing callus. I even loved that the ugly sound of a metal mailbox screeching open and closed would probably make me smile for the rest of my life.

Who knows? Maybe if I'd written a letter, I wouldn't have felt so restless that night, a feeling I thought might be helped by a jog.

I regretted it as soon as I stepped outside. It was as if the day's heat were trapped under some kind of invisible bubble that prevented it from dissipating. I forced myself to run down to the river in search of a slight breeze. Passing the Pig had become second nature, so I wasn't necessarily hoping to run into Jake as I huffed red-faced and sweat-soaked on West Eleventh Street. When I spotted him unlocking the restaurant door, I thought about turning back or attempting to jog by unnoticed, but instead I sucked in my stomach and said, "Hey."

When he didn't look up, I kept jogging, thinking that it was for the best we didn't see each other right then.

But after I passed him, I heard, "Hey, Cass!"

I turned and said, "Hey," again. He propped open the door with his foot and nodded me over with his head. "You've got to be dying in this heat. Come in. Let me get you a water."

"It *is* pretty miserable out here," I said.

It being a Monday, the restaurant was closed. I stretched a bit and wandered around, sipping my ice water and telling myself to leave while Jake futzed with some things behind the bar.

We chatted easily about nothing much—food trucks and competition and parking spaces, I think—though flashes of the kiss kept me on edge. Maybe he felt the same tension, because soon he was lighting a joint. Without the smells of food and people, the familiar aroma of Jake's excellent pot filled the space. When he offered it to me, I took it instinctively, joking about it not boding well to finish my jog. I wanted to take just a hit, for old times' sake, but I have to admit it was also to show Jake that I wasn't just a mom, that I was still cool. We passed it back and forth over the bar, me feeling lighter and freer with each puff. He offered me a beer.

"No, thanks. But do you have any chips or anything?"

"How about a sandwich?" he said, walking toward the kitchen and motioning for me to follow him. I stayed where I was on my barstool, though. I didn't trust myself to go into that kitchen with him. Instead, I stood up and walked out.

I floated home, feeling amazing. Why didn't I do this more often? I wondered. I wasn't stressed at all. Maybe I should be smoking during the day. Maybe I'd be a better mom if I were a little bit high for playground sessions or music class. I'd have to talk to Monica about this. My perception of depth, space, and time was a little off, but not so much as to be unsafe. In fact, I felt incredibly focused and present. What if I could bring this level of engagement to a game of statues or freeze tag? Forget Valium. This was the perfect "mother's little helper."

For a moment I thought about calling Jake to say goodbye and thanks, but I felt like there was something a bit sordid about what we'd done, and also like I didn't owe him anything. It piled on to my memories of his party, which made me feel silly and slutty and desperate, which in turn let me justify my rude exit and in a way let me feel like I had the upper hand.

By the time I got to my building, the pros list of being a stoner mom I'd been building up in my head came crashing down in a cloud of paranoia. Leo would know I was high. He'd know I'd been with Jake. He might be packing his bags right now. What if Jake—angry that I'd left without saying anything—had called Leo and told him what a floozy I was? Maybe I should walk around the block, I thought. It was eight forty-five, and I couldn't remember what time I'd left and whether that was so long ago as to raise suspicion. Did I smell like pot? Or like Jake's restaurant? I didn't have any money, or I would have gone to Amir's for some eyedrops and gum. I should have stayed for that sandwich.

But Leo barely looked up when I walked in. I went straight to the shower, and by the time I came out, he was busy doing something online.

"I got you a pad thai," he said.

"Ah. Perfect. Thanks." And that was all we said to each other for the rest of the night.

⸻❦⸻

Feeling tired and a tiny bit guilty about my dalliances the night before, I wasn't in the mood to make good on my promise to go visit our old neighbor Rachel and her two-year-old daughter, Brooke. They used to live on the fourth floor of our building before they moved across the river to Hoboken when Rachel was pregnant. But we had canceled and rescheduled four times already, so I figured it was best to get it over with.

The boys and I spent a rare morning indoors, and walked outside around eleven a.m. and into a wall of stink and humidity.

The PATH station was five blocks away, on Christopher Street, and then we had an eight-block walk to Rachel's place in Hoboken. Quinn helped me push the empty stroller while Joey skipped ahead. Within minutes, he'd stepped right into a big mushy pile of dog shit. I wrestled both of their already sticky and sweaty bodies into the stroller, promising chocolate milk for cooperation, took off Joey's shoe, tied it up in a plastic bag and tossed it in the bottom of the stroller.

Since it had opened six months ago, taking the place of our favorite corner bar, I had managed to avoid the Starbucks at West Tenth Street on principle. But it was too hot to go out of our way today, and I knew they had those boxes of organic chocolate milk. Plus, I'd seen many double strollers make it through those doors, so today it was a no-brainer.

They were out of chocolate milk, so I negotiated strawberry milks, and then changed one to vanilla milk, which I didn't even know existed until Joey asked for one, and then forgot to say "iced" when I ordered my chai tea latte. The stroller rocked back and forth as the boys wrestled, bonking each other on the head with beanbags shaped like bananas, screeching and yelping and not even hearing my hissed entreaties to stop it. The whole thing was pretty typical, but still my heart raced and my jaw clenched as I felt the line behind me growing longer. When Joey discovered that his milk box was missing a straw, he started sobbing as if he'd just watched a beloved relative savagely murdered. I asked for a new milk box as calmly as I could when the guy behind me in line exhaled loudly and muttered under his breath, "You gotta be kidding me."

Something inside of me snapped, and I spun on my heel so that my whole body was facing this guy, who was about my height and wearing a wool stocking hat in one-hundred-degree heat, and said, "Oh, fuck you." It was out of my mouth before I even realized what had happened, and I immediately felt shaky but powerful and a smidge relieved that I had finally done what I'd envisioned myself doing so many times and that I'd lived. An older, well-dressed woman with her five-dollar bill in hand, ready to order, was standing behind him and pretending not to notice me. I had a flash of Grandma Margie witnessing something like this and grew hot with shame.

Fortunately for me, the Starbucks worker handing me my new milk and iced chai burst into laughter and said with a flourish, "Well, there's a first time for everything," breaking the tension. I doubted it was a first, but the barista's reaction made it difficult for Wool Cap to make a next move, so he plastered a thin smile on his face and locked his gaze somewhere over my head, waiting his turn in silence. If Quinn and Joey heard what was happening, they gave no indication. The poor kids could probably make it five or six years before they heard the word "fuck" if we lived in, say, Connecticut. But this was New York, and most days they hear it a half-dozen times before lunch and, sadly, sometimes from their mother. The wool cap guy got his drink and skittered around us on the way out, letting the door shut right on the stroller's front wheel. But the barista—my new favorite neighborhood food-service worker—came out and propped open both of the doors so I could easily maneuver out.

On the quiet walk to the station, I tried my best to focus on the kindness of the barista. But I couldn't help reliving the confrontation with the wool cap guy, imagining more classy and intelligent ways I might have handled it.

⸺⬦⬦⬦⸺

Rachel Pfeiffer lived in a fifteen-hundred-square-foot ground-floor unit with a washer and dryer and a common indoor pool. I wouldn't let her tell me how much they paid for it because I couldn't bear to know. Not that I'd be tempted; it's been established that I'm too superficially proud of my New York address to ever move to New Jersey. Rachel was chomping at the bit to give me the grand tour, so we left the kids playing peacefully in the living room while she showed me around. In my apartment, the tour only requires craning your neck. But for her to show me the master bathroom with its soaking tub and double sinks, we had to walk down a pleasant hallway lined with framed family photos, past Brooke's room and the guest room, and through the master bedroom. The bathroom was a sight to behold. As soon as my bare feet touched the cool marble, I felt my internal temperature start to lower. I climbed into her giant bathtub and rested my still-sweating head on the cushy ledge designed for a Calgon moment. "This is fantastic, Rachel. It's like a real grown-up house!" I said, my eyes closed.

"Yeah, we figured it was about time," she said.

I was still in the tub when I heard the loud crash. I looked at Rachel and said, "What's that?"—refusing to panic just yet, in case she had a perfectly good explanation for what sounded like a boulder being thrown through a plate-glass window. Like, *Oh, yeah. That's why we paid only a quarter million for this place. We're right next door to a wrecking-ball testing facility.* But she was running for the door, so I scrambled out of the tub, and that's when the screaming started.

Quinn was standing in the middle of a pile of broken glass that had moments ago been the coffee table. A line of blood ran from his eyebrow, alongside his nose, and into his open, crying mouth. He was shrieking and staring at his hands, one of which was bleeding profusely. Joey, not bloody or screaming, was sitting on the floor and staring into his lap, where a puddle of urine had formed. Brooke appeared to be unharmed but was screaming even louder than Quinn. My heart split in two, half of it sinking to my stomach and the other half rising to my throat as I ran to Quinn. Yanking him up into my arms, I tried to cover the bleeding spots with the first thing I could grab, a cashmere throw strewn over the edge of the sofa.

Rachel called 911, and soon Quinn and I were in an ambulance on our way to the emergency room, while she followed in her car with Joey and Brooke. The paramedic fastened a tourniquet around Quinn's arm and carefully removed a few of the larger shards of glass from his eyebrows and scalp.

When we got to the ER and Rachel wasn't there yet, I was seized with irrational panic that she had gotten into a car accident with Joey, who wasn't in a car seat, and that I was going to see my other baby wheeled in on a stretcher. I couldn't bring myself to call Leo until I saw Joey and knew he was safe. While we waited, people kept coming in and out of the room, making both of us jumpy. Quinn cried on and off, asking the occasional question about what sort of machine the doctor would use on him, having not reacted well to the paramedic's quip that the doctor was going to "sew him up."

Rachel finally peeked her head in, and I ran into the hall and lifted Joey into my arms.

After I gave her an update on Quinn, she said, "I'm so sorry, Cass. I feel terrible."

"*I'm* sorry we destroyed your home. I can't believe he jumped through your coffee table."

"I'm sure it was an accident. I'm going to get home, though. Can I take Joey with me? He can stay with us until you're done here."

"No, thanks. I'll keep him here. Just let me know how much the table is and I'll pay for a new one."

"Oh, stop. Don't worry about that right now. Keep me posted on Quinn, okay?"

"Will do. See you."

Joey climbed up onto the hospital bed beside his brother and interlaced his fingers through Quinn's. He looked up at me with damp eyes and said, "It hurts, Mama." It wasn't a question. He felt his twin's pain. I sat on the swivel stool beside them, placing my hand over both of theirs and kissing their heads before calling Leo. I helped Joey change into clean pants from the change of clothes in my bag, and then a nurse came in and did a more thorough glass extraction and cleaning, patiently answering all of Quinn's questions.

"I have a three-year-old, too," she said, winking at me.

Her kindness brought a lump to my throat, and I felt the big August chip on my shoulder begin to dissolve. I found myself thinking about the wool cap guy and the barista and the nurse and how I wanted to be on the side of the barista and the nurse, not the wool cap guy. When the nurse and I made eye contact, I had to look away, deeply inhaling and digging my fingernails into my palms to stop myself from blubbering in front of the boys. Just then Leo was brought in by another nurse, and the tears started rolling down my face. Poor Leo must have assumed I had just gotten bad news, because he turned pale and searched my face for further clues, while walking quickly to Quinn.

"Bu-ud," he said.

"Daddy, I'm sorry," Quinn said, and started crying again.

Leo and I exchanged a look.

"I broke the table. I made a big, big, big mess," he continued through sobs.

"Did you do it on purpose, or was it an accident?" Leo said.

"A-a-a-accident."

"Well, if it's an accident, you don't have to say sorry. Nobody is mad at you—right, Mom?"

"That's right. I'm not mad, Quinn. Not one bit."

"Me neither," said Joey, who still had his fingers interlaced with his brother's.

When the doctor finally came in, he wasted no time on pleasantries. We were a long way from the pediatrician's office, where Quinn might have been called "big guy" and asked whether he had gotten into a fight with an alligator.

"Remove the brother from the table," was all he said.

Leo and I gave each other a *yikes* look, and Leo pulled Joey into his arms. The three of us huddled near the end of the gurney while the doctor worked in silence, the kind nurse by his side. I held Quinn's foot in my hand and laid my head on Leo's shoulder. It was the closest I'd felt to Leo in a long time. Knowing that he felt just how I did— full of fear and love—was a foreign and oddly thrilling sensation. All four of us, in fact, were united under a common goal. *Isn't this how family life should be?* I wondered. *Don't we all want the same things all the time? How do we replicate this feeling but swap out imminent danger for more love? Do we need to be against something to feel this solid? Or can we get it without one of us lying in a hospital bed?*

The doctor said that Quinn would need surgery to reconnect a severed nerve in his hand. We were there for nine more hours in the end. Joey said he wouldn't go home without Quinn and I didn't push him on it. I wanted us to leave the hospital as a family. So Leo kept Joey busy—a nap in an empty bed, wrestling on the grassy area outside, two movies on his laptop, and countless visits to the vending machine for Cheetos and candy—while I sat with Quinn, my heart in my throat. I hated myself for writing to Sid that I imagined life without the boys. I take it all back, I kept thinking. Please, please never let anything happen to them, I prayed to no one.

CHAPTER FOURTEEN

Singapore

July 27

Cassie,

Well, I finally confronted Adrian about the cheating. I'm not leaving quite yet, but relax, because we're not exactly together anyway. We see him fewer than ten days a month, and the rest of that time he's flying between Bangkok, Jakarta, and Kuala Lumpur. He's cried, groveled, declared his undying love, etc., etc. I surprised myself by being unmoved by the whole display. The truth is that I do love him and I am shattered over this, but despite the temptation to believe him and give this marriage another chance, to give Lulu a childhood with a mother and a father, I can see so clearly that he isn't really going to change. It's almost like I've been granted temporary clairvoyance. I feel kind of "in the zone" about the whole thing. I got this flash of him reciting the same apology

again and again, me having misgivings about his where-
abouts for the rest of my life. Oddly, I feel sorry for him,
which is not what I want to be feeling—good old-fashioned
anger would be more cathartic, I suspect. I do feel bad, really
bad, for Lulu and River. But I'm determined that Adrian's
wayward penis disrupt their life as little as possible. It seems
selfish and juvenile to leave in a huff. So we're staying for
now, and I'll figure out my next steps at some point. You
know what they say . . . It is what it is!

Love,
Sid

I couldn't believe how well she was handling this. And she knows
it drives me crazy when people say, "It is what it is," so she was even
making jokes.

I read back through all of the letters for earlier hints that she
and Adrian were in trouble. But instead I just found evidence of my
own bad behavior. I cringed as I read myself going on and on with
my stupid, selfish complaints while she was enduring something
truly wretched. But how do you listen better in a letter? I could
have asked more questions. Perhaps waited for answers before barreling through with every shallow observation in my head.

Between this and Quinn's accident, I had all the motivation I
needed: Things had to change; I had to change.

Over the next week, I felt like Michael Keaton in the "getting
stronger" montage in *Mr. Mom*. No more listlessly scrolling through
Facebook while I halfheartedly played dinosaurs with the boys. No
more being dragged out of bed by them at seven and placating them
with TV while I had my coffee and shower. I forced myself awake

when the alarm sounded at six and was ready to greet them with hugs by the time they awoke. I tried to talk the way Mrs. Pteranodon from *Dinosaur Train* talked to her dino kids. I begrudgingly made an effort to implement the strategies Jenna had outlined in her "Zen of Parenting" blog post. *There is only now,* I coached myself. And sometimes it worked. I became completely absorbed watching Joey spend five minutes eating a single peanut M&M as if it were an apple, falling a little bit more in love with him as he carefully chewed off the candy shell bit by bit so that by the time he reached the peanut, which he licked clean and then handed to me, his face and fingers were covered in chocolate. The fact that he either hadn't noticed or wasn't bothered that his brother had quietly polished off the rest of the bag helped me understand him a little better. I felt love and appreciation for Quinn then too, for being wily or kind enough not to gloat to his brother about eating all the candy. If I could be so moved by this seemingly mundane episode, I wondered what else I had missed while my face was buried in my phone.

When Quinn peed his pants in the stroller, I undressed him from the waist down, and when he wiggled free and started running away, casted hand and bandaged face, yelling, "I'm make-did! I'm make-did!" (his word for naked), I followed behind at a safe distance, enjoying the laughs and even the startled and disapproving looks from passersby. I did take out my phone, but only to film him.

I had taped a list to the fridge of things I imagined good moms did with their kids. I'd made my way through sidewalk chalk in our building's courtyard, homemade Play-Doh, and brown-bag puppets, all of which I'd proudly documented on Facebook as if they were normal activities for me.

"Make cookies" day had arrived, but I decided that cookies were a bit ambitious and switched to brownies from a mix. I set out the ingredients and measuring cups and then read the instructions aloud to the boys, forcing myself to let them do everything. I clenched my hands into fists and winced while offering encouraging words as milk sloshed out of the bowl and a good portion of the dry mix ended up on the counter. It's possible I gave them too much freedom, because when Joey picked up the bowl and Quinn began ushering the lumpy wet mix into the pan with a spatula, the bowl shot out of poor Joey's arms and landed upside down on the corner of the rug.

I slopped up what I could in one big swipe of a kitchen towel while refereeing a brief screaming match regarding whose fault it was. Leaving the rest of the mess on the floor, I took the boys back to the store and bought a new mix—something the Cassie of even two weeks ago would never have done.

As we commenced batch number two, I realized we didn't have an egg. The finished brownies were to be an emblem of my improved attitude and capabilities, and I was determined to see this project through with a smile on my face, even if the vein on my forehead was about to burst through my skin. I turned on the TV to distract the boys, ran across the hall, and knocked on Jenna's door. She didn't have eggs either, but she offered to watch Quinn and Joey while I ran to get some.

"That'd be great. You are a lifesaver," I said, and I meant it.

She called to Valentina, who was munching on what looked like endive while paging through a book.

"Okay, Mom," she said, and wiped her hands and face on a cloth napkin before getting up to follow her out the door.

Jenna and Valentina stood in the doorway to my kitchen/living room, surveying what must have seemed a foreign land—TV blaring, one boy standing on his head on the sofa while picking his nose, the other one, naked, huddled over the pile of spilled brownie mix, repeatedly dipping his finger in and licking it.

"Do you mind if I just pop this off?" Jenna asked in her best attempt to sound casual as she sidestepped the brownie spill and made her way to the TV, where she frantically groped, her fingers locating buttons underneath that I didn't even know existed, which only caused brightness and contrast screens to pop up.

"Noooo!" Joey shouted.

I sighed and reached around Jenna to press my finger against the red dot in the bottom-right corner of the set as Joey erupted in tears.

"Oh, I am sorry, kiddo. How about we do a puzzle?" Jenna said, her eyes scanning the room for something wooden or educational.

I hated that she made me feel like a bad mother in my own house, but before I broke my new vow to not hate Jenna, I quickly forced some undies onto Quinn and then scooped up the still wailing and shoeless—but thankfully clothed—Joey, grabbed my keys from the hook, and ran out the door, calling, "Be right back!"

"I wanna watch *Wonder Pets*!" His cries echoed through the marble corridor.

"I know, sweetie," I said, descending the stairs with him on my hip. "We can watch it later, okay?"

By the time I reached the main doors, he had calmed down enough for me to shimmy him around to my back. I let him hold a dollar and hand it to Amir in exchange for one egg. Like he does with everything, Amir put the egg in a little black plastic bag with a wad of napkins and handed it to Joey. I'd been meaning to talk to him about that. If I buy a can of Diet Coke, it does not need to be placed in a plastic bag with four napkins. But for now I was grateful

I'd yet to intervene, because it meant that Joey was able to transport the single egg upstairs without incident.

I thanked Jenna and hoped she would disappear, but she lingered for another mommy intervention.

"I forwarded you an invite for this 'Superfoods for Kids' workshop happening next week," she said.

"Sounds cool. Thanks," I said, choosing to ignore the implication that I was in need of a class on how to feed my children.

"It'll be amazing. It's being organized by Kendra Watts, the chef from Artichoke? And Brooke Klein, this awesome holistic-minded dietitian? Her daughter is in Valentina's kindergarten class."

"Will you be there?" I asked.

"Oh, I'm not sure. I think I sort of know most of what they're going to say."

"Mmmm," I said, both irritated and encouraged by her response.

I did actually want to go to the workshop, which promised to teach me fast, easy ways to incorporate "superfoods" into my kids' diets. I love food, and feeding my family delicious and healthy meals had long been on my to-do list. I'd always pictured myself as the kind of mom who would do that. Alas, food preparation and I had just never clicked thus far. So even though it fell on the coming Thursday, which was to be the first of Leo and my weekly date nights (another tactic of Operation Better Mom/Wife/Sister/Person), I RSVP'd yes.

The session—less of a workshop and more of a lecture—was at seven p.m. in the back room of the Cowgirl, a kitschy American restaurant on Hudson Street, and Leo met me there when it ended.

When I found him sitting at the bar, we decided to just get a table there. Our waiter wore tight dark jeans, a gingham shirt, and shimmery blue eye shadow, which made it hard not to smile each time I looked at him.

"How about next time we go someplace a little more adult?" I said, nodding to the stack of high chairs in the corner.

"Done. First rule of date night: no restaurants with high chairs," Leo said. Although, with the cost of paying Wanda—eighteen dollars an hour plus forty dollars for a car service home—our options were limited.

I told him all about the workshop, and I could tell he was impressed that his non-foodie wife was making an effort to feed the kids better food.

"I'm gonna do it. I am. I'm ordering FreshDirect tonight. Those boys are eating salmon cakes with Greek yogurt red pepper aioli and kale chips for dinner tomorrow." I pounded my index finger on the table to show I meant business.

The chef who led the workshop and who had bragged that her baby's first food was runny eggs—eliciting a dramatic inhale from a woman in the front row—had convinced me that I could go from a dinner rotation of cereal and milk, chicken nuggets, and Chinese takeout to preparing home-cooked meals from scratch every night and that it would be supereasy. The nutritionist delivered an ode to wild-caught salmon, which, even—especially—out of a can (a can!), was basically a ticket to Harvard.

"Here's to canned salmon," Leo said, raising his Ball jar of beer to mine.

Leo and I had the best conversation we'd had in months. (Not that it had much competition.) Sitting across from him and just talking was unusual, and, as depressing as that realization was, we were having fun. I ordered a second beer and told him about the sweetly earnest parents in the class—most of them either pregnant or with babies about to start on solids. The vigorous nodding, the copious note taking, the unabashedly ignorant questions: *Can you freeze food*

*in plastic containers? When can you start blueberries? Would cauliflower—
organic, of course—be a good first food?* We laughed at their opposition
to the show-offs in Leo's cheese classes, who were masters at coming
up with questions that aren't really questions at all but thinly veiled
attempts to demonstrate their knowledge. He has a theory that these
people come to the classes with the single goal of being heard on the
subject of cheese.

We reminisced about a "Mystery of the Caves" class he took
me to while we were dating, where we toured the cheese caves in
the shop's Bleecker Street basement. There were a few people in the
class asking such specific questions that they must have either been
working on their own cheese cave—in Manhattan!—or had come
in from the suburbs, or had researched the temperatures and conditions of cheese caves to the extent that they were able to challenge
the instructor on optimal temperatures and number of weeks to
properly age a Humboldt Fog or a Coupole.

"Oh, wait, we did have one of those," I said. "This lady who stood
in the back as if to monitor the speakers. She constantly interrupted
but never had a question. She was kind of a heckler, actually. But the
poor thing, her son has all kinds of food allergies—gluten, dairy,
nuts, you name it. She said she eliminated these foods one by one
from their whole family's diet, and it started curing them of all of
these random ailments."

"Like what?" Leo asked, automatically dubious of people who
claim to have food allergies, as if they were making it less easy for
him to refuse a food group on ethical grounds.

"Well, apparently her husband's eczema cleared up and her
older son stopped complaining of leg pain every day. So I started
thinking about my restless legs, and I'm going to try an elimination diet and see what happens."

Leo could barely contain his amusement. I was notorious for my undisciplined and dairy- and carb-rich diet; it wasn't unusual for me to have a bagel and cream cheese and a latte for breakfast, a slice of pizza and a Diet Coke for lunch, and a beef and cheese burrito for dinner, interspersed with snacks of cereal and milk. "Oh, really. When's this starting?" he said, nodding to the cheeseburger on my plate.

"Tomorrow."

As it turned out, it was dairy. I'm officially lactose intolerant. After a few false starts on a full elimination diet, I decided to start with dairy, which was hard, but within two weeks my legs were better. I couldn't believe it. I went to bed and fell asleep and didn't wake up kicking and twitching. I hadn't felt truly rested in years. To wake up in the morning and not immediately go through my day looking for a window where a nap might fit in was terrifically refreshing. I saw dairy as the poison in my body that was causing me to be such a slacker of a mom and wife, and as it left my system, so too did the apathy, the unfaithfulness, the general blah-ness I felt almost all of the time. I pictured my blood running pure red instead of a milk-tinged pink. And I have to admit, if Jenna hadn't sent me to that workshop, I wouldn't have found the cure and had that great date with Leo that renewed my hope in my marriage.

CHAPTER FIFTEEN

A week after the Hoboken disaster, I took Quinn to the neurologist to check the nerve endings on his hand. Mom had arrived the day before for a visit, so Joey stayed home with her. The waiting room was small and dark and devoid of any toys or books, so I handed him my phone to watch YouTube videos of toads catching flies in slow motion. Digging through a pile of *Cosmopolitan*s and *Good Housekeeping*s, I found a battered copy of *New York* magazine, which featured a two-page spread on Jake and his now-famous beer-and-bacon-braised Brussels sprouts. Forcing myself to skip past the article, I instead flipped to the back page for the Approval Matrix.

Had I not resisted the temptation to read the article on Jake, had I been remotely interested in what *Cosmo* says he's really thinking in bed, had I chosen to abide by my resolution to be more present with Quinn instead of handing him my phone, I might have remained blissfully in the dark for just a bit longer. Maybe even long enough for evidence of my improved behavior and mothering skills to show up in my letters. But this was the moment that the shutter closed on the snapshot of my life. There, in the Lowbrow/ Brilliant quadrant of the "oversimplified guide to who falls where on our taste hierarchies" from the editors of *New York*, right between a chubby nine-year-old in a tuxedo singing a tear-jerking rendition of the National Anthem and a new Muslim superhero movie, was this: *Our latest voyeuristic guilty pleasure, the Slow News Sisters.*

And there was a teeny-tiny picture of one of my letters. It was on my graph paper and I couldn't make out any of the words, but I recognized my writing and the big heart I had drawn at the bottom. For the second time that week, my heart dropped right out of my chest. I shoved the magazine in my bag, as if it were the only copy in the world.

"Mama, come on. That lady saying my name!" Quinn stood in front of me, pulling me by the hand. He sounded far away; my ears were ringing with some sort of internal alarm. When I started walking, my heart, having bounced off of my cushy pelvic floor, made its way up to my throat, and I felt like I might vomit it right out.

"Do you need to sit down?" I heard someone ask.

A woman was leading me by the arm to a chair inside the doctor's office, and I muttered something about low blood sugar and skipping breakfast. Quinn studied me silently, looking like he might cry. I knew I should pull it together and stop freaking him out, but I felt trapped inside a body that was unable to do anything but physically react to seeing what I had just seen. A nurse brought me a juice box, and I pretended that it was exactly what I needed. If only. I took a sip and offered some to Quinn. He pushed the juice back toward me. "Uh-uh. You drink," he said.

The nurse gave me a look, and I nodded at her. "I'm okay. Thank you so much." When she left the room, I took a deep inhale and slid the magazine out of the top of my bag to look at the date. It was this week's issue.

⸺⸱⟨∞⟩⸱⸺

The mind is a funny thing, isn't it, that it could come to the following explanation and hold on to it until midway through the subway ride home: It's simple, really. This is some kind of bizarre coincidence. It was a movie or a book or a TV show or something with the same name as my private blog.

What a coincidence. I muttered it like a mantra while leading Quinn to the Thirty-fourth Street station. I was gripping his forearm the way a clueless bachelor in a movie might hold on to a three-year-old he's been tasked with keeping safe for the day. In a daze, I led us onto an empty car on an otherwise packed train and then cursed my amateur mistake when the doors closed and we found ourselves alone on that express train with a ranting, awful-smelling person. I knew better than to try to get Quinn to move to another car—he was (rightfully) terrified of that space between the cars. So we sat as far away from him as we could, and I focused on distracting Quinn by softly singing "Baby Beluga" and fishing a stick of peppermint gum out of my bag, hoping the scent might alleviate the violent odor in some small way. Quinn watched me intently, not singing along. When I finished, he said, "Mama, are you happy with me?"

"Yes, sweetheart, I'm happy with you. Of course I'm happy with you. Are you happy with me?"

He rolled his eyes and said, "Yes."

"How's that finger feeling?" I managed, putting my arm around him and pulling him closer. He let his head fall into my lap and looked up at me.

175

"I'm all better. 'Member? Doctor said. I'm getting bigger and bigger and bigger, you know."

"I do know."

I glanced back at the man to make sure he had no plans of moving from his seat. While I rarely found encounters like this alarming, being alone with Quinn in that car and in the state I was in had me feeling vulnerable and uneasy. His pushcart had fallen over, and some empty water bottles and a beer can littered the floor. The beer had been full only moments ago, by the look of the fresh puddle making a small river down the middle of the car. The Velcro was undone and the tongues stuck out of his black shoes, which seemed about two sizes too small for his balloonlike feet.

We rattled through the Twenty-third Street station, and the rants grew louder. "Fucking spies! Fucking criminals!"

"Is he a bad guy?" asked Quinn.

"I'm not sure. Probably not. What do you think?"

"He smells like poop and pee."

"Yes, he does, honey," I said, finding my earphones in my bag and playing him "Here Comes the Sun" off my phone. He listened and pulled his T-shirt up over his nose.

"Goddamn secrets. Everyone knows. Stupid bitch."

And then my heart was in my throat again because my cerebral cortex, or whatever part of the brain it is that's in charge of grasping reality, kicked in. I woke up and smelled the poop and pee, and I was in deep shit.

CHAPTER SIXTEEN

We arrived home and shared the good news about Quinn's hand with Mom and Joey, who had their own good news: A trip to the toy store had garnered little Batman and Robin figures with accompanying Batmobiles and Batcycles. The boys immediately busied themselves, and Mom showed me a flyer she'd picked up for some famous storyteller coming to the bookstore. Great. We would definitely go, I promised, walking into my room.

"I just need to take care of something on the computer real quick," I hollered over my shoulder, leaving the door slightly ajar.

Typing "Slow News Sisters" into Google, I held my breath. After four entries dedicated to the Pointer Sisters' song "Slow Hand," my heart rate began to slow. Maybe it was just a coincidence. But then I saw the fifth link: *The Slow News Sisters*. I clicked on it, and there it was, my blog. It looked exactly how I had left it. *Can this be right?* I thought. Then I noticed a little gray "263" at the bottom of the most recent letter, clicked on it, and watched in horror as pages and pages of comments unfurled.

The comments were all dated in the past two weeks, but almost all of the letters had been commented on, going all the way back to January.

Yet another wave of panic washed over me, and I scrambled to find the privacy settings. The shock mixed with adrenaline had me struggling to remember basic computer skills, and I fumbled around until I found it. *Uncheck public, check private. Change password. Confirm password. There.*

I moved on to Twitter and searched for "SlowNewsSisters," where I discovered "#TeamCassie" and "#TeamSid." People were pitting us against each other. I was further befuddled when the tiny URLs took me right back to my blog, as if the doors were still wide-open. Was this because the computer knew it was me?

I had so many other questions, most of them beyond the scope of any Geek Squad. *I'm sure it was private and even regularly double-checked the settings, so how did this happen? Did one of the kids inadvertently make it public? Did Mom use my laptop and somehow press something? Did she see it? How could I have been so stupid as to think this could never happen? Who in the hell are GaryX and Kitty69 and HamsterSandwich, and why are they talking about Sid and me like they know us?*

One of the (many) things that surprised me was that despite the name of the blog, a lot of people didn't seem to be clear on the relationship between Sid and me, perhaps because of her name. There was a raging debate among a few of the commenters over whether we were sisters or a couple.

All this time, Mom had still been talking to me—asking questions about what the doctor said, telling me about a rude woman at the bookstore who had admonished Joey for not using his indoor voice—to and I made weak efforts to respond, but my scalp was buzzing and my ears were ringing, making communication difficult. I wanted to slam the door and curl into the fetal position, but Mom wouldn't stop with the small talk, so I closed my laptop, went to the bathroom to wash my hands and face, and rejoined her and the boys.

As if on cue, she said, "Oh, this is weird. I just had a voice mail from Joanne Stryker asking me if you and Sid were some famous sisters on the Internet. The Bad News Sisters? Isn't that the strangest thing?"

I produced a sort of guttural expression of confusion, hoping to summarily dismiss the topic. My apartment suddenly seemed even smaller than usual, and I longed to scurry down a hall to, say, find a ringing phone or investigate a crying child. But I had just come out of the bathroom, so there was nowhere to go. Looking around for something to put between us, the best I could do was open the fridge and stick my head inside. I eventually grabbed us each a can of Dr. Brown's black cherry soda. If Mom hadn't been there, I'd have mixed it with the Stoli from the freezer, but it wasn't even three o'clock on a Wednesday and I'd hate to give her something else to worry about.

I started shooting enthusiastic questions to the boys about what they were doing, with the aim of shifting Mom's attention to them. But my normally loquacious and needy little ones were of no help. They were in a new-toy trance, and all I could get out of them were dismissive grunts. If Mom found any sort of ironic satisfaction in that, she didn't let on. Unable to imagine getting through an afternoon of chatting with Mom, given my scrambling brain, I played my ace.

"Ugh. I'm not feeling well all of a sudden," I said, rubbing my eyes.

"Oh, hon," Mom said, coming over to feel my forehead. "I thought you looked a little peaked. Go lie down. Get some rest. I'll take the boys to the park and then we'll get dinner at the Hudson. I'll bring you some chicken soup. How's that sound?"

Mom could be a real gem sometimes. I think she might have a touch of that disorder where you want your children to be sick, because that's when she's at her best. Growing up, we stayed home from school whenever we had sore throats or looked flushed. I missed half of first grade before we figured out that I was allergic to cats and got rid of the stray we had taken in that summer. Sid and I joke that her version of heaven is for us to be mildly ill—sick enough to have to stay home, but well enough to play a game of Oh Hell or watch a Turner Classic Movie with her—lying on the sofa under crocheted afghans, asking meekly for chicken soup and ginger ale. I blame her for my inability to function when I have a cold. Leo's mom—while she doted on her boys regularly—did the opposite when they complained of a cold or a toothache. Toughness was expected, weakness not rewarded. So, while Leo expects a round of applause for unloading the dishwasher, he soldiers through a nasty case of the flu or a hangover with hardly a word.

I sat on my bed and stared at my closed laptop, unable to bring myself to take another peek. I felt like I might cry, but crying seemed too simple a reaction. The situation was so complex that I was not yet fully grasping it. I also worried that if I started to cry, it would be the loud blubbering sort that would attract the attention of Mom and the boys. If I could just write to Sid, I might be able to think clearly.

Writing to her had become my destressing ritual, its effects at least as great as a cigarette, a brisk jog, or breathing exercises. I retrieved a pen and a zebra notecard from the box under my bed, but for the first time since that inaugural letter to her back in January, I felt paralyzed, unable to let my pen mar the surface of that creamy mottled paper. Several minutes passed and I still had nothing. Suddenly, I remembered that I hadn't checked the mail since yesterday. By then Mom and the boys had left, so no one was there to see me sprinting though the apartment and down to the mailboxes like a maniac. Shaking, I turned the key in that metal box marked "2K" and lurched at the letter inside like it might scamper away. Taking the stairs back up two at a time, I was with it enough to know that Sid's letter wouldn't contain the panacea, but for a few minutes it could make me forget.

Singapore
August 2

Dear Cassie,

When it rains it pours, doesn't it? I'm feeling a bit foolish today. Susan, one of the helpers in my bank group, lied to me about her son needing an operation. I loaned her $400, and she disappeared. Then I noticed that all of the money in my bank was missing—I had one of those accordion files with a folder for each helper, and the whole thing is gone. I had $1,100 in there. The other helpers tell me she has a boyfriend in Malaysia whom she may have gone to live with. The money's not the problem—I can replace $1,500 without Adrian even noticing. But still, for this to happen while I'm dealing with an adulterous husband is just a bit much.

Of course, everyone is talking about it—the money, not the adultery (as far as I know!). The helpers at the playground are all abuzz, and the family who employed her is none too pleased with me, to say the least. Rumors are swirling about me funneling young women to Malaysia, I'm sure.

In related news, I have my first "frenemy" (one of River's girlfriends taught me that one). This mom in my condo—Bridget from Minneapolis—who resents me trying to help these women just stopped over to "make sure I was all right." But actually, it was to gloat. She was all, "I'm just relieved that you see now what they're capable of." Watching her stand there in her $900 sundress, her fake boobs, and her keratin-treated hair, having her "I told you so" moment, I felt—well, I felt nothing really. She's nothing to me, and having this confirmation of her mean spirit actually alleviates me of some of the guilt I have over being unable to be a friend to her.

The thing is, she's always popping up and acting overly familiar with me. Plopping down next to me at the pool, bringing over muffins (made by her helper) for no reason, stopping by with her little boy for a playdate. Sounds nice, right? But she constantly gossips and complains. We're the only Americans in our condo, and I think she assumed we were going to be good friends. When we went for coffee that first time, I knew immediately that was not to be. I was in the process of interviewing helpers and she was trying to give me advice, and it was the most bigoted stuff I've heard. I don't think she's all bad, just wrong about so many things and really sort of mean as a result. How do I get rid of her? I'm no good at this.

Love,
Sid

I let myself escape into her letter, and my heart ached for her. Stupid Adrian. Stupid Bridget. Stupid me. *When it rains, it pours*: oh, if you only knew, big sister. Knowing something about her that she didn't made me feel dirty and sad.

It crossed my mind to just call her and tell her exactly what had happened—that I chose the dumbest method imaginable to preserve our letters. That I wanted them to be saved only for us, all together, all in order, a complete and organized record of this beautiful experiment. But that something went wrong. I don't know how, but my private blog had become public. Very public, I'm afraid.

I knew she'd have trouble understanding, though. She didn't share my yen for order and control.

New York
August 11

Dear Sid,

I am so sorry to hear that. You are a trusting soul, and I love that about you. There are people out there who can't help but take advantage of that in a person (the helper), and there are people who are just fuckups (Adrian). Regarding this Bridget, oy! She sounds like a doozy. Since I can't do confrontations, I usually just freeze people out.

But what do I know—I have a frenemy too! And she's my first, too! How did we come all this way to have a high school relationship in our thirties? Her name is Jenna and she lives across the hall from me and thinks she's better than me because her kid eats broccoli. For some reason I can't not care—she drives me nuts! I find myself trying to compete with her and I hate it. And then sometimes I feel bad because I think she might just need a friend. But mostly I wish I could just erase her from my life.

I wonder if our frenemies would be friends. I would give anything to trade places with Bridget for a week or so—I'll plop down next to you at the pool and bring you muffins. And ol' Bridge can hang out here and receive a lifetime of free advice on child rearing, health and wellness, and general goodness from my building's foremost mommy blogger.

So what are you going to do about the stolen money? Did you call the police? Let me know if there's anything I can do to help. I don't know what that might be, but I'm here for you. And you know my couch and floor are all yours if you and the kids just want to get out of Dodge for a while. You can trade places with Jenna!

I've also been meaning to tell you that you're right about my life. It's not so bad. I've got myself a gratitude journal. I've signed up for this boot camp workout at seven a.m. before Leo leaves for work, and I have every intention of actually going to it. These sound like silly housewife-on-a-mission-to-change clichés. But what can I say? I'm too tired not to be a cliché. Not being a cliché is for the very few truly original people (you, for example) and the young who have the energy to fight being ordinary.

Love you.
—Cassie

Ah, that was just the fix I needed. That superfine black felt-tip was perfect on those notecards. Why hadn't I figured out that combination sooner? Basking in the warm glow of a back-and-forth with Sid, I curled up under the covers, closed my eyes, pictured old-fashioned TV static running through my brain, and fell fast asleep.

It was glorious, as naps go. I didn't stir until the boys were climbing on me, smelling of French fries and chocolate, at nearly six p.m. I had been in such a deep sleep that it took me a few seconds to figure out where I was. As I slid out of bed, doing my best to deflect their sticky hands from the clean sheets, a heaviness set in. *Something bad happened, didn't it? Or did I just have a bad dream?* And then I remembered, but I tried to push the reality back into the bad-dream part of my brain—it haunts you, yes, but no lasting harm's done.

In a haze, I made my way through bath, book, and bedtime with the boys, and then pizza and movie at home with Mom and Leo. It was Mom's last night in town, and we had talked about going to dinner just the two of us while Leo stayed in with the boys, but with my afternoon illness, she wouldn't hear of it.

Later that night, thanks to the nap, I couldn't sleep. My body tossed and turned but felt incapable of doing anything purposeful. Close to one a.m., I grabbed my iPhone from its spot under my pillow, just to double-check that the privacy reset had really worked. (Yes, I've read about the radiation shooting out of it and directly into my brain, but probable brain cancer is just another sacrifice of living in our fabulous apartment in our fabulous neighborhood with no room for suburban luxuries such as bedside tables. Our bed was nestled perfectly between two extra-tall dressers and beneath a to-the-ceiling Elfa shelving system, all cleverly concealed by curtains on the sides and a custom-made pull-down shade on the top. Standing back, the impression was that our bed was tucked back into a cozy nook surrounded by silver-gray silk curtains. But sleeping in our bed was exactly like sleeping in a closet.)

In fact, the longer I lay there, feeling the weight of my stupid clothes all around me, the higher my anxiety level climbed. I needed air. With Mom asleep on the couch, climbing out onto the fire escape was not an option. So I pulled on jeans and grabbed a bra from the hook on the back of my door, hastily securing it under the gray tank top I was sleeping in, and then reached under my pillow again to find a hair tie. I thought to take my laptop in case I needed full word-processing capabilities, stuffed it in my bag with the magazine, and as quietly as I could, snuck out the front door.

I figured I could get online at the Ostrich Lounge because it was next to a coffee shop with free Wi-Fi, so I headed there, knowing my disheveled appearance wouldn't raise an eyebrow. The Ostrich was the closest thing Hudson Street had to a dive bar, with a regular-people kind of clientele, a jukebox, and horrible bathrooms. A long and narrow space with booths on one side and the bar on the other, it had a gorgeous tin ceiling and ugly fake-wood-paneled walls.

The place was about half full, and I snagged the last barstool at the back and ordered a Stoli on the rocks with two lemon wedges. I checked the blog again, and it was indeed still private. I was the only one in the world who could see it now; still, the sight of it made me queasy and unsettled. I closed the laptop and got out my pen and paper. I thought I'd brainstorm a plan—a crisis-communications plan. Who do I tell, and when, and how? I jotted some nonsensical notes, and then started to wonder if I really needed to tell anyone. Hadn't I fixed the problem this afternoon? Maybe it would just go away.

The Sundays song that I associate with the beginning of this whole experiment started playing from the jukebox, and my eyes watered as I looked around the bar, half expecting Sid to be standing in the corner, smiling knowingly before she let me in on this elaborate joke she'd masterminded.

The bartender took it upon himself to serve me another drink, even though I hadn't asked. Grateful, I nodded at him and downed about half of it in one stinging go.

Then, to give my hands and brain something to do, I started jotting down the words to the song. I had a quick flashback to being thirteen or fourteen and writing down all of the lyrics to "It's the End of the World as We Know It (and I Feel Fine)," starting and stopping and rewinding my tape player over and over again and driving Sid crazy until she finally joined me. (*It does not go, "Donkey Kong foreign power!" Yes, it does!*) My eyes welled at the memory, but I forced the tears back and kept writing as fast as I could, clinging to a Sid-like notion that there was an explanation or a solution or—I don't know— a silver lining of some sort that would reveal itself to me if I only looked. Tears were threatening to drop on my paper, so I looked up at the shiny tin ceiling in an effort to stave them off, losing myself for a moment in the tiles' intricate pattern.

A familiar voice brought me back to earth.

"Drinking alone with your notebook again, Cassie?"

It was Jake. He smiled—extra warmly, I thought—and leaned in for a peck on the cheek.

I allowed it but didn't peck back. The bartender handed him a bottle of Sierra Nevada Pale Ale, his favorite, and shook his hand. While they exchanged pleasantries, I rapidly sipped my drink and told myself to pull it together.

He turned back to me and said, "So what is it with you and your notebook? You working again?"

"Ooh. Ooh. Not really. Sort of," I said, though I have no idea why, and quickly shoved it back into my bag.

"You all right, Cass?" he asked, looking at me closer.

"Yeah, yeah. I'm fine. I'm good," I said, glancing away for a second and hoping that my eyes were dry.

Jake motioned to the bartender, and then I had my own bottle of Sierra Nevada.

The buddy Jake had come with looked to be deep in conversation with a young woman near the front of the bar, which left Jake and me alone to chat. The topic I chose—how we'd gone years barely seeing each other and now every time I turn around, there he is . . . in a magazine, in my yoga class, on TV, at the corner bar—came off as more flirtatious than I'd meant it to. I was distracted and embarrassed, remembering how I'd ditched him at the restaurant and snippets of the drunken kiss. I wondered if he'd kissed me because he wanted to or because I was so obviously throwing myself at him, and if he'd (please, no!) seen the letters.

I noticed that there was a new song on the jukebox—"Under My Thumb" by the Rolling Stones—and I felt annoyed that he had made me miss what might have been a breakthrough moment during the Sundays song. I had a different sort of breakthrough then, despite the two vodkas and one beer in me, and thought about how this looked. I had just snuck out of my apartment, where my husband, children, and mother (for Christ's sake!) slept, while I drank at the corner bar with my ex, whom I had spent the last three months fantasizing about *and* whom I had recently made out with. I would finish my beer and split.

The conversation had meandered toward more banal topics, and he started telling me a story about his seafood supplier who keeps bringing him his home-pickled herring, but pickled herring is the one food in the whole world that Jake truly hates, and now he's in this situation where his white lie about how delicious the herring was has turned into this awkward and ongoing deception, and— missing a third possible breakthrough moment—all I could think was, *I should not be here. This is not who I am. I am Margie and Joe's granddaughter. I am Leo's wife. I am a mother. I should not be here.* I cut Jake off midsentence. I feared if I didn't seize this flash of prudence, there would be no turning back, because to be honest, I didn't want to leave.

"I'm sorry, Jake. I've got to get home." I touched him lightly on the arm, and a charge went through me. He reciprocated by cupping my elbow and drawing us an inch closer.

"Are you sure?" he said in a soft voice in my ear, leaving no question as to his intention.

A sexual advance from a new-old lover was exciting and seductive, and part of me—a big part of me, I'm afraid—didn't want to turn away from the feeling of that moment, of feeling desired and forgetting about all of my other problems. But I reclaimed my mind of ten seconds ago, shook myself loose from Jake's grasp, slid the two twenties out of my back pocket onto the bar, grabbed my bag, and headed for the door without another word. A group of people came in just as I reached the exit, and I found myself holding the door open for them, smiling and nodding and cursing my Midwestern manners while I resisted the impulse to glance over my shoulder.

Once outside, I felt the urge to run. Now, here's an urge I can give in to without hurting anyone, I thought, and so I started running. A middle-aged couple walking toward me hand in hand watched with concern. The woman seemed to be searching my face for signs of distress while the man strained to look past me— perhaps in case I was being chased. *Am I being chased? Did Jake come out after me?* I looked back, but the coast was clear.

"Everything's okay!" I yelled to the couple. It felt good, so I ran faster—as fast as I could down Hudson Street without losing my flip-flops. To the bouncer standing in front of Employees Only, also regarding me with curiosity, I yelled it again. "Everything is okay!"

To the women sitting outside the Henrietta Hudson, "It's okay! Everything's okay!" I rounded onto Morton Street, unlocked my door, and ran up the stairs two at a time.

When I got to my door, I took a few minutes to catch my breath, still muttering, *It's okay. Everything is okay.* With tears running down my face, I took a few shaky deep breaths to prevent a full-scale sob-fest, unlocked my door as quietly as I could with trembling hands, and stepping over the two creaky floorboards, tiptoed past my sleeping mother and back into bed with Leo. Lying there, I let my thoughts drift toward the more superficial elements at play here, such as being thankful for Mayor Bloomberg's smoking ban, without which I would never have been able to pull the whole thing off.

Mom's flight the next day was at noon out of LaGuardia. She was always nervous about getting to the airport on time, and I had assured her that if she left by ten she'd be fine. Yet she was packed and dressed for the day when the rest of us woke up at seven. As we went about our morning routine, she kept suggesting we go to the playground early, or put the boys in the stroller and go for a walk so we could talk. But I wasn't on my A game, and by the time we ate breakfast, saw Leo off to work, printed out her boarding pass, and had the boys ready to go, we had to put her in a cab. The boys and I walked her out, and when we got downstairs, she grabbed my arm and locked eyes with me.

"Talk to your husband, Cassandra," she said.

"Mo-om. What? Everything's okay," I said, sounding like a whiny teenager.

And then, with a sigh and a look that was either disappointment or plain weariness, she said, "I love you, honey," and came in for a big hug. She couldn't have known about the blog; she would have said something. She must have heard me come in last night and assumed the worst. I loaded her suitcase in the trunk of the cab while she said her goodbyes to the boys, and off she went, leaving me alone with my big, giant problem.

CHAPTER SEVENTEEN

Despite my proclamations to the contrary, everything was not okay. I died a thousand deaths before noon, physically crumpling at each flash of a catty revelation or unkind characterization of Leo's family that appeared in my letters. *How much did I say about Jenna? Was there anything about Mom that might hurt her to read?*

Question upon question piled up in my brain. I couldn't grasp the timeline of this whole thing. Was it over, or was it just beginning? It hadn't become real yet, because Leo and Sid hadn't seen it. Maybe they never would. But still, I had to do something about this, didn't I? There was damage to be undone, wasn't there?

I didn't trust myself to find the answers. What I needed was a third-party assessment: someone to explain to me what I'd done, how bad it was, and what I needed to do to fix it. My first two choices—Leo and Sid—were obviously out of the question, so I called Monica and set a noon playdate. We would bring lunch.

The next two and a half hours were rough. While the boys ran naked through the fountain at the Bleecker Street playground, I stole glances at the comments on the blog. Nothing new since last night, which meant my privacy lock worked. I could barely stand to read most of them. Lots of people were talking about me, and just as many were talking *to* me, which was strange. They were also talking to Sid about her letters. Some of the comments made me gasp out loud with bemusement or shock or even mirth.

"These girls seem nice but boring. I gave them a chance but going back to the *Real Housewives*."

Some kind souls came to my defense. "You are missing the point," wrote BarrioBabe. "This is about communication and sisters trying to navigate their lives while still staying close, not about manufactured drama."

Um, no. I wanted to correct them. *This is not "about" anything. This is nothing to you. Stop reading my letters! Stop having opinions about them!*

When Monica answered her door, she had the phone to her ear. Waving us in while she nodded vigorously and said, "Yes, uh-huh, nine twenty, sounds great."

I shushed the boys and tried to get them to enter like secret agents.

Pocketing her phone, she looked at me with eyes bulging. "You will never guess who that was."

"I'm not even going to try."

"Kathie Lee motherfucking Gifford," but she only mouthed the "motherfucking" part, not that the boys would have noticed. They were barreling in to join Ana and Jonny in the playroom in the back of the house.

"What? Why?" I said as we walked back to the kitchen.

"So in the Hamptons my Twitter feed was bursting with this stupid 'Dear mom on her phone' post written by some old man," said Monica. She handed me a glass of water and I leaned against the kitchen counter while she loaded the dishwasher. "You probably saw it." (I had, but hadn't clicked through to read it.) "He was admonishing every mother who ever used her phone in the park and saying they were basically missing their children's childhoods and demonstrating that their phones are more important than their children."

"Dick," I said.

"Complete asshole," said Monica. "Anyway, I wrote a response on my blog and it went viral."

There I was, dying to share my big news, and she beat me to the punch! I almost said, "Okay, great, but guess what happened to me!" But I couldn't. That would be shitty. First I had to work through forty-five minutes of her thing before we could get to my thing. I pride myself on being an actual conversationalist, not just a person who waits for her turn to say something, but I struggled that afternoon. Luckily, there weren't a lot of opportunities for my input.

"And now Kathie Lee and Hoda want to have me on the fourth hour of *The Today Show*," she continued. "Kathie Lee called me herself. She was all, 'You go, girl!' She said she read the post, too, and was wondering why all these moms were letting some old guy shame them, and then someone e-mailed her my post and she was all, 'Yes! Thank you!' So I'm going on tomorrow. I have to be there at nine twenty. Do you want to come with me? What should I wear?"

We were on our way to her bedroom when we were diverted by the kids, who needed a peace deal brokered over a plastic dinosaur. After hearing their arguments, Monica set her kitchen timer for five minutes, at which point Joey would have to give the toy to Jonny.

We sat with the kids and she pulled Ana onto her lap. "I mean, it's not like the guy doesn't have a point. Most of us *should* put the phone away more often, but the moms I know are awesome, regardless of how much time they spend staring at their phone. So I listed all of the things these moms he's judging might be doing on their phones—like making doctors' appointments for elderly parents; researching their child's autism; editing a blog post that needs to go live in the middle of playtime . . . They should be applauded, not shamed. Their kids get to run around and play outside while they get stuff done. Right?" And then, as if really looking at me for the first time, she said, "Cass? Is everything okay?

"Yeah, yeah. Sorry, I was sort of spacing out for a second there. I actually have a crazy story of my own."

"What's going on? Tell me." She lifted Ana off of her lap and shooed her away.

"All right. So, did I mention how I've been writing letters to my sister all year?"

"Yeah—you told me a while ago."

"So, yeah, it's been this great thing we've done all year, and I feel closer to her than I have since we were teenagers." I was stalling.

"So what's the problem?"

Ding! The timer sounded. With minimal cajoling, Joey handed the dinosaur to Jonny. "Okay, five minutes for you and then we eat lunch!" announced Monica, setting the timer again. She and I got up and went into the kitchen to set out the bagels and salads.

"All right, Cass, let's have it," she said, and handed me a stack of plates.

I set the pile of plates on the table, and it all came tumbling out in one breath.

"Wait a second—what?" said Monica.

"Well, in a nutshell, I had a private blog of all the letters between Sid and me. But it turns out it wasn't private, and it became super-popular for a couple weeks. So we both went viral, I guess."

"What's the blog called?"

"*The Slow News Sisters,*" I said.

She gasped and pulled up a note on her iPhone. It said, "*Slow News Sisters* blog."

"What the hell?" I said. "You've seen it?"

"No—I overheard two women talking about it at the market up in the Hamptons," she said, "so I made a note to check it out."

"Well, what were they saying?"

"Cass! I can't believe this is you. One of them was telling the other one she had to read it. That it was these two normal sisters writing these honest and real letters. Someone was being cheated on. Oh shit, it's not you, is it?"

"No. Wait, they said we were normal?"

"Does that surprise you?

"God, I don't know. I guess we are normal."

"So what did Sid say?"

"I haven't told her. You're the first person I've told."

"But you're going to tell her, right?"

"I don't know. I don't know what to do. I made it private again, so it's gone now, right? I mean, no one can see it anymore, right? That's what I need you to explain to me."

"Well, here's the thing. It's rare that you can one hundred percent erase something from the Internet. Remember that picture I took of that little girl taking a dump in a portable training potty in the middle of the playground at Chelsea Piers and it turned out to be Suri Cruise?"

"Yeah." I had a feeling that this little allegory was not going to end well for me.

"Her lawyer asked me to take down the photo, so I did, but Perez Hilton and Page Six had already reblogged it with a screen capture. I could only control what's on my site, so the legal team had to track down everyone who had reblogged the shot and linked to Perez or Page Six."

I took a deep breath. "So I'm fucked?"

"Maybe not. Did you delete the whole thing, or is it still up?"

"Still up. But private again."

She looked at me, narrowing her eyes and nodding in thought.

"I mean, you're probably okay, but it's hard to say for sure."

Then the timer dinged again and the kids came stampeding into the kitchen.

"Do you want to see it?" I said, once all the kids were settled with bagels and peanut butter and carrots and cucumber sticks.

"I'm dying to! But only if you're cool with it."

"I think I want you to—I need you to tell me how bad it is."

I handed her my phone, and she took her salad into the living room to eat and read on the couch while I dined with the kids. I plowed through my salad in a fit of nervous energy and then picked at the kids' bagels during the impossibly long time it takes them to finish the smallest amount of food.

The kids finished lunch and charged into the back room while I stayed put, awaiting a signal from Monica. When I heard her ask them about Play-Doh, I cleaned up the lunch dishes while she, presumably, continued to read.

Once the kitchen was spotless, I couldn't take it anymore and I went into the living room.

I looked at her expectantly.

"Cass. Wow."

"So what do I do?"

She got up and followed me back into the kitchen. "Well, you've got to tell Leo. And your sister."

"I was afraid you'd say that."

"Oh, come on! You and your sister are solid. What about you and Leo? Do you think a drunken kiss is enough to topple your marriage? And, Jesus, I was not prepared to read that part—I wish you would have warned me."

"Pretty major, right?"

"Well, unexpected, but what are we talking, a kiss? Or is there more?"

"No. No more," I said, though in my memory it was hardly just a kiss.

"I think that's something Leo can handle."

"But other than that, there's so much in those letters I would never want him to see—petty stuff about his family, stupid complaints about our marriage. Nothing I'd call a deal breaker on its own, but all added up, it would be hard to take. I mean, where do I even begin with him? Do I have him read everything?"

"I'd vote against doing that. What if you told him about the kiss, and the blog, and then asked him if he wanted to read it all?"

"I guess that could work," I said, though I wasn't convinced.

"It'll be all right, Cass. You just need to come clean. Dreading their reaction is the worst part."

The kids were still happily playing Play-Doh (a magical substance, as far as I'm concerned. I've often wondered if it contains a mild sedative, based on the uncharacteristically calm and content behavior my boys exhibit under its spell). We had moved from the kitchen to her bedroom during the course of our chat, and Monica was rifling through her closet for something to wear on *The Today Show*, while I lay on her bed, chewing apart my lip in thought.

I knew she was right about telling Leo and Sid. But now that I had stopped this runaway train, I had to gather my thoughts—or read an instruction manual—before I defused the bomb. Talking to Monica had helped a little, but it also made it clear that this was my mess to clean up, that no one was going to do it for me. I thought, if I could just get some time to think, I might be able to handle this situation with some delicacy and save my loved ones from pain and disgrace.

And then I remembered something. I scrambled for my phone and scrolled back through the letters until I found the one I was looking for: Sid said she was going to Bali for another yoga retreat on September first—today. (Or was it yesterday for her?) And Leo and I were scheduled to be at the Jersey Shore with his family tomorrow. When Leo wasn't working, he rarely checked his e-mail. His team could handle almost anything that arose but knew to phone him if there was an emergency. So as long as no one in his family found out about the blog, I was safe. Contemplating the idea of someone in his family finding out triggered another wave of panic. I needed to walk. I asked Monica if she'd keep the kids while I did a quick Duane Reade run.

Filling my basket with bubbles and sunscreen and car snacks, I weighed the pros and cons of the weekend away. I framed it like this: With Leo and Sid effectively sequestered, I'd gained a few more days of ignorant bliss for them—torturous anticipation for me, yes, but as long as none of the Costas knew, I could maintain the status quo.

Not that I had a choice in the matter. September third is my mother-in-law's birthday, and it goes without saying that all four of Mary Costa's boys will be together—with her—on Labor Day weekend. It is the one holiday she insists on, having given up on getting full attendance at Christmas or Easter years ago.

Besides, the boys loved seeing their cousins, Leo would get to spend time with all three of his brothers, and I would get to hang out with Emma.

I fetched the boys from Monica's and we walked home. It was one of those special days where the mailbox contained two letters from Sid, only instead of feeling the childlike joy that I'd felt the other few times this had happened, I felt anxious and guilty. Still, here they were. Once upstairs, I distributed iPads and decided to open the one with the earlier postmark and save the other one for later.

Singapore
August 20

Hey, Cass—

Oh no—I'm not calling the police about the missing money. I doubt my little bank operation was entirely legal, and if there's one thing Singaporeans are exacting about, it's their rules. I'm over it. It was just a really bad week. The Adrian mess still smarts, as I suspect it will for a long while, but this bank business isn't getting me down.

But listen, you aren't the only mom on a mission. I'm getting certified to teach yoga—six classes to go! And speaking of clichés, how was I not into yoga before now? It's right up my alley, and completely saving my sanity these days. One of my mantras is this: "The stronger you become, the gentler you will be." Cool, right? Think about it.

I really am so lucky to have the time for it. Rose is like family, and Lulu has a great time with her. Plus, River's officially on his "gap year." He's looking into volunteering in Cambodia or Vietnam, but for now he's around a lot, which is great. Oh, and NYU said they would let him defer until next year. I'm really hoping that he does so he'll have you around, but he's still considering a few other schools. You are a doll for offering your place to me. Believe me, I will keep it in mind—because yes, it would be beyond fun!!

Love you.
—Sid

And what could I do? I had to write her back. So the letters continued, though sans scanning and posting. By this point, every day that I let pass without fessing up meant that my stupid, yes—but innocent—mistake became a conscious lie.

New York
Sept 1

Sid,

The other day Leo and I had drinks with some old work friends of mine and I caught myself telling the story about the stitches and how the doctor couldn't believe we didn't want a plastic surgeon for Quinn's eyebrow gash, but Leo and I were both like, "No. Scars are cool. And he's already a twin, so this scar will be his thing. He'll be the one with the scar."

I'm getting good at that story, and Leo has heard me tell it to neighbors, friends, Amir at the bodega, his mom on the phone, and just about anyone who will listen. And he laughs and nods and even chips in at just the right moment every time.

So as I was telling the story for the twenty-fifth time, an equal parts wonderful and horrible thought occurred to me: Leo is Joe and Margie stock. I'm the problem. He is decent and kind and simple, and I'm a fucking mess. I mean, I don't let the guy finish his own stories if I've heard them before. I'm trying, though. The first step is admitting you have a problem, right?

Congrats on the yoga teacher thing. I hope you can teach me someday. I don't even think I told you about my disastrous attempt a few months ago. How awesome is River? Let me know what he decides to do with his year. I would be so happy to have him at NYU!

Xoxo,
Cass

When I'm trying to look on the bright side of challenging situations, I focus on the empathy it can teach me. When I was pregnant and couldn't tie my own shoes or walk up a flight of stairs without getting winded, I had compassion for obese people. When the boys were in the thick of the terrible twos, I understood those mothers who go berserk and plunge their cars off of cliffs. And when I became a deceptive and secretive ne'er-do-well, I gained empathy for blackmailers and backstabbers and those men in Lifetime movies who have two families in two different cities who know nothing about one another.

CHAPTER EIGHTEEN

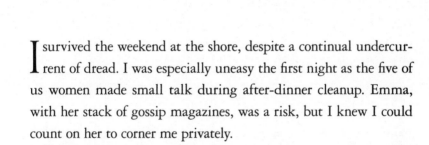

I survived the weekend at the shore, despite a continual undercurrent of dread. I was especially uneasy the first night as the five of us women made small talk during after-dinner cleanup. Emma, with her stack of gossip magazines, was a risk, but I knew I could count on her to corner me privately.

Becky was another story. She had lost major points in Leo's book when it was discovered that, in fact, she did not enjoy college football as much as she had let on while she and Rob were dating. As soon as they were married, it was clear all she wanted to do on Saturdays was watch bad reality TV. She was a fan of the *Real Housewives* franchise, and even knew one of the women from the New Jersey edition quite well—a fact that she loved to sprinkle into seemingly unrelated conversations. Becky wasn't my biggest fan because I couldn't bring myself to act impressed about her *Housewife* connections, and also because her younger sister once had a fling with Leo and carried a torch for him for quite some time after he started dating me. If Becky knew something about the blog, she would find a way to say it in front of the whole group—or, worse, tell Mary or Leo behind my back.

I made sure to offer up plenty of conversation topics, fearing a lull might give her or, heaven forbid, Mary, an opening to say, "Hey, that reminds me—those Slow News Sisters—is that you?" I found myself imagining ways in which I could seal the family off from reality. Stealing all the phones, computers, and iPads and hiding them until the end of the weekend, or maybe systematically knocking all the devices into the pool and blaming the kids—it all crossed my mind.

By the second night of our three-night stay, I had begun to relax, hopeful that the Costa family had remained insulated from the *Slow News Sisters* phenomenon, and starting to talk myself into the idea that it wasn't a phenomenon at all. And yet every time I saw someone scrolling through a phone, my stomach tensed.

As it turns out, Leo's uncle Sal was the one who had me quaking in my Havaianas. Uncle Sal is Mary's younger brother and the main reason for Emma's and my organized-crime suspicions. We call him Sawed-off Sal, on account of his missing the two last fingers on his left hand, which no one ever talks about. We've presented our theories to Leo and Stevie, and they laugh at us—but they've never denied it either.

At home, the worst time of day is between dinner and bedtime, when the boys are wound up and restless and my patience levels are at their lowest. But down at the shore house, it's different. With everyone fed and the kitchen cleaned, the kids always play peacefully, as if we adults had forgotten about bedtime and if they just don't draw too much attention to themselves, they'll be free to play all night. And they're right—we let them go until they can barely keep their eyes open and have to be carried off to bed half or totally asleep.

It happened during that relaxed postdinner period on our second evening. The dinner was cleaned up, the wives were relaxing, and every single male member of the family and a few of the girls were gathered at the wooded section at the edge of the yard where a garter snake was in the process of eating a toad. Poor Sophie, Emma's four-year-old daughter, ran back and forth from the moms to the dads, pleading for someone to save the toad. Mary was still futzing around in the kitchen, tidying here and there, while Alyssa and Becky retired to the two chaise longues in the yard.

The Costa house was two blocks from the beach, but the air smelled of salt and the sky turned orange as the sun sank lower into the clouds. Emma and I sat on the steps that go from the wooden deck down to the yard, discussing the possibility of adopting a more interesting signature drink, perhaps the Bellini. But that would have to wait until next time, because we were on the final sips of our last bottle of cheap sparkling wine. I went inside to fetch us a couple of beers and as I rounded back onto the patio, I came face-to-face with Sawed-off Sal.

He spread his arms and cocked his head to the side. "Doll! You shouldn't have!"

Usually, you can hear Sal before you see him and have time to deviate from your path, because he often wears one of those swishy nylon tracksuits. But today, in his oversized St. Francis Pancake Breakfast 1999 T-shirt over baggy black board shorts, he was able to catch me off guard. He did really clichéd things like go around with a toothpick in his mouth and wore a thick and shiny gold chain that matched the band of his Rolex. He dressed like a slob and accessorized like, well, like a Jersey gangster.

I handed him the Corona meant for Emma, but when I attempted to head back to the cooler, he said, "Whoa, whoa, what's your hurry, Wednesday?" (He thought Wednesday was a clever nickname for me, like he couldn't remember my surname or maybe I didn't deserve for him to since I was the only wife who hadn't taken the Costa name.) I tried to beckon Emma over to join us, but she was comforting Sophie, who had broken down into sobs over the toad's imminent swallowing.

"I heard something about you . . . What was it?" he said, though I clearly wasn't expected to answer. He did this humming thing to hold the floor between statements.

I shrugged and sipped my beer, waiting. To stave off a panic attack, I told myself that there was no way Sal would be the one to read the blog.

Mary hovered just behind him, tidying the glass patio table. She seemed to be straining to listen in, which set me ill at ease.

"Ah, forget it. I can't remember nothin' these days."

"Oh, well!" I said. "Maybe it'll come to you later."

"Oh—I know what it was. So you used to be a workin' girl, didn't you?"

"Yeah. My corner was 116th and Broadway. It's how Leo and I met," I deadpanned. I noticed Mary stifle a smile; she loved a bit of crude humor.

It took him a moment, but Sal's head jerked back and he let out a roar of laughter, his reaction a bit much for my lame joke. Behind him, Emma was sitting Sophie down with a bowl of ice cream at the table Mary had just cleaned. When she looked over at us, I gave her a "save me" look. But Emma just did her best goombah stance, cracking her knuckles and rolling her head around, quickly shifting to a self-neck massage when Mary reappeared with a dry cloth to finish off the table. When Mary saw that Sophie was about to mess it all up again, she shook her head and doubled back to fetch the Windex. *Poor Emma,* I thought. *There go another ten points from her daughter-in-law score.*

"You always were a funny one," he said finally. "No, no, I mean, what was it that you did when you worked? Was it something with the Internet or blogs?"

I felt the blood drain from my face. Now his ridiculous laughter fit seemed like the one the mob boss does to lull you into a false sense of security just before he offs you. He tongued his toothpick and stared at me, waiting for an answer.

Suddenly nervous, I replied, "I worked for a magazine. We did have a blog—"

"Reason I ask," he said, cutting me off. *Oh God, here it comes,* I thought. ". . . is that I been doing some writing. Like a memoir. Stories from growing up in the old neighborhood, that kinda stuff. I haven't been able to get a publisher, so Deena says I should just put it on the Internet. She figures way more people would read it than would read a book. Isn't that right, D?" he called over to his longtime girlfriend, who was crouched down, filming the toad-versus-snake battle on her phone. From the breathless reportage being shouted from the huddle, the toad had extracted a leg from the snake's mouth and looked to be making a slow break for it.

"What's that, Sally?" Deena yelled.

"That if I put my stuff on the Internet—as a blog or somethin'—lots more people would read it that way."

"Oh, definitely. Definitely," she said in her deep, husky voice, nodding affirmatively as she continued to film. "You gotta see this, Sally. This toad is gonna make it."

Ignoring her, he maintained eye contact with me. "So, Wednesday, you'll help me out?"

What I wanted to say was, *Not for all the tiramisu in Little Italy,* but instead out came, "Oh, it's really simple. But sure, I can help you get set up. Leo probably could, too, or even Stevie. So any of us, really, could help."

"Aw, Stevie and Leo are busy. They got jobs," he said.

Now it was my turn to laugh, which seemed like a good way to wrap this up, so I feigned a sudden interest in the toad's survival and joined the fray, promising to talk more about it later.

I spent the next day at the beach, building sand castles, playing chase with the waves, applying and reapplying sunscreen, and wondering whether Sal really did want to post his personal memoirs online or if he was just really bad at making threats.

We had packed a cooler with lunch, and after chicken-salad sandwiches, grapes, potato chips, and juice boxes, I retreated to the blanket under the umbrella and pulled out the letter from Sid I had saved as a treat.

Bintan, Indonesia
August 24

Darling Cassie,

We're in Bintan, Indonesia, right now—Lulu, River, and me. It's an hour's ferry ride away, and there's this old resort with tiny stone cottages right on the beach. It's just a bedroom and a bathroom, but we love coming here. The cottage is infested with ants, and the food at the restaurant is horrible, but we just walk and play on the beach all day, go to bed early, then do the exact same thing the next day and get the late ferry back to Singapore. Lulu's asleep inside, and I'm sitting on the porch while River sits on the beach and reads. It rained for an hour earlier, and River and Lulu and I played tag in the cool rain and then got into the ocean to warm up. The sand here is the extra-fine kind that seeps into everything—fingernails, bathing suits, hair, notebooks—it's everywhere and I love it!

Adrian's actually been kind of decent about this whole thing. I mean, he's a shit and possibly a sex addict, but he didn't try to deny it or cover anything up. He just faced the music and let me say everything I needed to say. He has crumpled and begged for forgiveness a few times, but he hasn't made excuses or tried to justify his actions in any way. And I guess in some small way, I respect that. In this freshman ethics seminar back in college, I remember my professor saying "Walk merrily to your execution." I always thought of that line when I did something stupid. Just live with the consequences of your actions and try to make the best of the situation. I think that's what Adrian's doing. It's funny that I'm just now fully getting what that meant.

Love,

Sid

I loved feeling like we were both at the beach at the same time, if on different ends of the earth. Of course, her letter had been written two weeks earlier, yet I'd come to see her life as unfolding in real time as the letters arrived.

But what was this about walking merrily to my execution? Did she know? Was she telling me to plaster a dumb smile on my face and come clean? While Leo and the boys buried Stevie in the sand,

I drifted in and out of sleep, dreaming that Sid had found out
about the blog and hired Uncle Sal to execute me.

The boys both fell asleep on the way home from the beach and
were up until nearly eleven p.m. that night. They rewarded us by
sleeping past nine the next morning. But at seven forty-five, I was
awoken by the buzz from my phone. It was the world's longest text
message from Rachel.

> Hi, Cass! Hope Quinn is on the mend. Brooke's been having
> nightmares so I took her to a therapist, who advised me to
> draw a picture book of the accident and emphasize how every-
> one is okay at the end. Not sure if your boys are similarly trau-
> matized, but it's been helpful, FYI. Anyhoo, I would really like
> to replace my Noguchi coffee table before Brett's 40th birth-
> day party next month. (Invite to come!) What would be easiest
> for you—to PayPal me $$ for the table plus the $100 for the
> cleanup crew? (Don't worry about the therapist bill—I'll take
> care of that.) If it's better for you to use a credit card, I can send
> you a link to the coffee table and you can order it for me online.
> Let me know—I'd love to get this taken care of ASAP. Thx so
> much! XO—Rachel

I found this incredibly annoying on several levels. First, that it
came through in four separate text messages, the final one being a
helpful link to the coffee table. Second, I had told her at the hospital
that of course we would pay for the coffee table, so she didn't need to
act like she was broaching uncharted territory. Third, I was secretly
hoping she would ignore my offer and take care of it herself, which
is what I would have done had a friend's child hurled himself
through a piece of glass in my apartment while I showed off my

giant bathtub. Fourth, Leo and I had been pinched financially lately, and this was not in the budget—especially if I was going to fly to Singapore to tell Sid about the blog face-to-face, which was becoming the only way I could imagine this going down.

Lying in bed, I followed the link to Design Within Reach, where the table was listed at $1,600. Leo wasn't in bed, so I crept out of the room with the boys still asleep in their Lightning McQueen sleeping bags on the floor. All of the adults were already up and drinking coffee in various places around the kitchen and adjoining den. I helped myself to a mug, sat at the big farmhouse table across from Leo, and told him about the text. Naturally, it became a whole family discussion.

Stevie, always the conspiracy theorist, piped up. "That's bullshit. I wouldn't pay that. I bet her table was a knockoff. What does Quinn weigh—thirty pounds, maybe? He's supposed to so easily shatter a sixteen-hundred-dollar coffee table? They're gonna use tempered glass on a table like that."

Then Becky chimed in with, "I don't understand how this even happened in the first place. Where were you?"

"Oh, you know, lounging in the tub," I said, with panache.

"And eating bonbons—right, dear?" Mary laughed. "Boys will be boys, Becky. These things happen."

I couldn't resist shooting Becky a rueful look. She had three girls and simply couldn't share the soldierlike bond that Mary and I did.

"Come on," Stevie said. "Let's go throw a watermelon through the patio table—that thing was three hundred bucks and I bet we couldn't break it."

"You will not," barked Mary.

"Your friend is pulling one over on you," said Stevie.

Leo just laughed, but I could tell Stevie's comments had his wheels spinning.

"Did it look real to you?" Leo asked.

Honestly, I had my doubts. "I don't know. But if it was a knock-off, she probably didn't know it," I said. I was tempted to jump on Stevie's bandwagon, if only to ally myself with Leo against a common enemy.

Then Sal spoke up. I hadn't even noticed he was there, but he was leaning in the doorway, filing his nails with a big pink emery board. "You need a designer table? Why didn't you say so? I got a guy."

"Of course you do," said Emma, smiling brightly at me, practically rubbing her hands together in anticipation of more mob clues.

Leo's always been a Boy Scout—he doesn't even download pirated music—but he looked at me with his thick black eyebrows raised to the sky, and I shrugged. We were in a tight spot, so why not avail ourselves of one of the perks of being related to a low-ranking official in the Italian-American organized-crime syndicate?

I spoke up. "Really?"

Emma jerked her head around and bulged her eyes at me. She was either thinking that this was finally our chance to find out for real if Sal lived up to our *Sopranos* fantasy, or just shocked that I was about to hop into it.

But what I was thinking was that maybe I was simply taking my natural place in the world. So far this year I had become a cheater and a liar. So why not a receiver of stolen goods?

Accepting my fate, I took the lead on making the arrangements with Sal. He said he could have it for me in a few days. I texted Rachel back and told her I'd order her the table this week, and felt the rush of satisfaction of having a project.

CHAPTER NINETEEN

Master of denial and avoidance that I was, I managed to parlay the few days I allotted for perspective into nearly two weeks, during which time I had come up with all kinds of explanations as to why this whole thing was a nonevent. It happened in August. A throwaway month. Nobody remembers things that happen in August. We were into September now. The city was running as it should, and everything was back to normal. The blog going viral was a blip. Fifteen minutes of fame? Try fifteen seconds. It was done. I still punished myself silently, but I saw no reason to upset Sid and Leo if this whole thing was blowing over.

There was one little problem with my line of thinking, though: After my initial total immersion, I had avoided the Internet as best I could while I instinctively hunkered down with my family. Knowing that my character might soon be called into question, I was too busy shoring up my key witnesses to root around the Web. Unfortunately, any dummy knows that just because you don't follow baseball doesn't mean they canceled the World Series.

My campaign wasn't totally manufactured, though. I was getting on with what I had set my mind to do before the awful discovery. I became playful and sentimental with the boys and more loving toward Leo. The constant undercurrent of fear and dread didn't work wonders for my patience levels, but it was offset by my determination to be remembered as a good person, should I be dragged away to jail for crimes against common decency.

My whole Jake fantasy disappeared as quickly as it had started. I suspect it would have died out on its own, but things getting real between us turned out to be a turnoff. I shifted my energies in that department to where they should have been all along: my marriage. I became bolder in bed with Leo, initiating sex at least as often as he did. Instead of feeling like we each had a heavy weight in us that rolled around under our skin, constantly pulling us down to the bed, I now visualized the backs of my hips and shoulders attached by long strings to the ceiling. The living room floor became our spot. With a solid wall and two doors between us and the kids, we had leeway for more than the hushed quickies our bedroom allowed. My self-preservation instincts led me to figure that if Leo found out, he'd be less likely to divorce a sexually available wife than the sexually distant one I'd been for longer than I cared to admit.

Simultaneously, I was bracing for the worst. I made myself a punishment playlist: Lots of Morrissey, Dylan's "Positively 4th Street" and "Don't Think Twice, It's All Right," Rihanna's "Take a Bow," Beyoncé's "Irreplaceable," plus some extra-angry Fiona Apple and Lily Allen, all of whom I'd imagined singing to me.

As if to further castigate me, Sid's letters kept coming in at a good clip.

Singapore
Sept 10

Cass,

First, I love that stitches story. Scars *are* cool! Send me a photo of Quinn and his badass scar, please. And don't beat yourself up. It takes an exceptional person to recognize her own failures in a relationship. I'd say you are going to be fine. You love Leo, right? He'll forgive you, Cass. I think you should tell him about the kiss.

XO, Sid

When Leo came home from work on Tuesday night two weeks after our return from the shore, the boys and I were sitting on the floor listening to Birds of Chicago and eating Peanut Butter Panda Puffs right out of the box.

I was nervous and distracted. Tonight was the night. I had to tell Leo. Instead of rehearsing my lines in my head, I was in a total daze, focusing on the loud rhythmic crunching in my head.

"Daddy!" the boys screamed, snapping me out of it.

Leo always got the rock-star greeting from the boys. The three of them collapsed in a hug-wrestle pile while I shoved the last of the cereal in the box into my mouth.

"Hey, you cheated!" Leo said, still smiling. He was looking at me.

Is this it? I thought while I blinked in confusion.

"Real food week," he said, nodding to the box of cereal, which I'd been clutching like a security blanket most of the day.

"What?" I said.

"Real food week! It was your idea. I thought we started this morning."

"Oh. I didn't realize we were really doing that. I thought we were just talking hypothetically," I said.

We'd exchanged e-mails yesterday regarding this. There was a blogger who'd pledged to feed her family only real food—nothing processed or artificial or packaged—for one hundred days. I had suggested we try it for a week—but not *this* week.

"Yeah, that sounds about right," Leo said, with a sudden edge.

"Leo. We can do the real food thing. I didn't realize it was that important to you."

Shit. How did this happen? These were not the conditions under which I imagined telling him what I needed to tell him. Things had been going so well between us. I opened my mouth to apologize, but he was busy getting the boys drinks of water and telling them about a huge rat he saw on the subway platform earlier.

There was a lot of information I had to relay to him, and I had to do it quickly—before the boys did, because *they* knew that I was leaving on an airplane to visit their aunt Sid in the morning, that I would be gone for four days and Grandma Rita would be here with them and Dad. They did not know the more crucial information—that thousands of strangers knew intimate details about Mommy and Daddy's marriage and that I'd made out with an ex-boyfriend and broadcast it to the world. Nor did they know about the troubling events of my day leading up to and just after my purchase of the single airline ticket. Still, I wanted to tell Leo everything myself before they could start spilling the beans.

"Sorry. I'm just irritated because I have to go back to Fourteenth Street in an hour," Leo said.

"Seriously? For how long?"

"Yeah—the new membership cards aren't scanning, so I've got to figure it out. No idea. Maybe an hour, maybe more. I just got the message but I was almost home, so I thought I'd come up and have dinner and say good night to the boys."

Dinner? Since when did I have dinner waiting for him when he came home? And now apparently there was some rule about it being "real."

"Uuuuh. The boys ate at the Hudson. I thought we'd just order Thai—I mean, or something more healthy?"

"That's all right. I'll pick something up on my way back."

<hr />

When Leo had left for work earlier that morning, I was still happily biding my time, with vague plans to tell him soon. But after the day I'd had, a confession moved to the front burner.

"I love starting the workweek on a Tuesday," he'd said on his way out.

"Oh my God—it's Tuesday. Wanda's coming today!"

"She is?"

"Yeah, just today and next week, until school starts. She needs the money, and we haven't been great about those weekly date nights I told her we'd be using her for."

"It's cool. Enjoy your day," he'd said, and left.

I calculated that once Wanda arrived, I'd drop the clothes off at the Chinese laundry on the corner, buy groceries, prep lunch and dinner, and maybe even squeeze in a quick pedicure.

But I didn't get the pedicure, nor did I drop off the laundry or even buy groceries. Because when Wanda left with the boys for the park, I decided to check my Yahoo account. Since I'd switched to Gmail for personal mail years ago, my Yahoo account was almost exclusively spam, but I still checked it and occasionally read the e-mails from BabyCenter or the West Village Parents.

I had forgotten that this was also the address I had used to set up the blog. There were four urgent e-mails from Fishfood, the blog's host, instructing me to check and reset my privacy settings because many of their blogs had their settings wiped out when a server crashed. *Ah, so that answers that,* I thought, taking a moment to imagine the brief panic followed by quick relief I'd have experienced had I read the e-mails in time. I didn't get to revel for long, though, because my in-box contained several personal e-mails with subject lines such as "Seeking Representation?"; "Book Deal and Speaking Opportunities"; "Introduction." Confused, I read a couple of them. They were from agents, one of whom outlined a plan for a speaking and talk-show tour. Another promised a lucrative book deal with one of a number of publishers.

The one I found most distressing was this:

Dear Cassie,

I am a producer with *It's All Relative*, a program on ALM Radio. We've been alerted to your blog, *The Slow News Sisters*. I would like to speak with you about doing an interview for our segment, which will focus on ways long-distance siblings stay connected. Jessica Ronan, author of the bestselling book *Sisterhood*, will participate. I hope that you will join us on air, as the story is pegged on the sudden popularity of your blog. Please let me know if you'd be interested in participating. And would you mind putting me in touch with your sister, Sid? I can't seem to find a valid e-mail address for her.

Regards,
Caroline Stein
Senior Producer, ALM

The e-mail was three weeks old, and I had two more recent e-mails from her, asking if the blog was down.

My family listens to ALM. It's on in the kitchen at my parents'—and my grandparents'—house around the clock. The little Tivoli radio on our windowsill was tuned to its local affiliate. This had to be stopped.

I grabbed that same box of Peanut Butter Panda Puffs off the table and started pacing. I finally worked out the perfect handful size and chewing pace so that I could get a fresh mouthful at the same spot where I turned on the ball of my foot each time, when I realized what I needed to do. I checked for flights to Singapore and bought a single ticket for $1,700, then called Mom and asked if she could come back to New York. She assumed I was going to be there for Sid, given the whole mess with Adrian, and I didn't correct her.

I had just completed purchasing Mom's ticket and was wondering what the chances were of Leo checking the credit card statement online today. I was about to search ALM Radio's website to confirm my hope that the story had gone forward without mentioning my blog, figuring that if not, I'd call Caroline Stein and beg her not to include me in her story, but the buzzer rang.

Assuming it was Wanda with the boys, I buzzed them up without checking the intercom. I was disappointed that they were home so soon, but when I opened the door and poked my head out, instead of Quinn's and Joey's voices, I heard heavy breathing and quiet cursing. A few moments later, up came Sal with the glass top for Rachel's coffee table.

"No, no, no, no, no! Sal! Not here. It goes to my friend's place in Hoboken. Remember?"

Ignoring my comment completely, he said, "Wednesday. There

is no way Quinn could have busted through this thing. It weighs sixty pounds at least."

"Sal, listen. This has to go to Hoboken. Not here."

"Hoboken? I just came from Hoboken! Why didn't you say so?"

He stopped in the hall and rested one side of the plate-glass oval on his knee. It wasn't even wrapped in anything.

"Be careful. Here, I'll help you get this back downstairs," I said, slipping on my flip-flops and rushing to grab a corner of the glass, which was indeed heavy and thick.

Out on the sidewalk, Sal and I stood facing each other, each holding a side of the tabletop and waiting for his ride to circle back around the block, when Jenna and Valentina approached. Jenna had been leaving notes on my door and sending me text messages, but I'd been ignoring her and didn't want to deal with her now.

"Oooh. Pretty," Valentina said, pointing at the glass, the side of which was sparkling blue in the morning sun. And then, before anyone realized what she was doing, she removed a sticker from the sheet she was holding and affixed it to the glass.

"What the fuck?" said Sal.

Jenna hurried to peel off the rainbow sticker, but not before holding up a hand to Sal and saying, "Please. Language." Sal just stared in astonishment.

As she picked away at the sticker, licking her thumb to get the last remnants of the adhesive off of the glass, Jenna said, "Valentina, do we put stickers on other people's glass?"

I shook my head at the sky, and Sal said exactly what I was thinking. "What a stupid thing to say."

"Sal, this is my neighbor, Jenna, and her daughter, Valentina."

"You know them?" he asked, disgusted that I would associate with such low-grade characters. I smiled and shrugged at Jenna, who stood there, mouth agape. "Leo's uncle," I said, by way of explanation. This was the most fun I'd ever had with Sal.

"Cassie, I've been trying to get in touch with you. Is everything okay?"

"Yeah—why?" I said.

"Oh—I'll talk to you about it later. But wait—you have a sister, right?"

"Yeah," I said.

"What's her name again?"

"Why?"

"Ride's here!" Sal interrupted.

I looked up to see Mary Costa's black Suburban pulling up.

I don't know who I was expecting—some crony of Sal's with a limp and a gold tooth, or even Deena. Mary was definitely a surprise.

"Okay, well, I'll talk to you later," said Jenna. And then, "Oh—your sister's name?"

I pretended not to hear her, which wasn't a stretch since Sal was shouting, "Bad news, Mar. We gotta take this thing back to Hoboken."

"Hoboken! We were just there!" Mary yelled back. "Hi, Cassie, sweetheart. Where are the boys?"

"They're at the park with the sitter. But wait. I thought you guys knew this table wasn't for me," I said.

"You said it was for your upstairs neighbor!" Mary yelled.

"Naw. I remember now. She did say this gal had moved to Hoboken," Sal yelled back, although Mary was now two feet in front of us.

I noticed Jenna and Valentina turning to leave.

Mary threw her hands up to the sky and then slapped her thighs like an umpire calling a play. She looked from Sal to me, and I got the impression that she was expecting an apology. Normally I would have obliged, but I had plenty of real apologizing to do, and I was not about to start handing them out for free.

"Arright, hon. You know where this thing needs to go? You hop in and show us the way," said Sal.

I let out a groan. But they were doing this for me, so I ran upstairs to get my phone and my purse. I had a sick feeling in my stomach that I hoped was hunger, so I grabbed the only food I had in the apartment—that box of Peanut Butter Panda Puffs—locked the door, and then ran back down and into the back of Mary's truck, not bothering to say anything to Jenna when we passed in the hall.

I texted Wanda, asking if she could stay an extra hour and maybe even later. And instead of wondering whether Mary was also a mobster and if she had ever transported any dead bodies in this very truck, I was anxious about the radio thing and what to do about Jenna, who almost definitely had seen the blog. The phrase "lucrative book deal" also bobbed around inside my head, tempering the stress and dread with a mysterious thrill.

"So, Wednesday, when are we gonna get to that blog?" Sal shouted. I reacted as if a tarantula had just landed on my shoulder. Luckily, I didn't have to speak, because Mary started in.

"Blogs," she said. "I don't get it. Why do people think their every thought needs to be out there for the world to see? It's ridiculous, if you ask me."

"No one asked you," Sal shot back. "Oh, Jesus, why the hell are you driving uptown? The Holland Tunnel is right around the corner!"

"I told you I hate the Holland Tunnel! When you drive, you can take whatever tunnel you want. Hell, take a boat, for all I care. I always take the Lincoln. So shut up and let me drive," Mary yelled.

He looked back at me and pointed at Mary. "Some things never change. She'll always be my big sister." I had to smile, because the subject had changed, and because I was thinking the same thing, that there are only a few people in the world you could talk that way to and not have it damage your relationship. If you're lucky, a sibling is one of them. In some ways, I envied the relationship Mary and Sal had. They saw each other all the time and seemed to have no secrets. Maybe they were a bit abrasive and careless with each other's feelings, but beneath it there was genuine affection.

Through the tunnel, I read Rachel's address off to Sal, who laboriously punched it in the GPS mounted to Mary's dashboard, even though I told them I knew how to get there.

I was still unsure as to the origins of the table and whether I was paying for it or not. "So how much do I owe you for the table?" I asked Sal.

"Don't worry about it. You help me set up my blog, and we'll call it even."

"My blog." Mary shook her head and snickered.

"Are you sure, Sal?" I asked.

"Sweetheart," Mary interjected. "If you're lucky enough to have people to help you out of a tough spot, just go with it."

Fair enough, I thought, and took out my phone and began searching ALM's website for "sisters," "communication," and "slow news." When nothing turned up, I started an e-mail.

Dear Caroline,

Thanks for your interest in my blog. I'm a huge fan of your program and completely tickled that I'm even on your radar. Unfortunately, I cannot participate in your segment. In fact, I'm writing to implore you not to even mention my blog. The truth is, it was never meant to be public. It's a long story involving privacy settings, a server crash, regret, etc. Maybe one day I'll be able to tell the whole story, but if I did it now, it would cause too much pain to the people I love. I hope you understand. Please let me know what you decide to do.

Kind regards,
Cassie Sunday

Once we got the table into Rachel's place, I felt fairly certain that hers had been a fake. The one we brought—a real one, or a very good counterfeit, with legitimate-looking papers from Herman Miller and a little signature on the side of the thick plate glass—looked significantly better than I remembered hers looking.

Rachel must have thought so, too, because she let out a gasp when we set it down. Then she started gushing. "Oh, thank you so much. It was really sweet of you to bring it over. I didn't realize how much I missed it until just now."

I suspected that she was slowly figuring this out and hadn't deliberately bilked me for a sixteen-hundred-dollar table, but still, I found the whole display so off-putting that I doubted our friendship would survive.

Mary asked Rachel where the Windex was and gave the table a shine herself before we went on our way.

I felt a bit sick over the whole thing. *Is Rachel purposefully duping us, or is she innocent? What is wrong with her that she'd let my mother-in-law clean her table? Are Mary and Sal sketchy or just helpful? Do I have only myself to blame, literally lying down on the job while my son seriously injured himself, setting this whole chain of events into motion?* At any rate, I couldn't bear to be around any one of those people a second longer. I convinced Mary and Sal to drop me at the PATH station and let me take the train back home, saving them the trip.

Before I went underground, I texted Leo to see if he could meet for lunch, so I could come clean to him before I left.

Sorry. Swamped all day. Hopefully not too late tonight, came his response.

Okay, I will just have to tell him tonight, I thought.

Stevie and Emma's place was just around the corner, so I decided to drop in on them. I might need Emma in my corner in the near future. If the family found out while I was in Singapore, she would need to be prepared.

U home? I texted her.

Yep. Need to talk to u.

I rang her doorbell, opened the door a crack, and immediately kicked myself for having been so engrossed in my phone that I hadn't noticed Mary's car parked outside. I could hear her talking right away. Emma appeared, shooing me back out, and hissed, "What is going on? Becky just showed up here, running her mouth about your diary being online. She's got everyone gathered at the computer."

"Who's at the door?" hollered Mary.

"None of your business," singsonged Emma, audible only to me.

"Nobody!" she yelled back next.

"Is it true?"

"Well. Sort of. But it's *gone.* I swear. So I don't know what she's showing them."

"Maybe you should get out of here," she said. "Becky wants your head. I'll call you when they leave."

When I exited the train back in Manhattan, I called Emma right away. She didn't answer but called me back two minutes later.

"So apparently Becky's friend e-mailed her a letter or something that she claims you wrote, where you call Becky a bitch and talk about having sex with Leo in a taxi. She said it was on some blog, but Becky couldn't find it."

"Fuck. What did Mary say?"

"She was like, 'Are you sure? That doesn't sound like Cassie.' But Becky's obsessed, so she's rooting around the Internet, trying to find this blog and prove that it's real. Honestly, everyone's kind of lost interest, and now it's just her sitting at the keyboard and texting her friend nonstop."

"Okay. Listen, it's all true. All of these letters between my sister and me *were* on the Internet—but they're gone now. Jesus. Do what you can to cover for me, would you? Leo doesn't even know yet. I'm telling him tonight. But there is a ton of incriminating shit on there. I'm going to Singapore tomorrow to talk to my sister about it."

"Oh my God. Okay, Cassie. I'll see what I can do."

"I love you."

"Love you, too, Cass. Can I help with the kids while you're in Singapore?"

"It's all right. My mom's coming."

"Okay, well, keep me posted on all of this."

"I'll tell you everything when I'm back."

⸺⧼∞⧽⸺

I was packed and ready by the time Mom arrived. I hadn't slept a wink the night before. Leo finally came home again well after midnight, and though I *had* managed to tell him that I was going to Singapore, he'd immediately assumed it was to be a shoulder to cry on for Sid, which put me in an awkward position. He seemed exhausted from his day, surprised that I was leaving on such short notice, and a touch annoyed that he and my mom were going to be roommates for the next four days. Instead of just telling him then, I suggested we meet for a coffee in Union Square before my three p.m. flight the next day.

During the short taxi ride to Union Square, I wished I'd chosen a less frumpy outfit than my old leggings and hoodie and taken the time to dry my hair or put makeup on my face, which bore the marks of sleep deprivation and stress. I sighed and shook my head; this was really a conversation I should have looked my best for. I was also worried that it would seem to Leo like I was squeezing him in for a hasty or offhand apology before Sid's. To be fair, I thought Sid deserved to know first; they were her letters, after all. Plus, I needed her on my side before I faced him. Of course nothing about any of this was going as planned but there was no way to delay telling him any longer, lest Becky or Jenna get to him first.

Leo and I found each other near the Gandhi statue and kissed hello. I handed him the coffee I'd just purchased from the Mud truck.

"Where's yours?" he asked.

"I didn't think I could carry two," I said, nodding to my roller bag.

"Hang on. I'll get you one," he said, running over to the truck. I stood there, scanning the benches for a place to sit where we'd have the most privacy. When he returned with my coffee, I led him to the spot I'd identified. Afraid that I'd lose my nerve if we started chatting about something else, I got right down to business.

"Okay," I said, taking a deep breath and looking him in the eyes. But the intimacy of that was too much, and I shifted my gaze to a bird's nest built into the "A" of the Shoe Mania store across the street. I stared at that nest hard and launched into a presentation of my misdeeds.

I was careful to be factual and get everything out so I had to do this only once. I covered setting up the blog with care to make it private, the server crashing, the reason I didn't see the e-mail alerting me to the problem, and then moved on to the blog going viral, the letters that contained sister-talk about our marriage and sex life, and the kiss with Jake.

At one point, Leo got a confused look on his face and turned around to see what I was staring at, prompting me to do the adult thing and look at him in the eyes again, just as I was getting to the part about the kiss.

"And that's what I needed to talk to you about," I finished. And then I added, "And why I'm going to Singapore. I have to tell Sid."

Leo opened his mouth to speak. I don't think he said anything, but I can't be sure because my heart was beating so loudly in my ears. Then, as if to check my hearing, he let out a short burplike sound, a quick stop that emanated from his throat.

Made nervous by his silence, I spoke again. "I know. The whole situation is crazy."

It sounded glib, and I immediately regretted saying it.

Leo didn't respond, so I continued.

"I need you to know that there is *nothing* going on with Jake. I deeply regret the kiss, which was a stupid mistake that I barely even remember." And then, realizing that I hadn't yet said the most important thing, I added, "I am sorry, Leo. I am so sorry." The more I said, the shakier I felt.

He made a praying gesture with his hands and then dug his index fingers into the corners of his eyes, pressing down hard. He gave a half exhale and said into his hands, "How could you be so stupid?"

"I know. I was so drunk. It's not an excuse, but this year has been really tough for me, with so little adult contact and the schlepping around in my mom clothes all the time, and we never had sex, and then I was around all these beautiful party people and I got caught up and made a really bad call. It was a terribly immature and thoughtless thing to do. I know." It all came out in one breath, and afterward I searched his face for a signal that he maybe sort of understood a little bit.

He was still quiet but looking at me like I was deranged. I started wondering if he'd ever strayed. He's good-looking, smart, and decent—a catch by any standard. *Maybe he's got other options. Maybe's he pursued them. Maybe he's been having amazing tantric sex with one—or several—of his hard-bodied gym girls. And if not, maybe I just gave him permission to do so.* I felt off-kilter and unable to trust my thought process.

When he finally spoke, his voice was cold. "No. Not the kiss. A blog, Cassie? A blog was the best place you could think of to store your private letters? Do you even know what a blog is? I mean, what's next? You wire our life savings to a guy trying to flee Nigeria?"

I reflexively snorted, an unbeautiful sound. He wasn't smiling. I thought about reminding him that I'd used a private blog without incident at the magazine for three years, but didn't want to seem argumentative. Instead I tried to look at it from his point of view. It was bad. I was not only his frumpy, haggard, cheating wife. I was also his stupid wife. I had offended his most basic sensibilities when I deemed the Internet a safe place to store my most private thoughts.

He got up and started walking away. I sat there watching him walk, feeling small and dumb and wondering if he was just taking a cooldown lap. But when he didn't circle back around, I unfroze myself and jogged after him, leaving my coffee on the bench and pulling my cheap wheelie carry-on behind me while hoisting my bag back onto my shoulder. I touched his arm and winced when he turned around with a look on his face like a teenage boy might give an embarrassing mom.

"What can I do?" I asked him, now near tears.

He shook his head. "Just. Leave me alone," he said.

"Okay." I gulped and nodded, as if we had a plan. But as the meaning of his words sank in, it became impossible not to cry.

"I need to get back to work," he said flatly.

I held my breath and went in for a hug, circling my arms around his back and under his arms, one of which he raised to limply pat my back. Releasing him, I told myself that a limp pat was better than nothing, and turned to go.

CHAPTER TWENTY

I spent ninety dollars in the Hudson News store at the airport, buying a big bottle of water, a couple of granola bars, a pack of Dramamine, a book of essays, and magazines—*People, Us Weekly, Monocle, Harper's, New York, Newsweek, InStyle, Nylon, Vogue, Elle Decor,* and *Dwell.* I may have gone a little overboard, but I was daunted by the twenty-four-hour flight ahead of me and desperate for some distraction from the mess at hand.

At the gate I had a moment of panic when I matched my flight number to that on the board, which read ZURICH. Afraid that in my haste, I had somehow purchased the wrong flight and wasn't even going to Singapore, I approached the gate agent. "Is this right? My final destination is Singapore. Shouldn't I be headed east?" The uniformed woman with perfect makeup and an ambiguous European accent quickly sorted me out—but not without first making me feel like an unworldly dummy. As it turns out, Singapore is so far away that you can jet either way around the globe and not have it affect your flight time by much. I was literally flying halfway around the world to tell my sister the truth and to ask for her forgiveness. If this wasn't a grand gesture, I didn't know what was.

Of course, Sid was no stranger to grand gestures. In high school, Jeremy Kowalski had her initials tattooed on his calf *after* they'd broken up; she'd been the subject of at least two songs by Tet Offensive, the high school band that played all the dances; and Ryan Wilcox once had six dozen daisies delivered to her at the frozen yogurt shop where she worked in order to persuade her to go to the prom with him. The point is, a phone call wasn't going to cut it.

By the time I landed in Switzerland, I'd watched two movies and four TED Talks, taken a nap, tried and failed to write Leo a letter, but not opened a single magazine, so I lugged the stack of them with me to the next flight. I passed a line of people in kiosks on their cell phones and wondered if I should call and tell her I was coming. *What if no one is home when I arrive? Where will I go? Perhaps I should have bought a Singapore guidebook instead of all of these magazines.* Wrestling with the unwieldy pile through the Zurich airport, wearing my ratty old clothes and carrying my canvas tote bag, I felt like a frumpy schoolteacher plodding down the corridor at an elite boarding school among her more sophisticated and better-dressed students and colleagues.

On board flight number two, I distractedly leafed through the *Us Weekly* back to front. When I had nearly finished, I came upon a quarter-page piece that read:

WILL THE REAL SLOW NEWS SISTERS PLEASE STAND UP?

In the wake of the sudden popularity and equally as sudden disappearance of the popular blog *Slow News Sisters*, which recorded the letters of two sisters navigating their troubled marriages and messy lives, several would-be SN sisters are popping up to take credit. Speculation also abounds that the blog was created by the PR department at Warner Bros. Entertainment, who is rumored to have a movie of the same name under development. We choose to believe that the Slow News Sisters are real, if only they would reveal themselves.

You would think that since I'd had some time to wrap my head around the situation and I'd already seen my blog on the pages of a magazine, I might have taken it in stride. But the wound was still fresh enough that any change in the wind was a painful reminder that this thing was real. At the same time, I was perversely indignant that other people were taking credit for it. I wondered if this is how Al Qaeda feels when Hezbollah claims to be the perpetrator of one of their bombings.

I arrived in Singapore at eight o'clock in the evening. I found a currency-exchange booth and handed over ten twenty-dollar bills in exchange for nearly three hundred slick pastel-colored Singapore dollars. The long line at Customs and Immigration moved quickly, and when I handed over my card with the little box for "pleasure" checked as the reason for my visit, I hoped it would play out that way.

Soon I was in a taxi, reciting the address I knew by heart to the driver. We drove down a wide palm-tree-lined boulevard, then onto an expressway that passed through what I presumed was downtown: buildings on my right, a giant Ferris wheel on my left. Then a mile or two of identical, prominently numbered apartment buildings, followed by a long, winding jungly road. The car slowed, and I gasped when I saw the TANGLIN PARK sign, a name I'd written so many times. My heart started beating faster, and the shot of confidence I'd gained from handling the airport like a pro seemed a distant memory and a ridiculous thing to congratulate myself over: With its huge signs in multiple languages and an intuitive layout, it would have been a breeze for anyone. I thought of a framed cross-stitch on the wall at a kitschy nautical-themed coffee shop near Leo's old apartment: SMOOTH SEAS DO NOT MAKE SKILLFUL SAILORS. I began to obsess over this saying, the full weight of the metaphor sinking in. In the scheme of things, my life had been remarkably smooth. No wonder I was so ill equipped to handle this whole disaster.

My hand shook as I rang the doorbell at Sid's place, and I held my breath at the *click-clack* of a lock being turned. When the door opened, I made an awkward little jazz-hands gesture and said, "Surprise!"

My nephew, River, stared at me, looking more confused than surprised.

"Whoa! Aunt Cassie! I didn't know you were coming!" We hugged, and he grabbed my bag from behind me and brought it inside. River, eighteen now, seemed even taller and more grown-up than when I'd seen him at Christmas.

"Nobody does. It's a . . . a surprise," I repeated.

"Oh, man, I wished you would have called. Mom isn't even here. She gets back from Bali tomorrow night."

"You're kidding!" I moaned. "That'll teach me to do something so impulsive," trying to give the appearance of nonchalance, even though I was jittery with anxiety. That meant I'd have only about twenty-four hours with her.

"Well, listen, I'm starving, and it's nine a.m. my time, so how about I buy you a late dinner and we can catch up?" I said.

River agreed and showed me to the guest room. The bed was

piled with meditation books and yoga magazines. "Oh, sorry, Aunt Cassie. I can move all of Mom's stuff off for you."

"No worries," I said, invoking one of Sid's trademark phrases. It sounded strange coming from my mouth, like when I swear in front of my parents. "I'll move it later. Just give me ten minutes to freshen up and I'll be ready."

"Cool," he said.

———⚮———

River and I walked out of their condo down a quiet and winding street dense with giant trees that looked like a sprawling and exotic version of what I knew to be oaks.

"This is the back way to a cluster of restaurants in some old British military barracks from World War II," he explained.

Though the sun had been down for hours, it must have been ninety degrees or more. The heavy air was reminiscent of the F train platform in August, but instead of garbage and urine, the smells were of plants and flowers (which may sound nice but makes the heat only slightly less oppressive).

River told me to watch out for tree snakes, which are known to drop down and scare the crap out of people. While mildly venomous, they almost never bite, he explained. I let out a nervous giggle that must have triggered some hidden reserve of mirth inside of me, because I was seized by a fit of deep laughter that lasted much longer than was appropriate, given the situation. Poor River didn't know what to make of me gripping his arm for support while I doubled over, shrieking. Wiping the tears from my face, which had combined with sweat and tinted moisturizer to form a paste, I was glad I had opted not to apply mascara.

"Just be careful what you wish for," I gasped finally.

"What do you mean?" he asked, starting to laugh a bit himself.

"It's just that I was complaining to your mom a few months ago that my life was boring."

"Okay," he said, eyeing me sideways and probably forever designating me his weird aunt Cassie.

I let out a last groan and composed myself. "And, well, now I'm trekking through a snake-infested jungle in a foreign country with my little nephew, who is suddenly a grown man. It's just . . . just not boring." What I didn't mention was that this was merely the icing on the cake of my life that could now be read about in *Us Weekly*, complete with adjectives including "troubled" and "messy."

After a few minutes we arrived at a charming and busy café. I don't know what I was expecting, but it didn't seem foreign at all. Its tasteful modern furniture, blackboard menu on the wall, and fashionable and ethnically diverse diners wouldn't have been out of place in any large US city.

"Inside or outside?" the hostess asked us.

"Inside!" I offered a little too quickly, feeling slightly ill from the heat.

We were led to a small table in the middle of the black-and-white space. When the server came, we both ordered burgers and waters, plus a local beer—a Tiger—for me.

"So you like it here?" I asked River.

"Yeah. It's cool."

"I don't know about *cool*," I said, motioning to my sweaty face and upper body, the aftereffects of my recent outburst combined with my encroaching jet lag making me a bit punch-drunk.

"Yeah. It took me about six months to stop sweating profusely every time I left the house. It's funny—the expats here are always coming and going, and you can tell a newcomer by how pink and sweaty they are."

By the time our food arrived, I had changed the subject to Sid.

"So I can't wait to see your mom. How is she doing?"

"She's good. Superbusy with all the stuff she does for the helpers—and she's gotten really into yoga." And then his voice changed a bit. "So, um, look, this is kind of awkward, Aunt Cassie, but there's something I feel like I should tell you."

"Okay," I said, tensing up.

"I saw the blog." Likely prompted by my deer-in-headlights expression, he added, "With all the letters."

"Oh," I said. I consciously shifted my demeanor. No longer the loopy and expressive aunt of five minutes ago, I needed to be serious, contrite. I put down my burger, wiped my hands and mouth, and took a sip of my beer, the familiar roar of panic surging through my body.

"Yeah," he said, wincing at me as if to indicate that we were going to have to talk about it.

I took a deep breath. "That's why I'm here. I took the blog down—in fact, it was never meant to be live in the first place."

He looked at me like I was nuts. "Then why did you do it?"

"I know it's hard to believe, but I'm not as smart as I look," I said, attempting a joke. I felt like a child being questioned by my father, which was disconcerting, considering I'd changed this kid's diaper. I was dying to turn the tables and grill him on how much exactly he'd read, how he'd found out about it, and what Sid knew. But he had the upper hand. So I went with it, offering my pathetic explanation, which I hoped would sound better by the time I gave it to Sid.

"It was meant to be private—I made it private, as a way to save them for posterity, but Fishfood's server crashed and I didn't realize it became public, and by the time I found out, it had blown up."

"Oh, man. That's crazy," he said.

"Yep. I still can't believe it. So has she seen it?"

"No. I was going to show her, actually. But when I went to bring it back up, it was gone. So I didn't bother—I figured it would be too hard to explain. You know Mom—she's old-school. She barely even e-mails."

"She is an original," I said, glad that the subject seemed to be changing but at the same time anxious to get a bit more information from him.

"Yeah—it's annoying sometimes when things I'm talking about go right over her head. But it's also cool in some ways. I mean, some of my friends' parents are their Facebook friends and friending all of their friends, and it can get kind of awkward."

"Hey, I'm your Facebook friend! You know you can unfriend me if you don't want your lame old aunt knowing all your business."

"Nah—that's all right. I think Mom feels better knowing you're there. She probably figures you'll tell her if I do anything totally stupid, like post a bunch of private letters on the Internet for the world to see."

I groaned and buried my head in my hands for a moment, and when I looked up, River and I made smiling eye contact. He was a cool kid: kind and charismatic like his mother, and tall and bright-eyed like his father. I wonder if he turned out how he was going to turn out, or if Sid's parenting was the secret. Sometimes when I read about boys from seemingly nice families who become date rapists or merciless bullies, I become terrified that I will somehow neglect to teach the boys basic human decency, or even if I do, they still won't turn out okay. That they shared DNA with River was a comforting thought.

———⊰⊱———

I had an awful night's sleep, tossing and turning and checking my phone incessantly for any response from Leo, to whom I'd sent at least five messages through various channels. Around four a.m., I switched on the light and penned a desperate letter to Leo. One of those letters you think you'll probably never send, but need to write anyway. It helped to settle my mind, and sleep eventually came sometime after I'd folded up the letter and stuck it inside my passport. When I emerged from the guest room late in the morning, River called to me from the living room.

"Aunt Cassie! Come check it out!" He waved me over, and I walked out to join him on the patio, grinning because Joey says, "Come check it out!" in almost the exact same way. He pointed to the balcony one floor up and across the way, where three black-and-white birds the size of house cats were perched. They looked like toucans but seemed to have two beaks—a shorter one that sloped up atop a longer one that sloped down.

"Those are hornbills. Ten years ago they were declared extinct, but they made a comeback somehow. And a group of them nests right around here—cool, right?"

"Yeah. Cool. Wow," I said as the trio clumsily took flight.

Sid's place was on the ground floor of one of a dozen identical six-story white stucco buildings centered around a courtyard with a playground, a swimming pool, and a meandering stream filled with giant goldfish. The whole place was overgrown with big green plants and a variety of trees.

"I talked to Mom," River said.

"Oh! When?" I asked, my heart pounding.

"She called earlier this morning. I told her you were here, and she freaked. She's trying to get on an earlier flight."

Then Lulu toddled up the stairs from the courtyard to the patio, a short, plump, brown-skinned woman with shiny jet-black hair a half step behind her, ready to pounce should Lulu stumble.

I squatted down to greet my niece, who wasn't sure she remembered me, and I mentally ticked another X in the "cons" column of our little communication experiment. Had we been Skyping all this time, Lulu would have at least recognized me.

"Good morning, ma'am!" said the woman following Lulu.

"Hi. You must be Rose. I'm Sid's sister, Cassie."

"Yes, ma'am. I can get you something to eat and drink, ma'am?"

All this *ma'am*ing was making me a bit uncomfortable, but I was enjoying listening to her accent. Leo and I'd had it all wrong when we imitated it all those months ago.

Three hours later, I had showered, eaten a lunch of cold carrot soup and fried rice prepared by Rose, discussed River's deferred acceptance to NYU, read *Dear Zoo* to Lulu seven or eight times, fed the fish, and pushed Lulu on the swing before Rose took her off for her nap. River left to go to a friend's house and Rose got busy sweeping the floors. I didn't know when exactly Sid was coming, but I sensed it was soon. Growing nervous again, I picked up a *Yoga Life* magazine and sat on her couch, hoping to glean a few relaxation techniques.

I saw her before she saw me. She looked radiant, like a tanned and thin backpacker yoga girl. Her long hair was in a single dark-honey-colored braid that ended between her shoulder blades. She wore tiny gold hoops in her ears, a white tank top, and a floor-length lightweight olive-colored skirt. I stood there beholding my beautiful sister, hardly believing I was related to this exquisite creature. She slid open the glass patio door, let out a scream, dropped her bags, and put both hands on her heart. I felt a catch in my throat and couldn't speak. I raised my hands, palms in, and waved them toward me, making a "come here" gesture while I walked to her. Sid has always been a full-body-contact, holds-on-a-few-seconds-too-long kind of hugger. I'm more of a quick sideways hugger, but I always made an exception for her.

"You're here," she said, drawing out the word "here."

I nodded hard into her shoulder, fighting back tears.

"Cass," she said, pushing me away by the shoulders to look at me head-on and then pulling me back into an embrace. "My beautiful sister." (I never liked it when she said things about my being beautiful because I felt that it brought into ironic focus the fact that I was clearly the less attractive one, but in that moment I didn't even think about it.)

Lulu shuffled in, bleary-eyed from her nap, and she and Sid went bonkers for each other. We all played and chatted and had lemongrass iced tea and fresh tropical fruit, which Rose brought out to the patio. When Sid helped Lulu out of her chair and set her up to play at her sand table, I took a deep breath.

"Sid, I have to talk to you about something," I said.

"Wait a sec," she said. She was craning her neck to look inside. I turned in my chair and saw that Rose was talking to a uniformed man at their door. She turned and walked toward us, and Sid got up and went inside. I followed her.

"Ma'am," said Rose. "This man, they are coming here, he ask to see you, ma'am."

"Thanks, Rose. Could you keep an eye on Lu for a minute?" And then to the man, "Hello there."

"Hello. You are Sidney Sunday?"

"Yes. Is everything okay?"

"May I come in, Ms. Sunday?"

"Who are you?" she asked politely, as if she simply needed a reminder.

"I am Mr. Goh, Ministry of Manpower." He flashed a badge.

Sid glanced back at me with a frown and invited him in. I hovered around the edge of the room while she sat at the dining table with him.

"Ms. Sunday, I regret to inform you that your dependent pass is being revoked."

He spoke in a rapid monotone; when he did occasionally stress a syllable, it was the opposite one that I would have stressed, so it took me a few extra seconds to understand what he was saying.

"Excuse me?" Sid said.

"It has come to our attention that you have been operating an unlicensed bank and interfering with the lives of some foreign domestic workers."

"Oh," she said, a bit lower.

"Ms. Sunday, we have chosen not to turn this matter over to the police, but I must insist that you relinquish your dependent pass and leave Singapore. You have until Monday."

"What about . . . ?"

"Your husband has been informed. We just came from his office. Your son, River, is eighteen, so he is free to stay. Your daughter can stay with your husband."

"She stays with me," she said quietly.

As if on cue, Adrian walked in the door, looking frantic. He sat next to Sid at the table and nodded hello to Mr. Goh. Sid got up, went into the other room, and came back to hand two identification cards over. Mr. Goh had some papers for Sid to sign, and she and Adrian murmured to each other over the paperwork.

Once Mr. Goh left, Adrian said, "We'll talk about this tonight, okay? I have to get back to a meeting." I don't think he even saw me standing there.

Meanwhile, I had a bad feeling. I wanted to get home, and I wanted

Sid to come with me. Adrian was on his way out the door, and I stepped onto the patio to call Singapore Airlines. For several hundred dollars I could change my flight to one leaving early the next morning; there were additional seats available.

"Hold on a minute," I said to the operator.

Sid was still standing at the door, now leaning back against it.

"Sid, I know this is sudden and you must be in shock, but what if we left together tomorrow? There's a six a.m. flight with space for us. I'll help you pack."

"Oh my God, Cassie," she said, clearly reeling.

"Hon, I know. Crazy. What do you say? The airline is on the phone."

"Uuuum. All right." She looked stunned but went to get passports and her credit card and handed them to me. I spent the next ten minutes booking flights for the four of us while she went into her room alone.

When I finished with the tickets, I knocked on her door. She said to come in, and when I did, I found her sitting on her bed, looking unperturbed under the circumstances.

"So it's done?" she asked.

"Yep. Just tell me what to do to help now."

"Let me call River first," she said.

Sid convinced River to come with us by promising to buy him a return ticket so he could come back and say goodbye to his friends. She then gave me some tasks and had a talk with Rose.

We didn't speak much for the rest of the day. There was too much to do in a short amount of time. At one point, Sid sat on the couch with a pen and some stationery I recognized. I didn't ask about it, but felt a guilt-tinged pang of jealousy, wondering if she was exchanging letters with anyone else. When she finished writing, she snapped a photo of the letter with her phone, folded it, and placed it in an envelope. *Has she been saving copies of all of the letters, too? Maybe she will understand what I did.* She stood up and noticed me watching her.

"Well, that was easier than I thought it'd be," she said.

"What?" I said.

"My Dear John letter to Adrian."

"How come you took a picture of it?"

"I don't know. Just seemed important."

A teary-eyed and red-faced Filipina was knocking at the patio door. When Sid waved at her, she tentatively opened the door and poked her head in. "Ma'am Sid?" she said.

"Hi, Sharon," Sid said. "Come in."

"Is it true, ma'am?" a shaky-voiced Sharon asked. "You are going to jail?"

"No! I'm just leaving Singapore. But I'm leaving early tomorrow. I'm sorry I'm not going to be able to say goodbye to everyone. Please give all of the girls big hugs for me, okay?" Sid's voice was quavering now, too, and she had tears in her eyes as she hugged the woman.

"Here, ma'am," Sharon said, thrusting an envelope into Sid's hands.

"What's this?"

"We took up a collection."

I heard change jingling in the envelope.

"That was fast," said Sid, now laughing a bit. "But, please, Sharon, I'm okay. I promise. I'm going back to America with my sister," she said, returning the envelope to Sharon.

No one ever had an easy time saying goodbye to Sid, and over the next hour a line of brown-skinned women appeared at the back door. I remembered an article I read on the *Huffington Post* I'd been meaning to write to Sid about. It said that Singaporeans were ranked to be the least emotional people in the world and Filipinos the most. Judging by the stone-faced Mr. Goh compared to the procession of women forming on the back patio, many of whom were sobbing, I didn't doubt it.

We packed all day, and Sid spent a lot of time on the phone and receiving visitors. She put Lulu to bed and Rose served us dinner, a chicken stir-fry. I was (again) preparing to tell her the news when Adrian came home.

Sid seemed surprised to see him.

"I thought you were flying to Jakarta," she said.

"I canceled my trip, obviously," he said. Then, "Cassie, hi. Nice to see you."

I gave him a flat, "Hey, Adrian," and then, because I didn't feel it was my place to inject any more drama, I got up and gave him a cursory hug. But he was dead to me already.

"I didn't know you were coming," he said.

Sid didn't say anything about my visit being a surprise to her, too, so I said, "Yeah," not wanting to waste any explanations on him and also enjoying the vague suggestion that maybe Sid had some secrets of her own. In the awkward silence that followed, I suddenly felt like a third wheel. Adrian clearly wanted to be alone with Sid. I excused myself to go take a shower and pack my bag.

An hour or so later, I came out into the living room, hoping to have that talk with Sid, but she and Adrian were deep in conversation on the back patio. I returned to my room, set my phone alarm for a three thirty a.m. wake-up, and logged into my Yahoo account. I responded to the dozen or so e-mails regarding the blog, politely declining to participate in anything that might prolong this train wreck. Although the thought of that "lucrative" book deal was still exciting, anytime I gave it more than twenty seconds of thought, I came to the same con-clusion: no fucking way. I also repeatedly checked the various mediums through which I'd reached out to Leo: no response or sign that he'd attempted to contact me via WhatsApp, Viber, iChat, Skype, or e-mail.

As I stared at my phone, the fog of dumbfoundedness, panic, and dread I'd been living in since that day in the waiting room began to lift, and I started to feel something even worse: anger. I was angry about the blog. It should have stayed private. It *would* have stayed private if not for that freak server crash. I did everything right. (Well, unless you count not checking my Yahoo account for two weeks.) Leo, of all people, should understand this. I was so frustrated that he saw me as foolish for trusting the blog's settings when I didn't see it as foolish at all. Just *not* paranoid.

I finally shut down my laptop and set my phone aside sometime around midnight. I hadn't heard any movement and wondered if Sid and Adrian were still talking. I worried that Adrian had talked Sid into staying together and hoped he wasn't hogging all of her forgive-ness. Did she have a finite amount? If so, I felt I should have first dibs. I also had a sense that things couldn't work out for *both* our mar-riages, and I wanted first dibs on that, too. I'm the worst, I know. But in my mind, Adrian was somehow the real bad guy, while I was just a stupid person who made a big mistake. Does every bad guy think this? I wondered. Am I any better than Adrian? I drifted off to sleep feeling like the smallest version of myself I'd ever been.

We'd been on the plane for four or five hours by the time Lulu and River were both asleep. Before Sid also decided to nap, I shifted in my seat and gave her arm a gentle squeeze.

"Hey, did everything go all right with Adrian last night?"

She let out a sigh and said, "I guess that depends on your definition of 'all right.'"

I laughed nervously. "Well, my bar is pretty low these days."

"We sketched out a plan for him to see Lulu every month, and I promised to come to Singapore later this year."

"So you're definitely splitting up?"

"Yep."

I squeezed her arm again, and we both sat in silence for a moment. Remembering how I'd felt the night before, I was ashamed. I just wanted to take all of her pain away. I wished I could go back in time and make Adrian a better husband and me a better—or at least a wiser—human being.

With that familiar feeling of dread, I launched into the speech I'd been preparing in my head since I sat down in seat 14C. "Sid, listen, there is something else we need to talk about."

Startled, she replied, "Oh my gosh. That's right." She rotated her body to face me. "Sorry, Cass. This is all so surreal. I've completely lost track of things. It seems like a million years ago River told me you were there at my house. Why did you come all this way? Are you okay?" Her eyes were searching mine.

"Yeah. But you know the letters?"

Sid started laughing. "Um, yes, I know the letters, Cassie."

I heard someone take a sharp inhale and then a head popped up over the seats in front of us. "Ohmigod, I'm sorry, but I have to ask. Are you the Slow News Sisters?"

An American woman—in her late twenties, if I'd had to guess—was studying our faces. She had kinky dark brown hair and a voice like a Valley girl with a sinus infection. I immediately felt a physical disdain toward her.

"What? The what? No," I spat, furious that this idiot was about to ruin everything.

"Oh, sorry. I just heard the names Sid and Cassie and you mentioned letters, and I had to ask. I'm obsessed with them. *Obsessed*," she said, her eyes bugging out. "You know what I'm talking about, right?"

"Uh-uh," I said, shaking my head "no" while shooting death rays with my eyes.

"But wait—this is so crazy! You have the same names as they do. You did say Cassie and Sid, right? And you're sisters, right? You've got to be. You look so much alike." I could see her wheels turning.

"Okay, thanks. We'll have to check that out," I said with finality, reaching for the in-flight magazine.

"Just Google 'Slow News Sisters.' The blog is down right now because one of the sisters is suing the other one, but hopefully it will be back up soon. Wait. Tell me the truth. Are you them?"

I wanted to roll up that magazine and thwack her like a fly. "Please. I don't mean to be rude, but could you leave us alone? This is starting to get weird," I said.

She gave me a mean look and popped back down without another word.

Sid looked at me, bewildered. *What the fuck?* she mouthed.

Even under the harsh little spotlight that shone from above her seat, Sid looked beautiful, and I'm not embarrassed to admit that I took a moment to revel in the fact that the horrible woman said that we looked alike. But I had to get down to business. I was determined to come clean to Sid before we got back to New York, even if I had to pull her into the bathroom to do it. Then I had a better idea. I fished my notebook and pen out of my bag and wrote, *I'm sorry,* then nudged her elbow and pointed to the notebook.

Sid looked at me quizzically, awaiting my next move.

I got the *Us Weekly* out of my bag and showed it to her.

She stared at it for several minutes, expressionless.

She looked at me and pointed to the magazine and then gestured to the two of us, a confused look on her face.

I nodded.

She pointed to the seat in front of us.

I nodded again.

She held the magazine close to her face and reread the paragraph and then laughed a deep and strangely Santa-esque "Ho-ho-ho-ho-ho," as if blending "No" with laughter and shaking her head. Not smiling, but really not frowning, either.

Shooting a dramatic look toward the seat in front of us, I thrust the pen at her.

No words . . . she wrote.

I grabbed the pen back and wrote, *I wanted to save the letters forever, so I scanned them and then started a* private, protected *blog that no one was supposed to ever see, but a freak computer glitch made it go viral for a few weeks. It's* private *again now.*

Before I passed the pen back to Sid, I made a frowny face, but she made no move to take it. She closed her eyes and rested her head on her chair. My heart pounded as I waited for a sign.

She grabbed the pen and wrote, *All of our letters?*

Yes.

On the Internet?

Yes. But not anymore.

She looked out the window for a long time. I watched her, but she didn't look back. After a few minutes, I nudged her and gave her my most pathetic "sorry" face. Sid took off her seat belt, stood up, and looked down at the woman in front of us. Satisfied that she was engrossed in her movie, she whispered to me, "I don't know what you want me to say."

Ouch. Those felt like angry words, although her tone was gentle. "I just want you to know how sorry I am for violating your privacy. I didn't mean to." I could feel tears threatening, and Sid laid her hand on my arm and sighed.

"It's not the end of the world, Cass. It's not like I'm never going to talk to you again. It's just a lot to take in."

Lulu woke up and needed a diaper change, so Sid took her to the bathroom and then spent the next forty minutes or so following her as she toddled up and down the aisle. I just sat there, feeling helpless. The small amount of relief that came from having told Sid was countered by the frustrating inability to talk it through and the discomfort of being physically trapped on this plane with a few hundred strangers.

We managed to squeeze in a few more mini conversations over the rest of the trip, but we weren't really talking. I couldn't even tell if Sid wanted to.

CHAPTER TWENTY-ONE

Reaching JFK after the decency of the Singapore airport was about the worst thing that could happen after twenty-four hours of flying with a heavy cloud of unfinished business hanging between Sid and me.

Tired, grimy, and restless, we were funneled into an airless and low corridor with no signs. A uniformed man with a thick New York accent appeared and started yelling, "US citizens on the left; foreign passport holders on the right." But his arms were waving to our left when he said right and our right when he said left, and everyone was packed in so tightly that trying to rearrange ourselves while jockeying for position with roller bags and strollers and oversized backpacks that never should have been allowed in the overhead bins to begin with was an exercise in futility.

Poor Lulu could almost taste her freedom and was head butting my thigh and whining and falling down and doing whatever she could to exorcise the demons of being on an airplane for an impossibly long time. Sid rubbed River's arm as we stood there, but he looked straight ahead, ignoring her. He was probably still mad that she'd made him leave Singapore so abruptly. Finally, the line started moving, and all I could think was what a cold welcome to our country this was. I wanted to apologize to the tourists and tell them that it wasn't going to be like this everywhere, maybe slip them some restaurant recommendations to make up for this degrading scene.

We arrived home at noon and received a much warmer welcome from Mom and the boys. Homemade signs festooned the slightly ajar front door, and the sounds of home drifted into the hallway: "Yet's 'ten I am Batman and you are a bad guy . . ."

I had never really been away from the boys before, and hearing those sweet voices brought tears to my eyes. I hugged them tightly, inhaling their delicious scents, and listened with all my being to their stories about the adventures they'd had with Grandma.

Mom had bagels and coffee and juice waiting for us, and we all sat around on the floor and ate and talked. Sid and I barely made eye contact, but we were too busy with the kids for it to be awkward. Plus, Mom was grilling Sid about her banishment from Singapore. After we ate, we all walked over to the small playground on Leroy Street.

If you ask me, Leroy Street in the fall is the most magical place in the city. The trees have all turned the same spectacular yellow, and with half of the leaves on the ground and half still on the trees, walking down Leroy—especially in late afternoon, when the sun is low—is like passing through a golden tunnel. I recalled Sid's letter about missing the seasons changing, and silently thanked Mother Nature for making my sister's homecoming so special.

Mom and River chased after the boys and Lulu. Sid linked her arm through mine, and a swell of relief rushed over me.

"Cass. It's so beautiful," she said.

"Isn't it?"

We walked, arms linked, for a few sidewalk squares, enveloped in the shimmering canopy. I felt proud of my city and relieved that it had redeemed itself after that horrid airport experience.

"I am so sorry," I said.

"You know, I don't think I'm mad at you. I'm not really sure how I feel."

"I was in shock for a while, too."

"You took the blog down, right?"

"Right."

"So we're, like, famous?"

"I don't know. I guess we were for a few days or weeks, but I think our fifteen minutes is coming to an end."

"But nobody knows what we look like, right?" Sid said.

"Right. Well, except that lady on the plane, I guess."

Sid let out a little chuckle. "Right," she said. We walked arm in arm, slowly, taking in the trees and the colors and our happy children running and playing. I wished that moment could last forever. I was accepted, forgiven, loved. Already my trip had been worthwhile.

Lulu fell fast asleep while Sid pushed her on the swing at the park, so I walked them back home while Mom and River and the boys strolled over to look at the boats on the river.

Once I cleared the dinosaurs off of Quinn's bed and closed the room-darkening curtains, Sid laid Lulu down and whispered to me, "What did Leo say?"

"Not much," I whispered back, feeling a catch in my throat.

We made it back out to the living room, and she peered into my eyes. "Cass? Are you okay?"

"I don't know," I said, and started to cry.

I had been pretty successful at pushing my anxiety about Leo to the back of my mind since boarding the plane in Singapore, but now, with my mission to come clean to Sid accomplished, the release of her forgiveness only reminded me that Leo's reaction had been far less placid.

"He's not speaking to me, but I don't even know what I'd say to him if he were."

By this point I was blubbering. "I mean, if you were him, what would you be most mad about? That I kissed Jake? That I aired our dirty laundry on the Internet? That I *trusted* the Internet?"

"Oh, Cass." She pulled me into an embrace and then walked me to the couch, guiding my head onto her shoulder. I felt so stupid. In the past thirty-six hours, she'd been thrown out of a country, left her cheating husband, said goodbye to a dozen friends she might never see again, had her trust betrayed by her sister, survived twenty-four hours on an airplane with a toddler, withstood a tiresome line of questioning from Mom and suggestions that she go to the embassy or the police to report her unfair treatment in Singapore, and not cracked once. Yet here I was, literally crying on *her* shoulder. I got up and grabbed a roll of toilet paper from the bathroom, sitting back down on the couch to dry my eyes and blow my nose, stuffing the damp little wads into the cardboard hole in the middle.

Sid tried to comfort me, but when I revealed that I'd told him everything only about twenty minutes before I'd left for the airport, squeezing him in like an afterthought, even she had to admit that it didn't look good for a loving reunion with him that day. "But he'll come around. Don't you think?" she asked.

We had to wait only a few hours to find out. We were all there, discussing whether to order Chinese food or walk up to have Mexican on Fourteenth Street, when Leo came home from work. He gave Sid and the kids all big hugs, but not me. My heart pounded in my ears and I self-consciously wondered who else had noticed the snub.

To keep the tears at bay, I busied myself with minutiae—wiping the countertop, separating the mail, putting shoes away—while he chatted with Sid and River. He was keenly interested in Sid's dramatic expulsion from Singapore (which meant he'd at least *read* the messages I'd sent).

When River asked him to weigh in on the Mexican-versus-Chinese-food debate, Leo said he wouldn't be joining us for dinner, that he was going to stay at his brother's place in Jersey for a few days. He worked the practical angle, but I knew what was really going on. Until then I hadn't really allowed myself to seriously imagine him leaving me, but hearing those words made my mouth go dry.

Mom spoke up first. "Oh, Leo. No, no, no, no. We think alike! I moved my flight to this evening. So you can stay!"

She put her hand on his shoulder and looked at me. "This poor guy has been sleeping on the couch. I'm sure he's ready to have his bed back."

"No—it's fine. I've already talked to Stevie." He nodded to Sid and me. "I'll let these guys have the run of the place. You know how they are together. I'd only be in the way."

"Oh, Leo. You really don't need to. We could get a hotel," said Sid.

"Don't be crazy," Leo said, giving Sid a sideways squeeze.

"Well, we'll be renting a car and driving back to Ohio in the next few days, so you'll have your home back soon."

I decided I should probably speak. "Are you sure, hon?" I said, wondering if anyone noticed that my voice was shaking.

Without looking at me, Leo crouched down and talked to Joey and Quinn.

"I get to have a sleepover tonight with my big brother Stevie while you guys have a sleepover with your cousins. How cool is that?"

"Cool!" Joey agreed.

"Mmmm. But, Daddy. That means you won't be here, at your home," Quinn said.

This was more than I could take. I made a beeline to the bathroom and splashed some water on my face while trying to stop imagining more conversations about Mommy and Daddy sleeping apart. I looked like I had aged ten years. A red and itchy spot—possibly a hive—had appeared on my cheek, and I rifled through my Kiehl's samples for something with "soothing" on the label. I could overhear River helping with the boys, asking if he could sleep in their room and talking about how much fun they'd have. God, he was a great kid. He probably knew why Leo was leaving; he'd read the letters, after all. I felt bad for him and mad at myself, because I knew he adored Leo and had surely been hoping to spend time with him. *Is he thinking that I should be the one leaving?* The thought added to my anxiety, and I had to sit down on the toilet and take a few deep breaths.

When I came out of the bathroom, Leo was nowhere to be seen. I made my way through the crowd in my living room and found him in the bedroom getting his things together. I wanted to break down and beg and sob when I saw the size of the bag he'd packed. Instead, I silently handed him the letter I'd written that first night in Singapore.

But after he left I found the envelope, unopened, on the bed.

———— ❧⟨∞⟩❧ ————

By eight thirty that evening, Mom was safely on her way to the airport and River had fallen asleep in Quinn's bed while reading him a dinosaur book. Sid and I took photos of them with our phones; they looked so cute and comfortable that we decided to leave River there. (Also because his other option was the living room couch.) Lulu had slept all afternoon, so she was awake but looking at books and babbling contentedly to herself—something I've never seen either of my sons do. Is independent, quiet play something I could teach them, or was it too late? I sighed and mentally added it to my list of failures. Even though I was exhausted, going to bed didn't appeal. Plus, I wanted to be around in case Sid felt like talking. She was organizing her luggage, which was piled high in the entryway, moving clothes around so she, Lulu, and River all had things in a single bag, saving them from the game of Jenga required each time they needed something from their luggage. I fixed us each a vodka and orange juice, concluding that it was the perfect drink when your body didn't know whether it was morning or evening. She leaned back and looked in at the *clink-clink* of ice cubes in the glasses.

"Nightcap?" I said.

"No, thanks. Do you have any tea?"

"Only peppermint."

"My favorite kind."

I turned the kettle on, feeling disappointed that she wasn't joining me for a drink.

When her tea was ready, I set it on the square edge of my couch on top of a book.

"How are *you*?" I said, leaning in the doorway and hovering over her.

She looked over her shoulder at me. "I was just going to ask you the same thing. But thanks. I'm okay."

"Are *we* okay?"

"Always," she said.

"You're sure you aren't mad? I think I'd be a little mad." I was trying to comprehend the gulf between hers and Leo's reactions. True, Leo had the kicker of minor adultery to contend with, but those were her letters, her private thoughts, and I'd shown them to the world.

"You're all I've got right now. I can't afford to be mad at you."

"That's not true," I said.

She shrugged and turned back to her suitcase, withdrawing a small pile of clothes before zipping the case back up and hoisting it back to the top of the pile. Then she got Lulu a sippy cup of milk and plopped on the sofa. "Do you want to talk about Leo, or do you need to sleep?" she asked.

I sat on the opposite end of the couch, turning my whole body to face her.

"No. I don't want to sleep yet. I just can't believe he's gone."

"Oh, Cass. He's just gone because we're here. He's not *gone-gone*."

"I mean, maybe that's part of it, but he's pissed. He's never left just because my family is here. He loves packing this place with people, and he loves you guys. He'd sleep on the floor—he doesn't care."

"Well, he's allowed to be mad. Give him a little time. You're just going to have to wait and see what he decides to do," she said.

"That seems a little passive," I said.

It occurred to me then that Sid had probably always been too passive. All her life, she's been presented with an endless stream of opportunities: People are constantly wanting to take her places or introduce her to people. As a side effect, she was never selective enough with her boyfriends. Being the kind of person who sees the good in everyone combined with a weakness for romantic gestures meant that she usually ended up with the guy who made the strongest play. Had she ever fought for anyone? Would she even know how? She'd always been larger than life, mythical and perfect to me, even as an adult. I'd chalked up her romantic hardships to bad luck. But could it be that I was better at relationships? This revelation—while immature and competitive—steeled my resolve to save my marriage. Not the noblest of motivators, perhaps, but I would take all the help I could get.

Lulu came over and handed Sid a book. We rearranged ourselves on the couch to make room for Lu, who sat on my lap as Sid read *Brown Bear, Brown Bear, What Do You See?* When she finished the book, Sid said, "All right, let's get you ready for bed."

"No bed!" came Lulu's reply. To her credit, it was about ten in the morning in Singapore and she had napped until dinnertime. I didn't see her going to sleep anytime soon, although Sid looked exhausted.

"Maybe a bath first." Sid scooped her up and carried her off to the bathroom.

Now all alone and midway through my second screwdriver, I was feeling helpless and frustrated about the Leo situation, but also buzzy from the globe-trotting and booze and sisterly forgiveness.

I texted Leo, *Make it to Stevie's?*

Instead of staring at my phone, hoping for a response, I opened the rejected letter. There was no sign that he'd read it, so I sat at my tiny hallway desk right outside of the bathroom listening to Sid and Lulu sing "I'm a Little Teapot," and scanned it in. If he didn't respond to my text or become open to contact by tomorrow, I'd e-mail it to him.

I did a "Slow News Sisters" search and skimmed the articles and message boards. Nothing much new, but still a disconcerting amount of chatter and speculation.

Sid and Lulu came out of the bathroom, and I quickly switched to the *New York Times*, so Sid wouldn't see what I was looking at. I kissed them both good night and stayed at the computer, skimming the headlines. In an effort to gain a modicum of perspective, I forced myself to read an article about sex trafficking and one about a couple of fire-fighters in Minnesota who died on their very first call. It was heart-rending. They were kids—twenty-two and twenty-three years old. One of them was engaged to be married and the other had recently lost his father to cancer. I pushed all of my selfish interests out of my head for a minute and tried to imagine what their families must be feeling.

The buzz from my phone made me stop breathing for a second as my mind lurched back into my own particular mess. The phone was on the kitchen counter, only about four steps away, but as I strode across the room, I processed a dozen or so thoughts, from best to worst possible responses, while also telling myself to just calm down because it might not even be from him.

It was from Leo. *Y* (for "yes") was all it said. So he had made it to Stevie's. Accepting the one-letter response as progress, I drained my screwdriver and went to sleep on the couch.

⸺⋆⟨∞⟩⋆⸺

Leo texted me again the next morning to say he'd stop by to visit the boys after work and before going to Stevie's, a routine he kept up for the next few days. He would come in and wrestle with the boys and play dinosaurs while I tried to interact at an appropriate level for someone being punished. After a while, he'd take them and River for pie at the Hudson and then bring them home, keeping his interactions with me purely perfunctory. In fact, he barely looked at me when he came and went. I'd been telling myself his absence was due to our overfull house, but I knew in my heart that was merely an excuse for him to avoid me. I had twice convinced Sid to stay a few days longer, fearing the hard truth I'd have to face if her exit didn't immediately lead to his homecoming.

Before long, the cold shoulder started to wear on me, and I half seriously thought about having Sid pass him a note with "Yes" and "No" check boxes, junior-high style. *Are you open to reconciliation? Will you come home? Are we getting divorced? Do you still love me?*

One morning three days into Leo's absence, Sid and I leaned against the windowsill in the children's room of the Hudson Park Library while Lulu and the twins played with the little slide, rocking horse, and assorted cast-off toys donated by neighbors.

"Mom keeps sending me listings for houses in their neighborhood," she said.

"So you're really going back to Ohio?"

"Well, yeah. Where else am I going to go?"

"Stay here!" I couldn't believe that anyone who'd spent time in New York wouldn't do everything they could to stay.

"Cass, oh my gosh, we have way overstayed our welcome. Your poor little apartment is bursting at the seams."

"You have not. I love having you here. I mean, don't get me wrong—an extra bedroom or two would make it a whole lot easier, but you can stay as long as you want."

"Thanks, hon. That's sweet. But we need to get going—and pretty soon. I'm looking forward to getting back. I've missed working."

"Couldn't you work here? Midwives and home births are all the rage—you'd probably be delivering celebrity babies over on Charles Street in no time."

"I'm just not a city girl, Cass. I move at a totally different pace than you do."

"I guess."

"Plus, if we leave, then Leo can come back."

"But what if he doesn't?"

"Oh, honey," she said, squeezing my arm. "This is hard. I know."

My phone buzzed. It was a rare message from Leo. He had some free time in an hour and wanted to see the boys. Could we meet him at Bleecker Playground?

Sure, I responded, resigned to my role as social secretary.

We went to the park a bit early so the kids could eat their snack—rice cakes and grapes—before Leo arrived. I wanted the boys to be at their best each time they saw Leo that week, so I always made sure their hands were clean, their noses were wiped, and they weren't hungry—hoping that their adorableness would outshine my failings and lure him home.

When he arrived, the boys both wanted to swing, so Leo and I stood beside each other pushing in silence. After an awkward minute, I told him about the plan Sid and I had set in motion the day before. "Hey, we were thinking about getting out of the city this weekend."

"Cool," he said.

"Yeah, the walls are kind of closing in on us at home. Sid's luggage alone is taking up half of the living room. She's headed back to Ohio next week, so we thought it would be a fun thing to do before she goes."

"Sounds good. You guys should go," he answered.

"Well, I was thinking we could *all* go."

"I'll think about it."

He was being so aloof, and while part of me understood that he needed time to process or heal or think or whatever, most of me wanted to burst into tears and hash it all out right then and there. Instead, we continued pushing in silence until it was time for him to get back to work. He said his goodbyes—extra warm for the boys, cool for me—and headed off.

That night after the kids were in bed, Sid and I ate a late pasta dinner and drank a bottle of red wine. Just as we sat down, my phone buzzed with good news from Jill, the broker I'd been e-mailing with for months about homes in Westchester County. I told her I needed a better feel for the area, and asked if she knew of anyone who would rent us their house for the weekend.

While we ate, Sid asked me about seeing Leo earlier, and in retelling it, my impatience and frustration with his inaccessibility grew stronger.

"What about that letter? Did you ever e-mail it to him?"

"No. I was sort of waiting for a glimmer of hope."

Lulu woke up crying then, and Sid went into the bedroom to comfort her. I sat and finished my wine, thinking about the letter. I needed to get it to him, I'd decided, but the energy between us was so stiff and formal that it became a nerve-racking decision, almost like confessing to a work colleague that you were in love with him.

I opened another bottle of wine and poured myself a glass, wishing Sid would reappear to cheer me on. As I sipped and waited, I began to feel less vulnerable and more agitated.

I took the bottle to the hallway desk and found the scanned letter I'd saved on my laptop. *Be bold*, I coached myself. And then, perhaps going a little too bold, I did something I'd thought about once or twice but quickly dismissed as too risky, too foolish: I uploaded the letter to the blog, made it public again, and sent Leo an urgent e-mail with the link. To be safe, I sent him a text that said, Check your e-mail. Thx.

I got up from the desk, feeling a bit shaky, and stood in the middle of the living room and finished my wine.

Dear Leo,

I'm sorry about so many things.

First, I deeply regret betraying you. Please know that kissing Jake wasn't about him or me having feelings for him. It was about me being a ridiculous, needy mess. And—while I arguably still am—I know that with you by my side, I'll come out of it.

I can see now that I've been in a downward spiral since I lost my job, and to a lesser extent since I had the boys. Being a mom to these two wild, amazing, beautiful creatures is hard work—and when I started doing it full-time, I was surprised (and embarrassed, to be honest) at just how unsuited I felt for the job.

I wasted so much time and energy being aggravated that my prekids marriage, lifestyle, body, career . . . all of it . . . was just gone. The irony is that I thought I wanted a change; what I didn't realize was everything had changed, yet there I was, trying like mad to cram my fatter, messier, truly altered self into my old life. Like an idiot fish, I was swimming upstream, fighting the natural current of life.

No wonder I was always exhausted and cranky. What I should have been doing was growing with you into a life that makes sense for who I've become—and am still becoming. (It's clear to me now that you've been doing this gracefully all along.)

God, what a loser I've been . . . Don't you worry though. Your wife's glory days are not behind her! I feel a second act coming on. If you'll give me the chance to build a loving, grown-up marriage with you, I can promise you that I will come out of this a better wife, a stronger mom, a wiser soul.

Also, I think maybe I got my midlife crisis out of the way a bit early. So there's that.

Please forgive me.

Your loving wife,
Cassie

Posting that letter was hard, and not just because I knew other people would read it and that it might backfire, but also because I wasn't sure I was saying the best things in order to win him back. I worried it was too much about me and wondered if I should have made it more of a love letter. But I wasn't firing on all cylinders when I wrote it, and I didn't want to wait until I was, because who knew when that might be?

Within thirty minutes, I had four comments, including: "Good luck, Cassie! Xoxo"; "Don't believe her, Leo. She only cares about herself. She obviously just doesn't want to be a single mom"; "You have a beautiful soul, and you deserve happiness. Everyone makes mistakes. If he is smart, Leo will forgive you"; and "Cassie, have you tried asking the Lord for help? See my blog *jesussaves* for helpful tips."

I was so spooked by the responses that I deleted all of the letters except mine to Leo. I nearly deleted that, too, but in my panicked (and slightly inebriated) state, I had convinced myself to at least try to achieve salvation through the thing that had brought me so much grief. I had even begun to wonder if the blog was what had alerted the authorities to Sid's bank operation. I couldn't shake the feeling that this blog owed me something. *Give me back my marriage, stupid!* I wanted to yell at the computer.

When Sid finally came out of the bedroom, I was pacing. She looked like she had fallen asleep in there and didn't have plans for remaining awake much longer.

"What's going on?" she asked.

When I told her what I'd done, her eyes went wide.

"Should I take it down?" I asked her imploringly, showing her the page open on my computer.

Blinking, she considered this, and in a groggy voice said, "Give him a chance to read it. It's kind of awesome and romantic."

I liked that thought, and I had convinced myself that it was necessary—desperate times, desperate measures and all that.

Sid and I sat together on the same little desk chair and watched in amazement as more comments rolled in, my mood brightening considerably, thanks to the mostly supportive remarks. I half expected to see a reciprocal comment appear from Leo himself.

Ten minutes later we were still sitting there in silence, staring at the screen. In the quiet, after the freaking out stopped, two realizations set in. One was that this public letter to Leo wasn't going to be the thing that won him back. The second was that something awesome was happening nonetheless. Goose bumps appeared on my arms as it came to me: These people *knew* me. That I never invited them in suddenly didn't matter. They were in, and they were rooting for me. I stopped feeling violated and started feeling validated. I had witnesses to my pain and my growth, and that was a powerful feeling. The vulnerability increased, yes, but as it did, a great love and acceptance welled up from deep inside of me. After what I'd been through, to find anything other than misery and embarrassment in a blog's comments section—a place most people rightfully think of as the Internet's seedy underbelly—was a shock. It was disorienting, this sensation of entering a physical place of peace, like stumbling onto a magnificent church in the middle of a war zone. And I was a sinner ready to join the saved. I could have climbed onto its altar and cried, *Here I am. I'm flawed and ugly and beautiful, too, but I'm doing my best and I will be okay.* I wanted to be sure Sid was feeling it, too, but I didn't know how to explain it to her without sounding completely nuts, so I poured us each another glass and said, "You know, I think our people here deserve to know you left Adrian."

"You're not serious."

"Come on. I did it!"

"You're drunk."

"A little bit."

She looked at me skeptically while I stared back at her with the slightly crazy, glassy gaze of a zealot. With a look more mischievous than anything else, she took out her phone and e-mailed me the photo of the letter.

"I never even gave this to him, you know. I only wrote it in case he didn't come home before we left."

Adrian,

You shouldn't find it a surprise that Lulu and River and I have left. We'll stay with Cassie and I'll be in touch. I'm sorry I didn't give you a chance to say goodbye to the kids. You are, of course, welcome to visit them anytime, but as you know, I can't stay in Singapore, and our marriage is over anyway. I assume you can transfer back to the Columbus office if you want to be closer to us.

Thank you for Lulu, who is a beautiful, beautiful gift. She is part you, so I could never hate you. I still have love for you and respect the way you faced the music when everything happened. But please know there is no chance of us getting back together. I wish you peace.

Love,
Sid

I posted that, and within an hour, we had fifty-some comments. The most amusing ones included marriage proposals to Sid, offers to "mess up" Adrian, you-go-girl notes, how-dare-you-take-a-man's-child-away comments, a handful of sob stories, and all kinds of advice. I watched her, to see if she would have the same reaction that I did. To my surprise, she started writing back to a few of the commenters, something I couldn't bring myself to do. We stayed up until two a.m., drinking wine and reading and responding to comments.

At one point we searched Twitter and discovered that #*SlowNews* was trending. It wasn't so much about our blog, though; people were snapping shots of their own handwritten letters and tagging them as #*SlowNews*.

The next day, despite four hours of sleep plus jet lag and a vague hangover, I had an idea. It had been stewing for a while—this notion that I should make lemonade out of the extraordinary lemon that was the *Slow News Sisters*. And in some ways I already had, but I wanted to pass along the gift I'd received. To widen the circle, so to speak. In many of the comments, I sensed a yearning to share. People poured out little pieces of their hearts under the guise of offering me advice or support or even criticism, but really they just wanted to be heard, to be seen. Other commenters wrote about how much they loved handwritten letters—the "art form," so many called it, and then, of course, the whole *Slow News* hashtag really got me thinking.

I walked to the dreaded post office on Varick Street, remembering to bring two forms of ID and two proofs of address, and signed up for a PO box. Back at home I deleted the letter to Leo and, with Sid's permission, hers to Adrian.

I put up a new post, explaining that we were turning the blog over: Anyone who wanted to say they were sorry could do it here. I couldn't guarantee clemency, but I could promise a safe space for admitting mistakes and asking forgiveness. At the very least, it could provide a few virtual nods of encouragement. To a person in deep trouble, that's an attractive offer. What I didn't admit was I had an inkling that if this became a thing, the biggest beneficiary of all would be me. It hardly seemed fair that this could be the case, but perhaps my punishment was complete.

While I was sitting at the computer, I received a text from Leo: *Thx for the letter. Take it down now, okay?*

Already did, I texted him back. Posting the letter had served an important purpose, if not the one I'd originally had in mind. Now it was time to officially close that public chapter of my life and do some making up—and growing up—outside the spotlight. I had no way of knowing whether Leo read the responses and how he felt if he had. But it didn't matter, because his experience with this whole thing was his own. Whether or not to forgive me was his choice alone, and I didn't want him to feel ganged up on. Those comments were for me, and they would hold me up, whispering in my ear that I could do it, while I went about the business of rebuilding my family.

CHAPTER TWENTY-TWO

On Friday we pulled up to the Westchester house in our rented minivan. It was a big refurbished barn with an attached silo sitting on a piece of land at least as big as Bleecker and Leroy Street playgrounds put together, and the boys immediately went nuts. River stayed outside with them while Sid and I found the key under the mat and unloaded the car.

The entry looked down onto a sunken living room with a fireplace and huge windows showing off the woods behind the house. It was even better than in the pictures Jill had sent. We plunked our bags down and walked through the open dining area to our right, which led to a big warm kitchen, where a cluster of copper pots hung from a rack over a cooking island. The kitchen led back to the living room. Although everything was open and bright, the wall of trees encircling the property gave the house a cozy and enclosed feeling. Immediately glad we'd decided to rent the house for the entire week, I looked forward to settling in.

The silo was actually a separate house with its own entrance. It had a circular living room, bathroom, kitchenette, and two bedrooms, all stacked atop one another. River was taken with it immediately, so Sid and Lulu took one bedroom while he took the other, which the boys were delighted to discover was accessible via a "secret" tunnel on the second-story landing of the main house.

We explored the house and woods, then all had dinner together. Once bedtime for the kids was done and River was in his room, Sid and I dumped a big bag of mail out on the living room floor and lost ourselves in other people's problems. In the four days since I'd posted the invitation to send letters in for the blog, I'd received close to three hundred responses.

Some of the apologies made us laugh, a few made us cry, and several made us cringe with discomfort. I'd heard Sid gasp, groan, and giggle through the letters, and she, me. We decided to curate them after reading a few we suspected to be rejected *Penthouse* submissions, describing adulterous trysts in graphic detail.

Sighing, I added to the to-scan pile one from a seventeen-year-old who'd cheated on his true love when he went on a college visit. When I glanced at Sid, she was sitting up straight and gripping a letter with both hands. She didn't appear to be breathing.

"Got yourself a good one there?" I said.

She didn't answer, and in fact didn't even seem to hear me. I kept watching her, and when she finally folded the paper back up, she said quietly, "It's from Kenny."

"Who's Kenny?" I said.

She said nothing but looked at me, waiting for it to sink in.

"Oh my God, *Kenny.*"

"Yep." She nodded in slow motion.

"Holy shit. What does he say?"

She handed me the letter and lay on the ground in what I now know as corpse pose.

Dear Sid,

I bet you never thought you'd hear from me again. This is an apology. I am sorry for so many things. I've thought about you a lot over the years, and about our child. I thought about calling you so many times, but the years slipped by and now here we are. You might want to throw this letter away, and I wouldn't blame you. You may have heard, but in case you're curious about me, I toured for the next year and then right around the time Jerry died, I spent seven months in jail after getting busted with just the wrong amount of LSD, and then six years working as a bison observer, counting and charting alone in the woods in Wyoming. I found great comfort in silence, and I studied meditation at a center in Montana. I married a nice woman I met at a silent retreat and we have a ten-year-old daughter named Robin. We divorced four years ago and she moved to New York with her new husband, so I moved out there to be closer to Robin. I've been writing music for a long time, and I run the occasional retreat at a meditation center in the Catskills.

Some famous singers recorded a few of my songs, and I've been able to make a living that way. You may have heard some— you know that song on the Subaru commercial where the family is driving through the woods at night? It's about you, actually. I've thought about you every day. I don't know why I ran away; I think it had something to do with how terrible a dad my father was. He died this year, and I've hardly been able to think about anything else but you and our son (I ran into Kelly Krieger at a show a year after I split and she told me you had a boy). I should have been there for you. I'm sure you have been an awesome mom, and maybe he has someone he knows as Dad—I don't know—but I would love to meet him. I understand if you can't allow that. I have a college fund for him that I'd like to give you. He doesn't need to know where it came from if you don't want him to.

My ex-wife told me about this blog and said that the women in it had the same names as you and your sister (yes, my ex knows all about you), but when I finally went to check it out, I saw this open call for apologies, and so I took it as a sign that I should write this and hope it finds you. I'm sorry for any hard times you've had that I might have helped with. I wish I had done things differently.

With love,
Kenny Fisher

The next day I asked Sid if she wanted me to post the letter.

"I don't know. We'd have to ask River," she said.

"Good point. So what did he say about the news?"

"He's intrigued. It's hard to say, really. He said he'd meet him. Kenny's coming here on Sunday."

She showed me the e-mail she sent him, which, like Kenny's letter, never did end up on the blog.

Kenny,

You're right. I never thought I'd hear from you. It was hard not to Google you over the years, but I didn't let myself do that. I let go of any anger I had toward you a long time ago. As it turns out, I'm good at forgiveness.

River is amazing. You really missed out, and I think that's punishment enough for a less-than-mature reaction to a big surprise many years ago. It sounds like you spent a lot of years searching and drifting. I feel sad about that, because I think knowing River might have saved you a lot of trouble. Being his mom has brought purpose and great love into my life. He is a kind and mature and open-minded young man, so maybe I did all right all by myself after all. Of course, Mom and Dad and Joe and Margie were incredible partners in raising him, so he and I are both fortunate that way.

I spoke to him about it and he said he'd meet you. And—surprise—we're renting a house not too far from where you live. There's a lovely hiking trail right out back, and I've always been big on walking when you need to have a difficult conversation. Don't feel the need to explain things to him unless he asks you to. Just take it slow. You have my blessing to enter River's life, but I don't presume to make decisions for him—and River knows that I'll support whatever kind of relationship (or non-relationship) he chooses to have with you.

—Sid

I spent Sunday morning working on the blog, and by lunchtime I'd scanned and uploaded sixty-some letters, none of them having anything to do with me. Good news for Leo and me, but many of my readers posted that they were disappointed that my correspondence with Sid would no longer be part of the site. Still, most people were supportive of the new direction, and new commenters were chiming in all the time, with seemingly no connection to the old blog. A handful of meanies forced me to post some rules, and I even banned a couple particularly nasty posters. It had consumed almost all of my time for the past three days, a welcome distraction from my own marital woes.

Kenny showed up right on time, at three o'clock. Sid noticed his car pulling up and went outside to meet him while River and I watched from the window.

"So that's him?" he said.

"That's him."

"Do you think I look like him?"

"Yeah—I've always thought so."

"It's weird that you know my dad and I don't."

"It is weird," was all I could think of to say.

We watched Sid and Kenny hug for a long time. It was a sober hug, like one you'd give a close friend at a funeral. Then they talked for a moment and Sid led Kenny up to the house.

"Ready?" I asked River.

"I guess so," he said.

Kenny's bigness filled the room immediately. He was slimmer, his face more angular, but his blue eyes were just as bright as I remembered. He seemed taller, and his thick, coarse hair had remained completely white, if a duller gray version of the yellowish mane he'd had when I knew him. There was something natty and put together about his casual outfit—blue corduroys with the wales going horizontally, a beat-up brown leather belt, and a plain white T-shirt. As he and Sid stood there beside each other, their energy and warmth compounded and added a charge to the air.

With a big soulful smile, he said in his gravelly voice, "Hi, River."

"Hi," River said.

"I'm Kenny. I'm your dad."

"Okay," he said, nodding his head and looking at his shoes.

A lump formed in my throat, and I looked over at Sid, whose eyes glistened.

"Riv, do you want to show Kenny the trails out back?" she said.

"Okay. Sure." River glanced at Kenny and said, "Uh. Follow me."

It was the first time I was ever aware of his teenagerness, and I felt a strong urge to go hug him, but I just stood there.

Kenny turned, beaming to Sid on his way out, his gratitude palpable. I felt myself being swept up in a tide of love and family togetherness, forgetting for a moment that my own little family wasn't doing so great. Sid and I stood in the front room and watched through the windows as Kenny and River walked out on the porch and turned toward the trails. Watching them go, I had an irrational internal alarm go off that Sid had just sent her son into the woods with a former drug dealer and inmate whom we really didn't know that much about. I looked over at her, wondering what she was thinking, but not wanting to puncture the silence with the wrong thing. We stood there even though there was nothing to see until a car appeared, turning in and pulling slowly up the gravel drive.

"Looks like Stevie's car," I said. When it stopped and Leo stepped out, I felt my heart growing and straining against its little shell like the Grinch's does when he finally grasps the real meaning of Christmas.

Sid kissed me on the cheek and said, "I'll go see how the boys are doing with those Legos."

I walked out to the front porch and waved hello to Leo.

"Hey, Cass," he said.

"Hi, honey. I'm really glad you're here."

"Where are the boys?" he asked.

"Playing Legos with Sid upstairs. They are going to be so happy to see you."

"Me too—I miss them."

"We all miss you."

"So I thought I'd stay here tonight," he said.

I immediately felt lighter. "Great. Listen, I'm not assuming anything, but I would really love to hug you right now," I said.

He opened his arms, and I went to him, turning my face sideways to rest against his chest. He smelled like different laundry detergent and Altoids. I wondered if he'd been smoking again. When he stroked my hair with one hand, I thought, *Okay. Everything is going to be okay.*

"Do you want to talk?" I asked him.

"I don't think so," he said, releasing me. But then he started talking anyway. "I really don't want to read your letters, Cass. So don't ask me about that again, okay?"

I nodded.

He continued. "But I fucking hate it that a million other people have read them. If you were having such a hard time, you should have talked to me about it. Not cheated with your ex. God, Cass, I fucking hate that you did that."

When someone uses the term "fucking hate" twice in ten seconds, it's not generally a good sign. Without speaking, I tried to convey with my eyes how much I agreed with everything he was saying.

He was looking over my head at the house now.

"Do you want to go in?" I asked.

We walked up the stairs in silence, but once we were inside, the tension began to fade and we both behaved seminormally.

"Cool place," Leo said.

"Isn't it great? The boys are loving all the hiding places."

"They're upstairs?" he asked, motioning to the staircase.

"Yeah. Come on, I'll show you," I said.

"That's all right. I'll find them," he said, and bounded upstairs.

Within seconds, I heard gleeful "Daddy!!!" sounds, and let myself shed a quick tear.

Sid came down and walked into the kitchen to get started on a sweet potato and kale chowder recipe we'd found in one of the books at the house to go with the chicken that was roasting in the oven.

"You okay?"

"Mm-hmm." I nodded, biting my lip, which she of course knew signaled that I was not okay, but she let it go and we stayed busy with silent food prep.

Sid and I were setting the table when River and Kenny came back in through the front door.

"Hey, guys!" Sid called, searching their faces for a sign of how things went.

"Hey!" they said in unison, then looked at each other and laughed, if a bit nervously.

"How was your hike?"

"Cool," River said.

"Yeah, cool," added Kenny.

Sid studied River's face for a few seconds, and then, as if she had derived his permission telepathically, asked Kenny if he'd like to stay for dinner.

"I'd love to," he said.

Then Kenny turned to me. "Cassie. It is great to see you. I'm sorry I didn't say hi earlier. It was kind of a big moment for me."

Before I could answer him, the doorbell rang twice and the door opened. "Hel-loo-ooo!" It was Jill, my real estate agent. With her loose spirals of orange hair and rosy cheeks, she was just plump and cheerful enough to qualify as jolly. "So what do you think?" she said when she found us gathered around the kitchen island. She placed a brown shopping bag down on the counter and from it removed two pies. "Miller's. Best in the county."

"Oh—thank you. How sweet. The place is great. Thanks for finding it on such short notice," I said.

"They're asking $795, which I know is higher than we discussed, but I think we could offer low," she said. "The seller is anxious."

I was confused. "It's for sale?"

"Yes, of course. What did you think you were doing here?" she said.

"Uuuh. Renting it for the week."

"No, no, no. I had to convince the seller to let you rent it. He doesn't normally do this, but I told him you were serious. And that you wouldn't mind me showing the house while you were here. The guy's wife left him, and he moved to his apartment in the city full-time. Says he never wants to see this place again. He doesn't even want the furniture. It comes with everything you see. Of course, we'll get everything carted away if you don't want it."

Before I had a chance to respond to Jill, we were interrupted by screams.

"Monster!!! Monster!!!" The boys and Leo came bounding up the basement stairs and spilled into the kitchen. They'd been giving Leo an extremely thorough tour of the place.

"It is *spooky* down there," Leo said, scooping up Joey and hanging him upside down by the legs, eliciting squeals of delight. "Perfect for a cheese cave, though," and then looked up and noticed the two strangers standing in the kitchen. He looked surprised but set Joey down and extended his hand to introduce himself to Jill and Kenny. I could tell he was expecting someone to tell him who these people were.

"Kenny is an old friend of Sid's," I said. "And Jill is who found us this house."

"Oh," he said, looking back and forth between them, "what a coincidence."

"Actually, no—hon. They aren't together," I felt the need to explain.

Nervous laughter from Jill and Kenny filled the silence while Leo continued to look confused. I hated that we all had information he didn't.

"Kenny is, um, *that* Kenny. You know, River's dad," I continued.

Leo visibly softened. "No way, man," he said, reaching out to shake Kenny's hand again, this time adding an arm grasp. "Great to meet you." His eyes then sought out River's. Grinning beatifically, he nodded his head at River, who returned the smile.

Quinn said, "River has a *dad*?"

"Yep," River said. "Everyone has a dad, but not everyone gets to know them and live with them like you guys. You're lucky that way."

Trying to ignore the prophetic overtones of River's sweet explanation, I led the next chorus of nervous laughter that propped up the whole awkward scene. Feeling weird about being the one to announce River and Kenny's relationship like that, I was trying to figure out whether my own less interesting but still secret relationship with Jill needed to be revealed at that moment. I looked over at her.

She was smirking, clearly enjoying the *Maury Povich* moment unfolding here in the kitchen. When she felt my eyes on her, she jolted out of her daze and said, "Anyhoo, Cassie, I should run. I'll give you a call tomorrow." She hurried out, yelling over her shoulder, "Enjoy, everyone!"

"Who was that again?" Leo asked after she left.

Timing is everything, isn't it? What could have been easily explained away any other time was now another secret that—if he saw it as a lie—could be a real problem. I was staring at the pies on the counter, thinking that maybe Leo should pick one up and throw it in my face. I would be surprised, but not mad. I deserved it. He'd immediately feel bad and come over to me but would slip in the blueberry mess on the floor, pulling me down with him. We'd be all messy and we'd hug and kiss and that would be the beginning of our road back to wedded bliss.

"Her name is Jill. She's a real estate agent up here. Um, why don't we take the boys out back for some fresh air and I'll explain?" I said, grabbing two beers from the fridge—Samuel Smith's, his favorite, which I had stocked in case he came. I handed him one and told the boys to find their shoes and jackets.

Quinn and Joey set to work gathering sticks for the campfire they'd been promised. Leo and I stood side by side, watching them and yelling out encouragement or "Careful! Don't swing that near your brother!" admonishments here and there. The air was crisp but not quite chilly, and leaves were starting to fall. It would be dark soon.

"So," I began.

The weary look on Leo's face spoke volumes about his expectations of me. The term "so over me" came to mind. I couldn't blame him. I was tired of my bullshit, too.

"Jill's been showing me some properties."

Leo's eyes went wide. "You were planning to move out?"

"Oh God. No, no, no, no," I said. "What happened was that I just started looking at bigger apartments for us for fun, and it kind of became a hobby that I never told you about for some reason."

That sounded bad. Nonetheless, I continued. "I started in Brooklyn, and before I knew it, on Tuesdays, when the boys were with Wanda, I was looking at places all the way out here. I only wanted to see if I could picture us ever moving out of the city."

"Jesus, Cass. I don't care. I mean, I kind of do *now*, but I didn't. I mean I wouldn't have cared. God, you and your secrets." Poor Leo was so irritated with me that he could barely get the words out. "We used to tell each other everything," he added, a touch of sadness in his voice.

I promised myself then that I was done with secrets.

"Honey. Leo. Let's put the boys in front of a movie and go out to dinner in town. We can talk. We'll be home by the time it's over, and Sid and River and Kenny can have a nice meal together."

"No, thanks," he said coolly. "I brought camping gear. I thought I'd pitch a tent with the boys in the yard tonight."

It was a sweet thing to do. One of their favorite bedtime stories was about a boy who goes camping with his dad, but all I could think was that it was a handy way for Leo to avoid the issue of sleeping in the same bed with me.

"In fact, hold on. I should put it up before it gets dark." He handed me his beer and jogged around to the front of the house, where his car was parked. When he returned, I showed him a nice flat patch in the yard, and he agreed it was a good place for the tent.

The boys were thrilled about the campout and wanted to help with the tent, but Leo did this whole funny mock-angry thing about the measly pile of sticks they'd gathered and told them that if they wanted a decent fire, they'd better find five times as many.

Shaking out the tent, he said, "So Rob said Becky is pretty pissed at you," though his voice was light and he even gave me a hint of a smile.

I placed both beers on the ground and went to help him with the tent.

"I know. Did Mary tell you about our talk?"

"You talked to my mom?"

"We had lunch last week. She confronted me about the blog. Apparently, Becky won't shut up about it."

"Sounds about right," he said.

I grabbed a pole and extended it while he did the same with the other.

"Anyway, your mom thinks I'm ridiculous, blogs in general are ridiculous, and that people who read them are the most ridiculous of all."

He laughed. "Which would make you less ridiculous than Becky, I guess."

"Works for me," I said.

We finished putting up the tent in silence. It felt good to be working together on something.

"Perfect," he said when it was done, and leaned down to grab our beers. He handed me one, and just as I was starting to relax, considering telling him about how well the new blog was doing, he said, "You know she knows about the whole Jake thing, right?"

I crumpled a bit and said, "I know. Did you tell her?"

"No. I wasn't going to say anything, because I didn't want her to hate you, but she dragged it out of poor Stevie."

Yes! I thought. *I'm in! He wouldn't care what his mom thought of me if he didn't plan on getting back together.*

"Well, it came up at lunch, and it was pretty brutal. I told her about some things I would happily have gone to my grave never telling anyone, let alone my mother-in-law, but your mom is tough, and pretty understanding, after all. She even told me to let her handle Becky."

"I guess that explains why she called me all, *Don't you divorce that girl!*"
"Really?"
"Yeah. You know she's always thought you were good for me."
"Actually, I did not know that."

We both took a long, slow swig and looked out into the forest.

River came out and handed us each a new beer, taking our empties. He and Leo shot the breeze for a few seconds, but despite the boost I'd just received, I couldn't bring myself to be light and chatty quite yet. River seemed to sense this and backed away as Kenny and Sid came out to join him.

River and Kenny carried the big picnic table out closer to the fire pit, with Sid following close behind, carrying a tablecloth and a basket of cutlery and napkins. While she set the table, River and Kenny went about building a fire with Quinn's and Joey's help.

It was a moving scene: River reunited with his dad, doing this iconic father-son thing, my own little boys bringing them sticks and struggling to lift the logs. I found it impossible not to melt a little bit.

Sid passed us on her way back to the house and must have noticed that we were both just standing there, watching everyone. "You did that, you know," she called over to me.

"Did what?"

"Brought them together," she said, and continued back toward the house.

I hadn't thought of that. It floored me for a second. This thing that until just days ago had seemed like the worst thing that ever happened to me had officially redeemed itself. River had his dad back.

Quinn and Joey came barreling into our legs then. Leo looked at me and said, "I *do* like it here."

The next morning I woke while it was still dark, uneasily aware that the boys were not in their bedroom but bolstered by that promising conversation with Leo. I was also anxious because the site had crashed last night. I'd called Monica, who seemed to think the crash was a good thing, indicating that traffic was too great for the free host we'd been using. She said she'd call her Web guy first thing in the morning and see if he could meet with me. I wished I could just talk to Leo about it, but I didn't want to distract him from the matter of our reunion, which I hoped was imminent.

I went downstairs and started the coffee machine, then made hot cocoa on the stove. When it was done, I parked with my coffee at the back table, watching out the window for signs of life in the tent.

Soon Sid and Lulu came down and joined me at the table. While Lulu snacked on dry Cheerios, I told Sid about the crash and asked if she could watch the boys later while I went into the city to get the site fixed and check the PO box.

I didn't mention the "real money" Monica had predicted the site could make or the marketing consultant she wanted to introduce me to, but it all weighed heavily on me as I stared out at the tent. I let the fleeting fantasy of owning this house run wild in my head, placing the garden and jungle gym in the yard, extending the deck, painting the bedrooms. I wanted to tell Sid, but I was worried that I couldn't articulate my longing for this house without sounding materialistic or whiny, or like I was putting the house before my family. But the thing was, the house had become inseparable from my vision of a happy ending to this whole thing.

Sid got busy with Lulu's breakfast, and I kept watch at the window. When I saw movement in the tent, I ran to pour the cocoa into the four mugs I'd set on the tray and rushed out to the yard before they could come inside.

Leo was unzipping the tent as I stood there inches from the opening, smiling and holding my tray and feeling just a little silly and desperate.

"Hey," he said sleepily, stepping into his boots.

The sight of him first thing in the morning was not something I'd experienced in almost two weeks, and it filled me with emotion. The tray of steaming-hot beverages prevented it, but I longed to wrap my arms around him and nestle my head into his neck.

"Cocoa?" I said.

The boys stumbled out, and Leo helped them put their shoes on before they stepped onto the dewy grass.

We sat around the fire pit, the boys bundled in their sleeping bags, and sipped from our steaming mugs for only a couple minutes before Joey had to pee. I took him in and then brought him back, trading him for Quinn and bringing Leo a coffee. Soon the boys were cold and wanted breakfast, so I told them to go on in. There were muffins and bananas on the table.

"We'll be there in a few minutes," I promised. "Aunt Sid and Lulu are in the kitchen. Go ahead."

When they were gone I turned to Leo, but he spoke first. "So I told the boys last night. I'm taking the week off of work and getting away for a bit."

"Getting away?"

"Yeah. Stevie has to drive up to Boston for meetings, so I'm going to keep him company. I'll be back Friday."

We were supposed to be out of the house on Saturday morning, and I'd hoped to have some things between us resolved by then, things like, *Where do I go when I leave here?*

"And then?"

"I don't know. I need to think." Then he said something about needing to get to Midtown by nine thirty and asked if I minded taking down the tent once the condensation dried.

"Sure. Take care, hon."

"Bye, Cass," he said, turning and walking toward the house.

CHAPTER TWENTY-THREE

On Thursday night I sat out back around the fire with Sid, feeling blue that my time with her was coming to an end, that things with Leo were still unresolved, and about the threats and intimidation I'd employed to get the boys to stay in their beds that night. Jill and another Realtor had come to the house with prospective buyers on two separate occasions that week, and while the meeting with the Web people had gone well, it would take some time to integrate advertising and even more time to know if I'd really make any money from it. In other words, it was time to let go of the house.

On the upside, I'd picked up almost four hundred letters from the PO box, and had been so wrapped up in the blog that until now I hadn't had time to preemptively mourn this house or my marriage, both of which seemed to be slipping away.

"I love it here," Sid said, sighing.

"Me too. Our little halfway house for upper-middle-class women with broken marriages."

She giggled.

"Honestly, I'm not sure I'm ready to be rereleased into society," I said, taking a sip of peppermint tea and adding, "Why are you making me drink tea? I want wine."

Ignoring this, she said, "So a couple of days ago, I got a settlement from Adrian."

"Really?"

"Yeah. It was about six times what I thought it would be when he told me he wanted us to 'be comfortable,'" she said, making air quotes.

"You're kidding," I said.

"No. I tried to get him to take some of it back. I don't want guilt money from him. Plus, we don't need much—now that River's college is taken care of . . ."

"Keep the money!" I interrupted. "Think of it as his penalty for treating you so badly."

"He wouldn't take it back. So yeah, I'm keeping it."

"Hold on. We really do need some wine."

I went to fetch a bottle of red and two glasses from the kitchen and hurried back outside. I was excited for Sid and glad we'd have something else to do other than sit around feeling sad.

I kept trying to get her to tell me exactly how much she had, so we could start allocating it. I wanted to play a version of the game where you say all the things you'd do if you won the lottery. But she was rambling about farmers' markets and schools and the cool yoga studio in town when it dawned on me: *Oh my God, she's buying this house.*

I wish I could say my happiness was pure, but frustratingly, it churned up some complicated if-I-can't-have-it-then-no-one-can type of feelings.

"Cass? Are you listening?"

"You're buying this house," I said, hoping my voice relayed only good feelings.

"So what do you think?" She was looking at me expectantly.

"I think it's great. It's amazing. I'll see you all the time."

"Well, yeah."

"Yeah." I nodded. I was shocked, and happy, but also felt an ugly pit growing in my stomach. Having survived high school with nary a boyfriend squabble, here I was fighting back a jealous urge to yell "Mine!" over a piece of real estate.

"Cass, are you hearing me? I want us all to live here together. Your family and Mine. There's more than enough room, especially with the silo."

"Sid!"

The mood had gone from subdued to hysterical. We were standing up and screaming at each other. I felt like a guest on *The Oprah Winfrey Show* who had just been given a new car out of the blue. Confused and elated, I asked her to walk me through it once more, hoping I'd missed the part where she'd talked to Leo and convinced him to come back. But even on her second explanation, I was distracted by the sinking feeling that even if Leo were open to reconciliation, he'd balk at the idea of Sid buying us a house.

"We'll pay rent, of course," I said.

"Sure. We'll figure it all out," she said.

By the time we'd finished the wine, I'd grown more determined than ever to put my family back together. I just hoped that Leo was missing me as much as I missed him. I'd find out soon enough. He was due back from Boston tomorrow.

Lying in my bed later, I checked the blog and my e-mail from my phone, as had become my presleep ritual. Minutes later I shot up and trotted down the hall to Sid's room, still clutching my phone.

"Sid? Are you sleeping?"

"Cass? What is it?"

"Can I talk to you for a minute?"

"Sure—come on in."

I sat on the edge of her bed. "I don't want you to buy this house for us. I want to help, too."

"Of course. Of course you can."

"No—I mean, I met with a Web marketing consultant the other day. She's doing a reader survey and site-traffic analysis."

"Okay." She looked confused.

"Well, it's too soon to really know for sure, but I just read an e-mail from her, and she thinks the blog can generate a few thousand a month—hopefully more. Enough to cover the mortgage payments, right?"

And with that, we had a plan. A plan I felt good about presenting to Leo.

CHAPTER TWENTY-FOUR

I woke the next morning to the sound of Joey's favorite game being played on my phone. "Hey, guys," I said. "Good morning."

Joey said nothing but climbed into bed with me, fingers and eyes glued to my phone. I pulled him close and planted several kisses on the top of his head while he continued to play. Quinn was drinking from the water glass on my bedside table. When he finished, he looked at me and said, "Mama, do we live here now?"

I wondered for a moment if he'd been spying on Sid and me last night.

"Well, would you like it if we lived here?"

"Not New York City?" he said.

"We could take the train into the city and visit anytime we want. It's only forty minutes to our apartment."

"Can Dad live here, too?"

Gulp. "Yes."

"Then yes. Come on. Let's go get Dad."

There was no note of silliness in his voice. He meant business.

I texted Leo. Boys eager to see you. When you do get home?

Should be at the apt by 5.

We'll meet you there for dinner. Cool?

Cool.

Since this was Quinn's idea and because I was afraid that without the boys, Leo wouldn't meet me, I didn't consider going alone.

When we got to the apartment, Quinn and Joey dumped out a basket of dinosaurs and starting playing. I called for pizza and then washed my face and applied some blush and mascara. I went to the bedroom and found a simple black tank dress I knew Leo liked. Not wanting to look like I was trying too hard, I put on a denim shirt over the dress and tied my hair into my signature sloppy half bun, half ponytail. I found an iffy bag of baby carrots in the fridge, pulled the table out from the wall, and added the stepstool as a fourth chair. I was setting the table, considering lighting some candles, when I heard Leo's keys jingle in the lock. Nervous, I started rearranging the place settings so I'd be busy when he came in. This moment was the most afraid I could remember feeling during those harrowing few months.

Leo barely had the door open when the boys launched themselves at him. I couldn't see him from where I was hunched over the table, but I heard him say, "Hey, guys! What an awesome surprise. I thought I'd have to wait until tomorrow to see you."

I made my way over to the entryway and leaned against the doorframe, hoping for some eye contact or maybe even a quick unstilted conversation about how his trip had gone.

"Yay! Dad's back," I said, and immediately winced because I

worried that Leo would think I meant *back* back, and presumptuous was the last thing I was going for.

"Daddy, we are here to get you," said Quinn.

I guess Quinn and I should have gone over the game plan ahead of time, because I wasn't expecting him to just blurt it out like that. I had loosely planned on talking to Leo privately while the boys watched TV after pizza.

"Get me?" said Leo, as he pulled Quinn close for a hair tousle.

Leo looked back and forth between the boys while I tried to figure out how to insert myself into this conversation. With no better ideas, I decided to follow Quinn's lead.

"That's right," I added matter-of-factly. "We'd like you to come back with us. For good."

There. I'd said it. Leo stood up, looking (understandably) confused. The last he knew, the kids and I were meant to vacate the house and be back in the city—for good—tomorrow, his own place of residence TBD.

Quickly, I told him about the blog's advertising plan and Sid's financial windfall. We were technically still renting the house, but if everything went as planned, Sid, Leo, and I would soon own the house together. For the boys' sake, I made it seem like the big decision here was whether or not to move. But, of course, the bigger question—that I couldn't ask in front of the kids—was, *Will you come back to me?*

When I finished, Quinn and Leo stood looking at me while Joey retreated to the bedroom. Leo didn't say anything, but he stared at me, an unreadable expression on his face. I fought my nervous instinct to keep talking, to sell him on the schools, the easy walk to the train station and quick commute, my hope that he'd help me run the blog and get a less demanding job closer to our new home, my openness to selling the apartment if we needed to. None of that mattered if he didn't want to get back together. I forced myself to look back at him in silence, awaiting his answer to my unasked question.

The stare down continued for a few more seconds, until Leo broke into a slow smile. We hadn't made real eye contact in quite some time, and it had a thrilling effect. *Say it*, I thought. *Say something that tells me yes.*

Joey came back out of the bedroom, dragging a grocery bag filled with a random assortment of Leo's clothes, and held it out to Leo. "So let's go," he said.

"Okay, bud," Leo said, taking the bag from him. "Let's go."

We stood there, looking around at one another, me wondering if Leo's "Okay, bud," was my "yes," when the buzzer rang.

I had forgotten about the pizza. With shaky hands, I paid the delivery guy, then set the pizza on the table and went to the bathroom. When I came out, Leo was helping the boys put their shoes and coats on.

My heart pounded as we walked purposefully up Hudson Street. I wanted to ask Leo, *Are we officially back together, or are you just going along with this for the kids' sake?* Instead I went with, "Are we really going to let this pizza get cold?"

"Mom's right, guys," Leo said. "Let's grab this bench and eat."

On the bench outside of Hudson Bagels, with the huge open pizza box covering all four of our laps, I felt happy. When I lifted the cheese off of my slice and slopped it back into the box, I noticed Leo smile and shake his head—my lactose intolerance still a newish development—in what seemed closer to affection than annoyance, which heartened me considerably.

"So how's the pizza in Westchester?" asked Leo.

This was my signal that it was really happening, my "yes." Sitting there on that bench, on my way out of the city I thought I'd never leave with the husband I thought I might, I realized I had been wrong about both. The city was easy to leave. The husband's the one who nearly left me, and whom I learned I wanted to keep more than anything.

CHAPTER TWENTY-FIVE

The boys both fell asleep on the train, and we carried them the three blocks to the house, depositing them into their beds in the room beside mine. In the quiet hallway, I whispered, "Let's talk," and Leo followed me into my room, where we found ourselves truly alone together for the first time in many weeks.

I needed to officially win him back on my own, and had prepared a speech in my head on the train. But the charge between us was something I hadn't felt in a very long time, so instead of presenting my case for reconciliation, I did something that terrified me.

"Sit down," I said, then turned the bedside lamp on and the overhead light off.

Leo sat on the bed, and neither of us spoke. I stood before him and started unbuttoning my dress from the top down. Thankfully, I had worn decent underwear and a matching bra—from the Gap, maybe, but lacy and black, and doing the trick, it seemed. When I slid out of the armholes and let the dress fall to the ground, Leo was looking at me in a way I remembered from when we were dating.

My stomach, with its frown of a belly button and slack white flesh, was like a third person in the room: He'd seen flashes of it, but not head-on like this since before the twins were born (and it was an entirely different body part). *This is it,* I coached myself: *No more hiding. No more apathy. No more lazy, indifferent sex.* I undid my bra and—as gracefully as possible—stepped out of my underwear. I said nothing, but stood there as not quite the girl he married but, hopefully, the woman he still loved.

"Cass," he said, holding out his hand as if to answer my doubts.

My uncharacteristically bold seduction combined with the unfamiliar bed plus the fact that we hadn't been together in several weeks all added up to a fantastically foreign yet familiar series of touches and sounds and sensations.

Afterward, Leo nuzzled my neck and said, "So that's what they call makeup sex."

I blinked back tears and kissed him again before laying my head on his chest. "So we're made-up? You forgive me?"

"Yes. Thanks for coming to get me."

I just smiled and hugged him tight.

CHAPTER TWENTY-SIX

Sunnyvale, New York
December 12

Dear Sid,

Surprise! My fingers are crossed that this will make it to you. I've taken the extra precaution of mailing it express. I hope your Singapore visit is going well. Things here are great—so much news to share! The crew looks to be making progress on Creekside Homebirth. They finished the roof yesterday—just in time, it appears, because this morning it snowed.

I booked two speaking engagements for January, a "letter writers alliance" and a bloggers conference. I'm completely intimidated. I need you to help me with what I'm going to say.

Kenny stopped by today to say that his parents are going to make it for Christmas Eve, and Monica and TJ and the kids are definitely coming, so it looks like we will have quite a crew. I went to the big Target today (bliss!) and got new bedding for the two back rooms for Mom and Dad and Joe and Margie. Leo and I have the perfect tree in mind—we can cut it down when you get home.

Leo is over the moon because his buddies from Murray's came out to taste his young goat cheese and they told him if he can make enough, they will sell it in the shop. Needless to say, he's out goat shopping right now! The boys will be so excited.

You'll be proud of me: I've only sent Leo four texts this week. Four! I have so much to tell him when he gets home every day, I practically knock the boys out of my way to reach him first.

Do you realize that Christmas Eve is the anniversary of our little letter-writing experiment? (Actually, "little" is the wrong word. "Metamorphic," "gargantuan," "transformative" would all be more fitting.) The deal was a year, and I know we've taken a few months off (justifiably, considering we see each other every day), but I wanted to honor our pact and close out the year with this.

Thank you, Sid, for making this happen. What a fulfilling journey it has been, and what a delight to get to know you again. Living with you has brought more harmony, balance, and happiness into my life than I ever imagined. Your support has made me a better mom. And yet . . . it's hard to think about the joy this year has brought without also acknowledging the havoc I wreaked on my life, your life, Leo's life, and perhaps a few others. But I daresay we've all come out of it in one piece! Having my most private self become totally public turned out to be horrifying, yes, but ultimately liberating. I have no idea where I'd be today if it weren't for the tumult of the past year, but I can guarantee you I wouldn't be as happy as I am right now, with goats in my barn, a birthing suite in my yard, a cheese cave in my basement, and a house full of people I love and cherish.

Soak up that warm weather and then hurry home, my dear. I miss you. Kisses to Lu and Riv!

Love you so much.

—Cassie